ANOTHER TIME, ANOTHER PLACE

JO LOVETT

Boldwood

First published in Great Britain in 2023 by Boldwood Books Ltd.

Cover Design by Head Design Ltd

Cover Photography: Shutterstock

A CIP catalogue record for this book is available from the British Library.

Paperback ISBN 978-1-78513-501-9

Large Print ISBN 978-1-78513-497-5

Hardback ISBN 978-1-78513-496-8

Ebook ISBN 978-1-78513-494-4

Kindle ISBN 978-1-78513-495-1

Audio CD ISBN 978-1-78513-502-6

MP3 CD ISBN 978-1-78513-499-9

Digital audio download ISBN 978-1-78513-493-7

Boldwood Books Ltd
23 Bowerdean Street
London SW6 3TN
www.boldwoodbooks.com

To Oliver

1

LIV

July 2014

If fate's going to strike, you don't expect it to be next to some recycling bins at a bus terminus on Putney Heath.

I've been hefting bags of clothes into the recycling chute in front of me for what feels like several minutes now and my biceps are killing me. I should really go to the gym more often (ever). In my defence, the chute's high and you have to lift a really heavy handle with one hand while you put the bag in with the other. Also, I've put a *lot* of bags in.

The large number of bags is directly linked to what I now realise is my very bad habit of loving a bargain. Looking on the bright side about my enforced move out of London tomorrow, clearing out my flat has forced me to recognise that after approximately thirty-seven disastrous – although amazingly priced – sale bargains I should have learnt some lessons. (There's *always* a good reason that they're reduced.)

Another bright side is that I have to move to Paris. Paris! I should be very excited. Everyone wants to live in Paris. I *am* very excited. Just also a bit daunted. I've lived in London my whole life (apart from three years at university in Newcastle but that was easy because my twin sister did the same degree as me). I've always been lucky enough to be surrounded by family and friends, and it feels like it's going to be a challenge not knowing anyone at all.

The biggest bright side is that I'm getting away from my arse of a boss and even bigger arse of an ex-colleague. I don't have any caveats about that; I'm just delighted.

Someone behind me clears their throat and I realise I've been staring at my last bag – containing a heavy neon-yellow dress and a purple mohair bolero jacket, both unbelievable bargains but quite unwearable – for ages. Whoops. I should hurry up. No one wants to have to queue at the (quite smelly) recycling bank on a summery Friday evening. Why does it smell, actually, when it's only clothes and shoes? Have people been putting household rubbish in? Rude.

Anyway.

'Sorry.' I pick up the final bag and hoist it effortlessly (not really – I almost squeak in discomfort at the pull on my arm muscles) into the bin, and stand back to give the man behind me access to the chute. I almost gasp out loud as he flashes me a smile, because in that moment it's like everything else fades away and he's all I can see.

I've never in my life had such an intense reaction to just a smile.

It's wide, it's crooked, it displays almost-but-not-completely-perfect teeth, it transforms the rest of his face, and it makes your own lips start to widen in response. My lips, anyway; I think it might just be me whose knees turn to jelly at the sight of it. I know it sounds utterly ridiculous, but it's like I have some connection with him in the space of a split second. It does sound utterly ridiculous. I'm probably just feeling over-emotional because tomorrow morning I'm leaving my entire life as I know it behind and moving to France.

I realise that I'm staring, blocking the man's access to the recycling bin.

Recycling is why he's here. He is not here to smile at me. I move out of his way, rubbing my arms to smooth the tiny hairs that have risen, wondering how I'm suddenly shivering when it's still so warm, the evening sun high in the sky with no cloud in sight.

As I move, I take in more details of the man surrounding the smile. He's around my age, maybe two or three years older, so he's probably late twenties. He's tallish and broadish, and wearing a light grey T-shirt and khaki cargo shorts; he has ruffled mid-brown hair, tanned skin and, again, the smile.

I feel as though everything about him is amazing. I wouldn't be surprised to hear 'Love is All Around' playing behind me and see hearts floating through the air. I can almost *smell* the gorgeousness of him. I mean, not really. He could have the most wonderful manly scent ever, or equally the most disgusting BO, and I wouldn't be able to smell it above the delightful combination of putrid bin and the diesel fumes the red bus just to my left is pumping out, but I *feel* like he smells gorgeous.

I am literally on the brink of saying something along the lines of, 'Hi, my name's Liv. Would you like to go for dinner with me? Right now?' Or just, 'Well, *hello*.' Like my mouth is literally opening to ask him out. Which is bizarre, because I never make the first move. The last time I did was in Year Twelve with a new boy and that did not end well (Ned Morgan – nice name, nice face, really not a nice personality as it turned out).

Instead, I feel myself give a weird smile (I think I started by aiming for slightly flirty but panicked) and hear myself say, 'Enjoy your recycling,' and immediately give myself an internal eye-roll. Not that much better than 'Well, *hello*'.

'Thanks.' His voice is deep, holds a laugh, and gets me somewhere right inside.

And I'm staring at him again. He clearly just wants to do his recycling.

'Bye then.' Why? Why am I saying goodbye to him?

He smiles again and lifts his two bags in, fast, one after the other, and I turn to begin the walk across the grass back to my car, hoping that it isn't obvious that I'm practically drooling at the way the muscles in his upper arms flexed as he worked the chute.

I hear the light slap of his flip flops on the tarmac behind me, and then... he catches me up, definitely, definitely on purpose and says, 'Which way are you going?'

He has just asked *me* which way I'm going. As in he is definitely making conversation with me. Maybe he felt some kind of connection too. Maybe he's suggesting that the two of us go somewhere this evening. Maybe he just felt the same insane connection, like fate has pulled us together. Maybe…

Maybe not. I'm leaving tomorrow. And this evening my sister, Frankie, and my best friend, Sulwe, are coming over and we're getting takeaway. If fate *has* pulled me and this man together, it has very bad timing. Given that we're using the same clothes recycling bank, we probably live reasonably close to each other, so this could have happened any time. And that is one reason that I do not believe in fate.

'I'm just…' As I point towards my car, not totally sure where I'm going with the end of my sentence, I hear a noise from inside the little hut we're passing. I stop for a moment. 'Was that a cat?'

I move closer to the hut and listen. Yes, there it is again. We always had cats when I was growing up and the miaow of a miserable one is very recognisable. 'I think there's a cat with a problem in there.'

'Yep, I think you're right,' the man agrees in his lovely deep voice.

The door of the hut is slightly ajar; I push it and go inside. As I pause to let my eyes adjust to the dark so that I don't trip over any of the immense clutter in front of me (the owner of this hut is not a tidy person), I note two things. One, the sound is definitely the miaow of a hurt or scared cat and it's coming from the back of the hut, and two, the man has followed me inside.

I can make out a shelving unit at the back. As I advance cautiously, two green eyes stare at me from the very top shelf. I'm not cautious enough and I yelp as I stub my toe on something and then scream as something wispy catches my face. The cat's eyes widen and its miaow increases and then just stops. I've clearly terrified it. And obviously there was no need to scream because the thing that brushed my face must have been a cobweb and there is nothing wrong with spiders. Nothing wrong at all. Unlike rats and mice. I hear a little scuffly sound and have to swallow another scream. What if there are rats or mice in here?

'Are you okay?' I love the concern in the man's voice and now I'm feeling a lot better. Of course there aren't small furry creatures in here, and even if there are, it's fine. *Fine*. We are large humans. Mice (eurgh) and rats (actual vomit) are way smaller than us. We will be okay.

'Totally fine, thank you. I just banged my foot on something and then walked into what I think must be a cobweb. I'm not so sure the cat's fine, though.'

As I'm speaking, I continue to move forwards, my hands outstretched, and now I've made it to the shelves. I look up.

'It's stuck in something.'

'Cricket helmet,' the man says. The cat miaows plaintively again as if it's relieved someone's correctly diagnosed its predicament. 'I'm thinking I need to get it out.'

I nod. There's no way I can reach up there without climbing halfway up the shelves and they really don't look like they could support my weight. I move to my right to go past the man just as he moves to his left and then we both stop, and then I move left while he goes right and then we both stop again. We both laugh, kind of awkwardly, but we're also being a bit flirty, which I have to say I *love*, and then he says, 'You go.'

'Why thank you.'

Eek, no, that just sounded embarrassingly coy. I try not to shake my head at myself, and step to my right around him as he stands still. As I inch past, our chests are almost within touching distance and, honestly, I feel almost fluttery. Or giddy. This is ridiculous. Also, I admit, hugely exciting.

'Great, then,' I say with cringeworthy forced nonchalance, and come close to clapping my hands together before I realise that that would a) make me look very peculiar and b) scare the cat again. I gather my wits and say, 'Why don't I put my phone torch on so you can see properly?'

'Good plan.' He's already reaching up towards the cat, who's shrinking back as much as a cat that's stuck in a cricket helmet can. I can't help but notice the breadth of the man's shoulders, and almost shiver at the tenderness with which he extracts the cat-filled helmet from the other junk on the shelf, speaking gently to the little thing as he does so. As he lifts the helmet down, the cat wriggles but it's still stuck inside it. The man – I can't believe I still don't know his name; I feel like we've lived an actual experience together now – holds the helmet while I carefully reach in and try to dislodge the cat. It's tricky and I'm scared that it's injured or that I'm going to hurt it, but suddenly, as I reach a hand round the silky fur and delicate bones of its back and bottom, it's free.

It's clearly uninjured, and it isn't waiting around; it leaps out of my hands and sprints for the door.

As it leaves, it knocks the door, which swings closed with a clunking sound, like a lock clicking into place.

We both spend a good couple of seconds staring at the closed door by the light of my phone torch before moving towards it. I'm in front and get there first, in three steps. There's no handle on the inside, so I give it a push. And a harder push. Nothing. No give.

'Shall I?' the man asks. I nod.

I squeeze to the side as he gives the door a couple of pushes of his own.

'Okay,' he says. 'I think it's time for a serious shoulder shove now.' He limbers up a bit and I try not to snigger, because it's rare to see a real door-shouldering and the whole thing seems very silly, and then he gives the door an almighty ramming. 'Ow.' He rubs his shoulder. 'The door hasn't moved at *all*.'

We both stand and look at it for a moment, and then at each other.

I speak first. 'I think we might be locked in.'

'Yes.' He pauses and then sticks his hand out. 'I'm Ben Jones.'

I take the hand and shake it. 'Liv Murphy.'

It's odd that discovering we're locked in has turned us all business-meeting-style formal.

'Good to meet you.'

'Likewise.'

'Although maybe it would have been better under different circumstances,' Ben says.

'No, this is *lovely*,' I say. Ben laughs – which makes me smile – and then I say, 'I'm thinking we should phone for help.' I lift my phone from the top of the pile of cones I'd propped it on to give us a steady light while we tried to open the door. 'Shit. I have no reception. Do you?'

'Didn't bring my phone.'

'You didn't bring your phone?' I'm stunned. Who goes anywhere without their phone?

'Maybe we can get a signal somewhere else.' He picks my phone up and starts moving around the hut with it while I admire his solid thighs and capable-looking forearms.

Five minutes later I'm still enjoying watching him but he's looking quite frustrated because there's apparently no signal anywhere.

He wipes a bead of sweat from his forehead and says, 'Okay, using your phone doesn't seem to be an option.'

'Maybe we should shout for help? There are loads of people down by the buses and the recycling.'

'True. On the count of three?'

I nod and he counts.

Our first yell isn't that loud; we're both a bit too inhibited about it.

Ben shakes his head. 'That was pathetic. We need to give it some welly.'

'Okay. I apologise in advance if I split your ear drums.'

'Apology accepted. One, two, three.'

And we yell. And we are loud.

I'm closer to the door. I put my ear to it, expecting to hear sounds of people coming to our rescue, and... nothing.

Still nothing. Hmm.

'What about...?' I'm wracking my brain but not getting a lot of inspiration. 'Maybe the owner of the hut will be along soon.'

'Yeah, it's definitely well-cared-for and well-tended. The owner probably comes and sits in here with a newspaper and a cigar every evening to watch the traffic go by.' Ben accompanies his sarcasm with a big arm gesture at the total tip surrounding us.

'You never know. They might decide that this evening's perfect for a spring clean.'

Ben nods, his face very serious. 'You're right. It's a sunny Friday evening in July and you don't think to yourself that you'd like to go to the pub or sit outside or just go for a walk, you think aha, now's the time to sort out all the broken sports kit in the bus terminus hut.' He looks around using the light of my phone torch. 'Guessing it's used by a cricket club.'

'And maybe some fly tippers too.' I point at some big boxes in the corner.

'Wow.' Ben's eyes open wide. 'Grim.'

I bask in the mutual smile we share, before remembering that we should be focusing on the situation we're in. 'The door was open, though. Hopefully the person who left it open will come along soon.'

'Hopefully,' Ben says, although he isn't looking hopeful.

And then we just sit down on some boxes and stare at each other for a bit. I feel like my mind's struggling to process the facts and it looks like Ben's is too.

'So how are we going to get out?' I ask.

Ben shrugs in a very un-reassuring way. 'Dunno.'

2

LIV

My mind still isn't working properly, as if it's a clockwork toy whose wind-up mechanism is being turned too slowly. I can't think of any sensible next steps. I can't even decide whether I think we're in a *really* bad situation, or only *quite* a bad one.

I just keep coming back to the thought that we can't be locked in a hut together with no obvious escape route. This kind of thing does not happen to people in London in the twenty-first century.

And that's when I wonder: maybe there's a reason that it's happened. Maybe Ben and I are meant to be. Maybe this is our meet cute. Maybe we'll be rescued very soon but not before we've discovered that we really like each other and we'll start a relationship and in sixty years' time we'll be telling our grandchildren about this.

'We have food.' Ben's been looking around while I've been practically planning our wedding (I'm thinking Cotswolds – I've always liked it there). He picks up a family-sized box of cereal bars and another one containing KitKats. 'At least we're not going to starve.'

I drag my mind back from pondering good honeymoon destinations to consider our current shed situation, and begin to look around too.

'There's water,' I say after a few seconds.

Ben follows my pointing finger with his eyes and then we both say, 'Eeew,' at the same time. There are six little bottles, the 330 ml size, and they've all been opened and partially drunk.

'So, no water,' I say.

'We'd really better hope we aren't locked in for so long that drinking those becomes our best option. It's *hot* in here.' Ben does a fanning motion with his hand.

'Yeah, I'm thinking let's shout again?'

Ben agrees that's a good plan. I count us down, we both produce mammoth yells and... again, nothing.

We share an oh-fuck-what-shall-we-do-now-I-don't-know moment and then I focus back on my phone. 'Oh my goodness. My phone's only on four per cent now. I should switch it off in case we need the torch later.'

The second the light is gone everything feels completely different. It's dark, properly pitch black. I can't even see Ben's outline, or the outline of anything at all.

Neither of us is speaking, and suddenly I'm terrified. What if I misjudged Ben like I've misjudged all attractive men from Ned Morgan in the sixth form to most recently Max in my office? The gorgeous, charming ones always turn out to be total arses. What if Ben got me in here on purpose? What if he's a murderer?

No. He is not a murderer. He could not possibly have engineered this. No one could be that clever. Also, I'm pretty sure he doesn't have a weapon on him. It can't be possible to conceal a gun or an axe when you're wearing a T-shirt, shorts and flip flops. A knife, though?

No. He is not going to kill me. Obviously.

I hope.

'Are you okay?' Ben's voice cuts through my panic and I gasp very over-loudly. 'I can hear your breathing. Is the dark getting to you? I'm definitely feeling that everything seems worse now.'

'It is a bit,' I admit.

'I'm sure our eyes will adjust soon. In the meantime, maybe we should have a cereal bar each? Otherwise you're definitely going to be hearing some seriously loud stomach-rumbling from this direction pretty soon.'

Now Ben mentions it, I'm a bit peckish too. I think of the Indian takeaway Frankie, Sulwe and I were planning for later and almost whimper with longing.

We switch the torch back on for a second and Ben reaches for the box of cereal bars. As he passes one to me my fingers brush his, for only the briefest of moments, but I still feel my breath catch. There's something incredibly intimate about sitting here in this tiny space together, especially once the torch is off again. It's as though all my senses are heightened, like my entire body's on full alert. I mean, maybe I'm just describing how anyone would feel being alone in the dark with someone they've only just met yet fancy the pants off, but it genuinely does feel kind of special.

We sit and munch away in the darkness. Chomping on cereal bars together makes the whole situation seem both less sinister, and less romantic, due to the chewing sounds. It's also quite weird eating without being able to see the food at all.

'When you think about it,' I say between mouthfuls, 'you don't really eat in the dark a lot.'

'No, you don't. Reminds me of a restaurant I read about recently where they blindfold you so you only experience the smell and taste.'

'I love that idea. I wonder if they tell you what you're eating. It has to be so strange otherwise. Like when people make cakes that look savoury like steak and chips or pizza.'

'Okay, now I really want steak and chips.' Ben sounds as though he's shunting around on the big box of junk he's sitting on. 'Mind if we switch the light on again for a second? Maybe there's some more food.'

'Pretty sure if there's any meat in here it'll be a maggot-ridden health hazard.' I shine the phone torch around.

'Very true, but imagine if there were some crisps or dried fruit.'

'Mmm, yes. I could really do with some smoky bacon Walkers right now.'

'Not salt and vinegar Pringles?'

'Yes!' I beam at Ben. 'Those are even better. All that gorgeous vinegary grease.'

'Exactly. One taste and it's like you're eating chips out of newspaper on the beach in Brighton.'

'Yes!' I'm beaming even more. I love a man who has excellent taste in crisps.

We both peer around the hut, as if we're going to be able to conjure the Pringles up.

'Wow,' I say after a few moments, awed. 'It truly is the hut that got forgotten in time. Some of this is *antique* junk.'

'I know. The newer stuff, like the cricket kit, must get used. The rest of it, though... no words.'

'What would you do with it if this hut were yours?' I ask, turning the phone off again.

'Well, first I'd fumigate it, obviously.'

'Obviously,' I agree.

'And then... I don't know. Call me un-forward-thinking but I haven't given a huge amount of thought to what I'd do with a hut in an open-air bus terminus. Maybe I'd turn it into a storage facility and rent lockers out to bus passengers. Or maybe set up a little shop selling stuff that people on the move need. Like bottles of water and portable phone chargers and umbrellas.'

I shake my head in the dark. 'Café.'

'Really? There are a *lot* of fumes and concrete out there, though.'

'Customers don't mind fumes. Think how many people are really happy to sit on the pavement of a busy road outside a restaurant right next to lots of traffic. And the fumes are mainly on the other side of the turning circle. And people sometimes have ages to wait for buses, or they get off and they're thirsty. We could do takeaway too. I know the hut looks shabby but there's a lot you could do with the interior if you painted the panelling and then you could put an awning outside and tables underneath. And actually this is a very scenic location if you sit on the grassy side of the hut, and there are no other cafés for literally miles, just a couple of pubs. And those pubs do very well.'

'You've almost convinced me to hunt down the owner of the hut and try and get a business loan.'

There's a hint of a laugh in Ben's voice. I smile. 'I think it could be an amazing opportunity.'

'So would you like to set up your own café? Or do you in fact already have your own café? Or work in one?' It seems as though Ben instinctively understands me and I feel my heart swell a little.

'I actually would like to set up a café or restaurant.'

Our conversation meanders through café ownership to our favourite holiday destinations and Ben's ambition to cycle round Europe (I've never been *that* keen on cycling but all of a sudden I'm imagining a fitter, Spandex-clad version of myself marvelling at his pert behind as we pedal in tandem). I almost forget about the fact I'm sitting in the dark on an uncomfortable box being poked in the bottom by some unidentified objects, possibly trapped for a very long time and about to miss my train to Paris tomorrow.

I'm enjoying our conversation so much that when there's a scuffle, definitely involving tiny feet, I only climb onto the top of the box I've been sitting on and scream, rather than having a full-blown mouse-related meltdown.

I say mouse... I bloody hope it's nothing *bigger* than a mouse.

'Seriously.' Ben's jumped to his feet too, and has reached out to hold my arm and is steadying me as I wobble. 'People should pack their junk better in case a woman with a mouse phobia gets locked in here and has to leap onto a box.' The sound of his voice is already making me feel better. 'I'm sure it's gone now.'

'Really?'

'Definitely. It will have escaped through a hole somewhere and will already be happily reunited with its little mouse friends far away on the heath.'

I practise some deep breathing and let myself believe him and decide to clamber back down to the floor. Ben's still holding me and now that my mouse terror has receded, I'm incredibly aware that his hand is cupping my elbow and we're standing very close together.

I swallow hard. If I put my other hand out, I could touch his chest. I can feel my own heaving far more than it ought to be.

We're both completely stationary (apart from my galloping heart and the chest heaving). I sense his breathing quickening and him moving slightly closer to me, and I moisten my lips. Are we going to...? Should we...? Ben's still clasping my elbow and shoots of sensation are spreading through my arm to the rest of my body from his touch.

'I...' I say, suddenly feeling like the moment's too much, too charged.

'Of course.' Ben moves away from me sharply – I can't see in the dark what he's done but I feel that he's pretty much leapt backwards – and catches something with his leg, I think, and staggers. There's a lot of clattering. I reach out, fast, to help him, and my hand encounters some part of him – I'm not sure what, but it feels, frankly, *weird*, quite hard but not boney – and he says, 'Eurmph. That's my eye.'

Oh. Not really the kind of physical contact I was imagining only a couple of minutes ago. I can still sense where he was touching me on the elbow. Who knew that an elbow could be such a centre of erotic feeling? And why, really why, am I thinking about anything erotic when I've just poked him in the eye?

'Sorry, sorry, sorry,' I say.

'Not at all.'

'I'll put the light on and we can sort ourselves out.'

Where's my phone though? I sit down, gingerly, and begin to feel around. I encounter what must be Ben's bare, flip-flopped foot; he grunts and I squeak.

This is not good. I definitely need to calm down. Lust and panic are not good emotions to experience in a hut. I withdraw both my hands and count to ten.

'You okay?' From the sounds he's just made and from where his voice is coming from, I think he must be sitting down again.

'Yes, yes I am,' I say. I think I'm trying to convince myself. I remember why I was feeling around with my hands. 'I still don't know where my phone is, though.'

'It was between us, wasn't it? So hopefully it's still there. I'll reach down.' It sounds as though he's rummaging on the floor between our boxes. I tense. What if he touches my leg?

There's no touch.

'Got it,' he says, in a triumphant tone. To be fair, we haven't had a lot of wins since we got trapped in here.

'Cool,' I say. It isn't a *big* win, given the lack of reception and the fact that it's about to die. But it's still good to have found it.

We lapse into silence. I don't know what Ben's thinking about. I do know what I'm thinking about: him, and his proximity, and the fact that he touched my arm, and I poked him in the eye and touched his foot. I'm pretty sure he has very nice feet.

'So what would you have been doing otherwise this evening?' Ben asks after a while. I smile in the dark. Hopefully he's asking that because he wants to check that I don't have a partner.

'Well. Long story.'

'Hang on, let me check my watch. Nope, I'm good. I think I can spare a few hours out of the night to hear this.'

'Ha.' I pause, not sure where to begin. I haven't actually mentioned anything personal yet. I mean, yes personal in the sense that Ben now knows my favourite foods (snacks, fruit, veg, starter, main course *and* dessert), my favourite music, my favourite author, my favourite holiday destinations, and I know all of his too, plus we've both told some anecdotes; we haven't really talked about our actual *lives* though.

'Basically.' I decide to dive straight in with the biggie. Right now I feel as though we almost have an unspoken understanding that maybe this could be the start of something – I mean, you just don't normally talk this much and in this way to a complete stranger if it isn't going anywhere, even on a train (I do end up talking to people a lot on long train journeys) – and I feel weirdly as though I've been a bit dishonest in not mentioning that I'm not actually going to be around in London for the foreseeable. 'I was going to be finishing packing up the last few bits of my stuff and having takeaway with my sister and best friend because I'm moving to Paris tomorrow.'

There's silence for a few seconds and then Ben, suddenly sounding sort of careful, and without the laugh that's been hovering on the edge of his voice the whole time we've been in here, says, 'Oh, wow, that's exciting. For… long?'

'It's a secondment from my job.' Secondment feels like a euphemism because I had no choice but to go. I feel a small stress headache starting just at the thought, and hurry some more words out to try to push the stress away. 'It's for two years. It's obviously very exciting. Paris is such an amazing city. And not too far. I mean, it's quicker to get to than Scotland, and Cornwall, for example. I'll be back home a lot.' Not to sound too desperate to go down the we-could-definitely-date-because-Paris-is-*close* road or anything.

'Wow.' Ben sounds almost disappointed, which I can't help feeling pleased about, because I'm disappointed too. 'Do you speak French?'

'Nope. I mean, a bit. I did do it at A-level, but that's eight years ago now and I haven't really spoken any since. I think I'll be sorted if anyone asks me directions to the supermarket – but only if it's opposite the cinema – and I can definitely buy croissants and ask how much a single train ticket to La Rochelle is, but I'm going to be a bit buggered if I need to have any actual conversation. Which is cool. I'm looking forward to learning a lot more French.'

I am. I'm also genuinely looking forward to getting to know Paris properly and meeting new people. It's just that it feels huge leaving London, and, stupidly, even huger now I've met Ben.

'And what made you decide to move to France?' Ben clearly has no idea what a loaded question he's asked.

'Um.' I haven't told anyone other than Frankie and Sulwe about it. It's humiliating and embarrassing and also I'm not sure I've yet totally reached the stage where I can talk about it without crying from anger at the sheer horribleness and incredible injustice of it. I haven't even told my mum, although that's been more to spare her from any more distress after losing my dad at the beginning of the year than because I couldn't talk to her about it. But suddenly I want to tell Ben.

Maybe it's the fact that, even though it feels like we've known each other for a lot longer than just one evening, I do know that he's a complete stranger and sometimes it's easier to tell strangers stuff. Or maybe it's the fact that I just instinctively like him so much. Or maybe it's the darkness, like when as a teenager it's easier to talk to your parents about awkward stuff when you're sitting in the car together both staring straight ahead instead of looking at each other. I don't know. But I do begin to tell him.

'I had a difficult incident at work. Someone more senior than me asked me out. We went on one date, during which I discovered that he wasn't as nice as I'd thought he was, so I did the whole "I've had a lovely time, thank you so much, but I'm not sure if I'm ready for a relationship" thing.'

I stop talking, because I don't like it when my voice wavers with the anger that I would really like to have overcome by now.

'Normally I'd make a weak joke at this point but I'm pretty sure this isn't going anywhere great.' Ben's voice is grim.

It sounds like he's imagining truly terrible things, not just unacceptably bad things, and I rush to reassure him. 'Not great, but it could have been worse.'

Ben puts his hand out and touches my knee very briefly and there's just something so gorgeous about the gesture, like an expression of solidarity. I love the way he's waiting patiently for me to speak, or not, letting me choose.

But I feel now as though I ought to give him all the details, to stop his imagination running wild. I find that I actually want to tell him.

'I thought he was okay about the way we'd left things,' I continue, 'but the next week we had some work drinks and he, and several of our other colleagues, just kept on giving me more and more to drink and I'm not sure exactly what happened but I do know that they added quite a lot of neat vodka to the cocktails I had. So I was a bit drunk.'

I sense Ben tensing. 'God.' His voice sounds hollow. 'I'm so sorry.'

'It really wasn't as bad as it could have been,' I reassure him again, or perhaps I'm reassuring myself. 'I mean, it really wasn't good, but it could have been worse. Basically, as I was leaving the foyer, Max tried to kiss me and we had a bit of a struggle.'

'Fucker.' The quietness with which Ben says the word makes it even stronger somehow. I nod in the darkness. I know now that I'm going to give him full details. I *knew* that he wouldn't be one of them, but you do get those sexual predator apologists, like my boss in fact, the people who go down the whole 'boys will be boys; it was just a bit of fun; don't make such a mountain out of a molehill' route. Total arses who do not respect women.

'Yes,' I say. 'He didn't get to do whatever he might or might not have done next, because at that point a woman stepped out from behind these big stone pillars we have – it's quite a fancy atrium kind of foyer – and she started screaming. I discovered that she was his fiancée.'

'God,' Ben says as I pause for breath.

'Yep. I'd obviously had no idea that he had a partner or I wouldn't have gone on the one date we went on. Anyway. She punched me in the face.' I'm powering through the story now; it's made much easier by Ben's obvious sympathy and the way he waits for me to gather my thoughts and sum up what happened rather than just splurging unnecessary details. 'She was really going for it but luckily a security guard popped up from nowhere and pulled her off me. He then mopped up the blood and got me a cab.'

'And I assume Max was long gone by then?' Ben's voice is tight and hard.

'Of course. I went home in the cab and Frankie' – I've already told Ben lots about my sister (she crops up in a lot of my stories) so I don't need to explain who she is – 'took me to A&E the next morning. I was actually fine, no bones broken, just a black eye.'

'That's just awful. I'm so, so sorry.' Ben's voice sounds even tighter. I sense him doing something with his arms, maybe clenching his fists. 'I... Did you decide to move to Paris because of that? I truly hope that you *wanted* to make the move and didn't feel that you had to go.'

He's hit the nail very much on the head.

'Nope. I really did *not* want to go.' I can't believe I've finally admitted it aloud. I stop speaking, try to get myself back under control.

'Hey, please don't feel you have to tell me if you don't want to talk about it. I won't be at all offended. It's your story and if you want to tell me I'm here to listen and if you don't then please don't feel that you have to.' Ben's views on consent – extending to what I choose to talk about – are apparently very different from those of certain arseholes in my office.

'Thank you.' Against all the odds, I'm smiling a little, because in the middle of me telling my horrible – but sadly age-old and not unusual – story, Ben's reaffirming the belief I like to stick to, that most men are decent. My father was a lovely, kind, decent man. There are others. And honestly, now I'm going to have a wobbly voice again.

I take a couple of beats before saying, 'When I was back at work, I was called in to see my boss, and he tried to fire me because the fiancée made a complaint and they'd viewed the footage on CCTV. I insisted on watching the footage with them and you can clearly see that Max followed me and turned me round and tried to kiss me and I tried to push him away, but my boss wasn't having any of it.' I'm on a roll now. I can totally do this part. I'm just stating facts. 'Long story short, I threatened to sue for unfair dismissal and in the end we agreed that I'd take a secondment to their Paris office. And I'm still furious, with both of them, but also with myself for not standing up to them better. I shouldn't be going to Paris, Max should. Well, actually, I think he should have been fired, and the fiancée arrested for assault. But anyway, I couldn't carry on working for my boss or with Max after that, and I thought I should be pragmatic and accept the Paris offer, because there aren't many other jobs around at the moment.'

'That is... outrageous. I'm so sorry. This kind of thing should not still be happening in the twenty-first century. Well, ever, obviously. But I thought things had improved.'

'Yeah, apparently sexual equality hasn't really spread as far as you'd hope. But you know what? It's fine. I mean, it's shitty, but Paris will be an amazing experience, I'm sure.' I can't let myself become negative and dwell on the extreme injustice of the situation any longer. I need to accept that it's happened, leave it in the past, and embrace the opportunity.

Echoing my thoughts, Ben says, 'You're right. It's shit that it happened but I'm sure Paris will be fantastic.'

'Thank you,' I say. 'And thank you for listening. I'm a complete stranger and I just dumped a long story on you. I kind of want to apologise for that.'

'Really no need to.'

'Thank you,' I say again. 'Anyway.' I'm suddenly uncomfortable about how much I've been talking about the Max thing. 'You're right. This is a good opportunity for me to get something different on my CV and then maybe have the chance to change career path. My current job is not that exciting.'

During our strictly-light conversation, before Ben asked about my move to Paris, we didn't touch on our respective careers. I should ask about Ben's job.

'What do you do?' Ben asks before I get my question out.

'I work in finance for a sanitary product and toilet paper company. Which is almost exactly as fascinating as it sounds.'

There's a long pause and then Ben says, his voice a bit odd, I'm not sure why, 'And you'd rather set up a café?'

'Yes. Or work in recipe development. Or both. Anyway. That's a lot about me. What about you?' There's so much I'd love to find out about him. 'First off, what would you have been doing this evening if you hadn't had the good fortune to get trapped in this dream of a hut?'

There's a very long pause, and then Ben says, 'I was just planning a quiet evening in with my girlfriend.'

3

LIV

I jerk backwards in the dark like I've just been physically slapped by his words.

Girlfriend? *Girlfriend*?

Oh my *God*. I was *convinced* he was flirting with me. I was definitely flirting with him and I really thought it was mutual.

He definitely had the air of a man who was chatting me up, even before we made it into the hut. I think. I mean, he didn't *have* to catch up with me and ask me which way I was going. And he's been so friendly, and nice, and *surely* quite flirty while we've been in here.

If he *was* flirting with me, he's an arse. He's just been very sympathetic in a seemingly very authentic way about what a fuckhead Max was. And part of Max's fuckheadedness was going out with me while he had a fiancée. Chatting someone up in a bus terminus and then being very friendly with them in a hut when in fact you have a girlfriend is fairly fuck-heady too.

Ben seems really nice, though. I think I must have completely misread things and imagined flirting where there was none. God. I really hope he just thinks I'm a very friendly person and has no idea I was convinced that fate brought us together and that I was practically planning what we'd name our children.

I've been silent for far too long. I need to react in a normal way and ignore the fact that my face is aching from the effort of not allowing a tear to leak out (I am so pathetic).

'Will she not be wondering where you are?' I ask, pleased that my voice sounds so steady. 'Did you mention that you were planning to come here?'

'I didn't tell her I was coming. She might wonder, but probably not for a while.' His voice sounds quite weird and raspy. 'We left it quite loose for this evening.'

'Won't she text you to check where you are, though? And maybe look for you when you don't reply?'

Now that I know that Ben is clearly not The One, I'm exceptionally keen to get out of here as soon as possible.

There's another pause and then he says, 'I'm not a big texter.'

Right.

Great, then.

Neither of us says anything for a while and then there's a noise outside.

'Oh my goodness.' I stand up and start yelling, 'Help! In the hut!'

Ben starts shouting too.

And then someone bangs on the door. I think, anyway.

'Was that like when a dehydrated person sees a mirage in the desert or was that the sound of an actual rescuer?' I say.

'Rescuer,' he confirms.

'It's me,' shouts Sulwe from the other side of the door.

'Sulwe!' I scream. 'We're locked in.'

She rattles the door a bit. 'Yes, you are. There's no key. Hang on. I'm calling for help.'

'Is she calling 999, do you think?' Ben asks.

'Don't know.' I really don't care who she calls as long as she gets us out of here quickly.

Now that help's on its way, I'm allowing myself to admit that I'm nearly as desperate for the loo as I am to get away from Ben. If help hadn't arrived I think I'd have had to have considered weeing in a bottle, which I don't think would be easy, even in bright light, let alone darkness, and would clearly not be something I would want to do in front of anyone, including Ben.

'Help's on its way,' Sulwe hollers from outside.

'Thank you so much. Who did you call?'

'My nephew asked me for a key picking kit for his birthday last month, so I called my brother. He's driving over from Clapham with it now. His wife says that she'd be really happy for us to keep the kit because he's already trashed three locks in their house.' She's still shouting, like there's a ten-foot wall between us rather than just a door.

'I think we can hear you even if you don't shout,' Ben tells Sulwe at normal volume.

'Okay, great,' she replies at less of a yell. 'Who am I speaking to?'

'I'm Ben.'

'And how do you know Liv, Ben?'

'We don't know each other,' I say, fast, because I don't want to hear whatever Ben's answer might be. It's okay for me to say we don't know each other but for some reason I don't want to hear him confirm it. I feel like I've run the gamut of a lot of emotions in this hut and I don't want that to be dismissed by someone else as nothing. Even though it really was nothing.

I fill Sulwe in on the saving-cat-got-trapped-in-shed facts and then she fills me in on the where's-Liv-worried-something-terrible's-happened-she-did-mention-taking-some-clothes-to-be-recycled thought process she'd been through on her way to finding us. Apparently it's now quarter past ten and they've been searching for me since half past eight. How is it only quarter past ten? I'd have guessed at least midnight.

'Frankie's waiting at your flat,' she tells me. 'She was searching all the Roehampton clothes banks. We didn't know which one you'd have gone to. Oh look. Yaaaaay. He's here.'

And within a couple of minutes, Sulwe's brother, Yemi, has demonstrated that the lock picking kit does indeed work, thank goodness, and that it does indeed trash the lock.

And Ben and I emerge from the shed.

I don't really want to look at him because I just want to forget that this evening ever happened. I'm still not sure whether I should be extremely embarrassed or extremely pissed off with Ben but I do know that I really did not enjoy the girlfriend revelation. I sneak a glance at him and, yes, he's gorgeous. Properly, properly gorgeous. And properly, properly taken.

He gives me a (gut-punchingly attractive) half smile as I say, 'Bye, then.'

So weird. I feel like this is some kind of gigantic leave-taking. Like in the space of what I now know was two and three-quarter hours we ran through an entire relationship from mutual attraction to getting together to facing the world together to splitting up. All in my head of course and all one-sided. I am ridiculous.

'Bye. Good luck in Paris,' says Ben, just as Sulwe says really loudly in my ear, 'He is *hot*. You *really* lucked out there.'

I ignore Sulwe and say, 'Thank you!' to Ben. I sound far too exclamatory and fake-chirpy. I need to leave. 'Bye.' I turn and start walking across the terminus with Sulwe towards where my car's parked.

4

BEN

Three months later – October 2014

Red traffic light. I slow to a crawl and then stop in the queue. God, that was a long day. I roll my shoulders and then my neck.

Out of the corner of my eye I catch movement in the car just in front of me to my left. I focus on the woman in the driving seat and find myself smiling. She's seat-dancing, really going for it: shoulders and arms in exaggerated rhythmic movements, hands tapping her wheel, head rocking. I can sense even from behind that she must be smiling, singing along. It's contagious and I begin to move in time with the music myself. I then realise that she must be listening to the same song on the same radio station as me.

My smile widens and I look more closely at her. There's something familiar about the curve of her neck and shoulder in her bright green top, and the way she has her curly dark brown hair piled up high on her head.

It's Liv. The girl from the hut.

I shake my head. I'm probably imagining it. I've thought way more about her since then than has been good for my sanity. Have I now got to the stage where my mind starts painting her image onto other women?

That was a bad evening. To feel that level of connection with someone and to begin to imagine that – maybe – it could be the start of something... and then to realise that there could never be anything between us.

I *could* beep. She'd look round. I could wave. I could scribble my number on a piece of paper and hold it up for her. Or I could just scribble, "Fancy a drink? Meet me round the corner?" Or just smile and gesticulate. Roll my window down and shout.

But I know I can't do any of that.

The traffic lights change and Liv, swaying now to the ballad that's just started to play, rolls forward and turns left.

I point my car straight ahead, and continue in the opposite direction.

5

LIV

Two months later – December 2014

'How long will you be?'

This has to be literally the tenth time in twenty minutes that Frankie's asked me the same question, even though I'm almost ready and she is not. I'm fascinated: she's never this jittery.

'What about this one?' She twirls for me, in what's the fourth – or fifth? I can't remember – top she's tried on this evening, a very nice ivory-coloured silky shirt, very classic.

'I really like that one,' I tell her.

She actually looks good – stunning – in everything. We're twins but we aren't identical. When we first meet people, they really do struggle to believe we're even sisters. She got our father's height and green eyes, and our mother's sleek, straight but thick, glossy black hair, which she has in the most amazing swishy long bob. I got our mother's height (she's short) and dark brown eyes and our father's mad curls; the one good thing about my hair is that it's never lacking in volume, sometimes insane amounts.

She opens her mouth but I cut her off before she can ask again how long I'm going to be. 'And I'll be completely ready a lot faster if you don't keep asking me.'

I accompany my grumble with a smile because it's actually very cute how much she cares about this evening. It's also very surprising, barely credible in fact.

I'm meeting Frankie's latest girlfriend, Nella. Frankie averages about six 'serious' relationships a year, and in the past twelve months, off the top of my head, I can think of at least three other people that she's dated *and* introduced me to. There was a very Ken (as in Barbie)-like man who worked in IT. I think his name was Joe. There was a lovely musician called Davide, who I really liked. There was a woman called Sarah who always dressed in grey and brown (it looked better than it sounds), wore scarlet lipstick, worked in fashion and would have seemed like pure evil if she hadn't had this very endearing quality of taking the piss out of herself (along with everyone else) the whole time.

Frankie's always been the epitome of insouciance on the occasions when she's introduced me to her new partners. But right now she's the epitome of bricking herself.

I give up on trying to brush my hair into any semblance of sophistication and bunch it up with a scrunchie on top of my head.

'Okay, so will you be long?' She gives the blouse a little tug. 'Are you *sure* this top looks okay?'

'No, and definitely yes.' I reach for her and give her an air-hug so that I don't crease the immaculate ivory top. 'You look gorgeous and I'm looking forward to meeting Nella. This evening is going to be amazing.'

Frankie's face softens into a smile. 'It *is* going to be amazing. I know I'm being a little bit antsy but I just want you and her to hit it off.' The glow in her eyes as she speaks is new to me: I've never before seen her look so... in love. Right now, Frankie's reminding me of the way Mum used to be when Dad was due home after he'd been away a while for work (he worked on oil rigs for most of our childhood and would be gone for weeks at a time). As in, totally besotted, eyes sparkling, lips curling up at the sides whenever the person's name is mentioned.

I feel a twinge of something that I can't decipher.

It definitely isn't envy. I only want good things for Frankie; I don't think there's anything in the entire universe I'd begrudge for her or be envious of in her. Even the way she can get caught in very heavy rain without looking shit afterwards, and her amazing ability to eat and drink whatever she likes, get no sleep, do no exercise and still look and function exactly the same (perfect) day in day out.

I think hard about the twinge and decide that it's discomfort. Double discomfort. One, because Xavier, the man I've dated a few times in Paris, does not make me feel very jittery, certainly not like this. He makes me feel... I don't know. Pleasant, maybe. And the second part of my discomfort is the realisation that the only time in my life so far I've experienced jitters that can compare to those Frankie is displaying right now was in that hut with Ben, right before I found out he had a girlfriend.

It has been five months since I moved to Paris and I still catch myself thinking about him. I shouldn't.

'Will you be long?' I ask, picking up my bag, feeling smug that I'm turning the are-you-ready tables on her.

'I'm ready.' She does a final mirror-pout before linking her arm through mine as we go out of her front door. I lean into her for a minute as we turn along the road. It's good to be home for the weekend. After some serious initial homesickness, I've settled quite well in Paris; I've met some very nice people who are becoming proper friends and I'm loving the food and the culture. It is starting to feel a bit like home to me, but when I'm *home* home, seeing my family and old friends, I know that nowhere but here, where nearly all my favourite people are, could ever be actual home.

Fifteen minutes later we're outside the pub where we're meeting Nella. As we walk towards the double-doored entrance, several men emerge. And for a moment, obviously because I was thinking about him a few minutes ago, when we were getting changed, and then when we walked past the bus terminus on our way up here, I imagine that I hear Ben's voice amongst the group. I shake my head. This is ridiculous. It's happened to me before when I've been back in London for a weekend; I often imagine that I've caught a glimpse of him in the distance. I know that we totally *might* bump into each other because he lives near here (or he did when we got stuck in the hut), but the chances are slim.

I tell myself of course it won't be Ben, I'm just being silly.

The men come closer and fuckity fuck fuck fuck, one of them *is* Ben. I recognise him instantly. My heart's hammering as if it wants to break through my ribs and my breath's catching.

No. It does not matter if I see him. We are nothing to each other. Just two people who got trapped together once in a very silly incident.

I'm just going to keep my gaze slightly averted and be very engrossed in Frankie's remarkably interesting conversation on... What *is* she talking about? I can't remember at all. Doesn't matter. I will just smile and laugh and walk past Ben, very nothing-to-see-here.

'What is it?' says Frankie, as we're literally about one metre away from the men, their little group of four and the two of us both slightly squeezing to each side so that we don't get too close to each other as we pass on the way in. She's always had an unerring instinct for asking me loud, embarrassing questions at awkward times, from a Christmas-tree-chocolate theft incident when we were five, through the moment when she mentioned right in front of our old GCSE Chemistry teacher that I'd snogged his son at a party, to right now.

'Nothing!' My voice is far too jolly.

Frankie opens her mouth and I know that she's about to say something about how I'm being odd, which I really do not want her to do, because Ben *will* hear, as he's still only a few feet away. I open my own mouth to rush in with an inane question to distract her when – bugger – Ben says, 'Liv!'

The sound of my name on his lips makes me feel... simultaneously hairs-on-end alert and just pissed off that his voice has any effect on me.

'Hi Ben.' I do not want to talk to him because I don't like that I find him so attractive when I know he has a girlfriend. And what is there to say? *I* really *liked you during that couple of hours we spent together... until I discovered that you were taken*.

So I do a nice-to-see-you-and-goodbye smile and barrel forward, closing in on Frankie so I can quickly make it into the safety of the pub's interior. And then, at the exact moment that I get within touching distance of the double doors, Ben says, in his just-this-side-of-uncomfortably-deep voice, 'How's Paris?' And I get this definite impression that he *wants* to talk to me, like before, in the shed.

Frankie's head pops round. Which is weird, because now she's staring straight into my face, from only about six inches away, because I did not turn round. She stares harder at me and I stare back and then she nods over my shoulder, like she thinks I didn't hear the question. I carry on with the staring for a good couple of seconds, while she raises her perfectly plucked eyebrows, and then I decide that the best thing to do would be to have a very short conversation with Ben.

I turn towards him and say, 'It's great, thanks.' I risk a little look directly at him, and almost shiver, because yep, still gorgeous. Gorgeous in a winter way now, all muffled up in a puffa jacket and scarf, his hair still nicely ruffled. I do not want to find him attractive.

'See you inside,' Frankie says into my ear and out of the corner of my eye I see her disappear into the pub.

'Bye then.' I give Ben a wide but totally fake smile and reach out for the door handle.

'So are you happy there?' he persists. 'Or did you decide to come back?'

'Yep, all good. I'm loving it.' I gave him an even wider fake smile. 'Lovely to bump into you. Hope all's good with you too. I need to catch up with my sister. Have a good evening.' And I march myself through the doors and into the pub.

The wall of heat that meets me from the pub's ferocious central heating and fire has me tugging my scarf from round my neck and – I'm pretty sure – turning tomato-coloured. I can't help feeling pleased that Ben remembered about Paris, and a small part of me wants to sprint back outside and engage him in conversation and find out how he is. But I know I shouldn't. He has a girlfriend, so we could never be friends, not when he makes me feel like this.

A piercing sound penetrates my thoughts and I look round. It turns out that Frankie's screeching my name and windmilling both arms as if she's doing her best to get an entire stadium going on a Mexican wave.

'Who was that?' she says as I put my scarf down and sit on the chair opposite her. 'He was *gorgeous*. And the *tension* between you. How have I never met him?'

Unlike Frankie, I don't have dozens and dozens of exes, and she's met everyone I've ever been out with for more than a few dates (even Xavier one of the weekends she came over to visit me in Paris). She hasn't met any of my first-date disasters, though, like Max at work, or Ben. Whoops, no, the hut evening was not a date. I'm losing my mind.

'Seriously, who?' she repeats. 'I can't believe I haven't met him before.'

'Um.' I didn't tell anyone, not even Frankie and Sulwe, the story about the flirting followed by the girlfriend revelation, because it just made me feel kind of stupid and embarrassed; and coming hard on the heels of the Max thing I didn't need to talk any more about myself. I really don't like holding things back from Frankie, though. I mean, I never do. And right now she's staring at me, clearly perplexed by my silence.

'He's the man I got locked in the hut with.' I pull the wine list from behind a little vase containing a twiggy thing and some holly and begin to look very carefully through the four different white by-the-glass options there are.

'Oh. You didn't tell me he was *hot*.'

'Ha. No. Is he?' I'm trying to be nonchalant but by the incredulous look on Frankie's face I don't think I'm being very convincing.

And then her eyes light up and her mouth curves into a big smile aimed over my shoulder. I turn, and see a medium height, medium build, mid-brown-haired, medium kind of everything woman walking towards us. She has to be Nella, going by the way Frankie's looking her, but I would never have picked her out as Frankie's type; every single partner she's ever dated has had film star looks. And Nella doesn't look like a film star, she just looks *nice* (so in my book way better than most film stars).

'You must be Liv,' Nella greets me in the most gorgeous Irish accent. And then her face is transformed by a full-on Julia Roberts-style smile. Already I'm catching a glimpse of what Frankie sees in her; she's immediately likeable.

Two hours later, the three of us have barely stopped talking, and I can almost imagine not minding too much having to share my twin with someone if they become serious. Nella truly is lovely.

On the way home, when Frankie suggests stopping at the kebab hut that she says has just sprung up at the bus terminus and is doing a roaring trade, I'm very annoyed. That was *my* business idea, and they've messed it up because, according to Frankie, they're only open in the evenings, which is insane because surely more passengers travel by day. Also, it's *the* hut. I smile and agree to go for a kebab, though, determined not to let the Ben thing affect my life at *all* any more.

* * *

I'm stuck at home for a couple of days to get over the food poisoning the kebab gives me (yep, it seems like that hut is my actual nemesis). Once I'm back out and about for the Christmas period, I have further sightings of Ben and I begin to wonder whether fate is trying to tell me something I don't understand.

On 23 December I glimpse what I'm sure is the back of his head across a sea of shoppers disappearing out of the doors at the opposite end of the Sainsbury's just off Putney High Street. I only realise that my grip on the bag of Brussels sprouts I was holding has slackened when I hear an elderly lady next to me ask (for apparently a third time) if I'm alright, and look down to discover that the bag has split and the sprouts are rolling around all over the place.

I ignore a store assistant hollering a health and safety warning that only 'fully trained personnel' can clear the sprouts up, crouching down and (according to him) taking my actual life in my hands as I begin to gather them up. I can't go home without them (Mum loves sprouts and she's coming to Frankie's flat for an early Christmas dinner this evening), and this was the last bag, and also it's an excuse to hide from probable-Ben. And then, obviously, I can't help myself trying to peek out of the front window of the store to check whether it *was* him.

I can't see him any more but I'm pretty sure it was.

I walk home with my shop-floor-germ-dusted sprouts, trying hard not to look out for Ben amongst the people dotting the pavement ahead of me. I really hope I'm going to reach a stage where I can carry on normal life when I'm home in London without constantly thinking about bloody Ben. It's absolutely ridiculous. Yes, he's attractive, but he has a girlfriend and, also, I remind myself, I'm kind of seeing Xavier. Ben is not for me.

Mum arrives for dinner on the dot of seven – she's always extremely punctual – carrying the most ginormous Christmas cake (homemade), a chocolate log (homemade), a *lot* of mince pies (homemade) and a red-leafed bougainvillea (grown by her from a cutting).

'Hello, my darlings.' She pulls us both into a big hug and sniffs loudly but when she finally lets us go her eyes are dry and she's even managed a big smile. She's only fifty-four, far, far too young to be a widow, but she's doing brilliantly. Seemingly, anyway. I'm pretty sure she's putting on a brave face for us, and I'm also sure that she avoids us when things get too much for her because she doesn't want to dump her emotions on us. And right back at her, I don't want to make *her* feel miserable in any way, so I've been keeping my problems to myself since Dad died at the beginning of the year – at the age of fifty-seven, from a very sudden heart attack shovelling snow. Incredibly shocking (to the extent that the first thing Mum said about it was, 'It wasn't even supposed to fucking snow this weekend,' before she burst into the most hideous screaming wail I've ever heard) and not helped when about seventy-five per cent of all the well-meaning people we've spoken to have said, 'Best way for him to go.' So, no, I haven't been telling her anything negative. No word about the whole Max-nightmare-nearly-fired-from-job being the reason for my Paris move, for example.

To hear me talk now to Mum I am the most Pollyanna girl you could meet.

Everything's wonderful!

I was so lucky to get selected for the Paris opportunity!

I love working in finance!

'That's a lot of pudding for the three of us.' Frankie gives Mum one final squeeze and then takes the cake, log and mince pies from her, and I rescue the bougainvillea just before she accidentally tips some soil out of its pot.

'You'll need pudding for Christmas Day.' Mum knows that Frankie can't cook and that I can – I've heard her boasting to her friends about my cooking – but she still doesn't believe I can cook for actual important events like Christmas.

I look at her and catch a slight chin wobble, and realise that she's having second thoughts about her holiday plans.

Mum's two sisters asked her a couple of months ago if she'd like to go on a trip to Dublin, where their parents hailed from, and have a fancy Christmas lunch in a posh hotel there. She put up a token fight about how could they all leave their families to fend for themselves over the festive period, and they pointed out that of the nine children they have between them, the youngest is our cousin Luce, who's only two years younger than us and is a fully qualified teacher who's capable of keeping twenty-eight seven-year-olds under control just with this weird follow-my-clapping-rhythm thing that she does. Plus, they made the point that both their husbands would happily have a little break from a traditional Christmas to pursue their own interests (probably involving a pub in one case and golf in the other), and so she caved almost immediately.

I'm pretty sure that in theory she's absolutely horrified about being away from her daughters on Christmas Day but in practice she's sure that we would have spent the day feeling like there was a big empty space at the table if we just had a meal with the three of us and she'd struggle to hold it together. A very hard rock and an equally desperately hard place.

It does make me wonder if love is all it's cracked up to be. I mean, of course it is. Mum and Dad had the most amazing relationship. Yes, they had their little arguments (in particular, Dad used to lose stuff *all* the time) but that just made them stronger; there was always a lot of hand holding and, as we got older, spontaneous pub meals, just the two of them. But now Mum is a shadow of her former self. And she has a lot of life still to live.

I look into her eyes and feel the most enormous rush of love for her. For as long as I can remember, she's worn black eyeliner and mascara. She used to always wear bright red lipstick until we were about fifteen and then she switched to a nude one (partly due to fashion and partly due to age, she told us when Frankie asked why). She has fine lines at the corners of her eyes now and her face has filled out a little around the jaw but she's still beautiful. She's my mother and I want so much for her to be happy again.

I focus on the puddings so that I'm not overwhelmed by yet another rush of emotion.

'They look delicious,' I say, swallowing down the most enormous lump in my throat. 'And in return, I've only adulterated half the sprouts.' Mum likes her Christmas vegetables fancy except for her sprouts. Those she likes to have plain. I hate them, so every Christmas since I was about sixteen I've tried to sneak things like chopped chorizo and chestnuts into them. It's a constant tussle.

'No truer love for your mother than that.' She smiles at me and I smile back, my eyes really wide open, because if she isn't going to let any tears spill, neither am I.

And we don't, or at least not while we're together; we manage a truly lovely evening, just the three of us. I suspect tears are shed in each of our three separate bedrooms afterwards, but we don't mention them to each other. I presume that one day we'll be used to it being the three of us, no Dad, and eventually his absence won't make us want to cry that often any more, and right now that thought just makes me sob more.

* * *

Frankie and I haven't told Mum that we've discussed it and agreed that we can't bear to do Christmas with *two* big empty spaces at the table. But also we aren't up for doing one with friends this year, so we've booked ourselves into a restaurant on a boat on the river for lunch, and it's genuinely really nice.

When we get home, we stuff our over-full selves with some of Mum's mince pies and brandy cream while we watch the *Strictly* Christmas special followed by *Home Alone*, and around the time where Kevin's mum finally makes it onto a plane back towards New York, Frankie says, 'Hopefully the new year will be a new year for Mum. And us. Onwards and upwards.'

'Definitely,' I say, not trusting myself to say anything more than that. And then I despise myself because at that moment, when clearly we're thinking and talking about Mum and Dad, Ben pops into my head and I think that I need not to think about him ever again. Or if I do think about him, I need not to care.

* * *

I definitely catch sight of the side of his face on the twenty-seventh as I'm getting on a number ninety-three bus on Putney Hill and he's getting off at the same stop. And, actually, I'm pleased to say that it doesn't make me twitch. I manage not to hide, I manage not to even want to crane over my shoulder, I just pay at the card reader and sit down at the back of the bus.

As I watch the shops on Putney High Street go (slowly) by, I can't help having a little think about fate again, though, because, really, how many times do you bump into any given person normally?

6

LIV

Four days later, it's New Year's Eve and I'm sitting outside a pub on Putney Embankment next to the river with my friends. I love them all and I love that I'm here with them right now, and I'm going to miss them hugely when I go back to Paris the day after tomorrow, but, if I'm honest, I've been warmer. In fact, I'm absolutely bloody freezing. Why does anyone want to sit outside when it's literally six degrees and a bit foggy?

My friend Emmie plonks some pitchers of still-steaming mulled wine down in the middle of the table and we all start pouring.

'You know?' says Nella as we all chug our drinks. 'I saw an amazing fire inside when I popped to the loo.' She inches a bit in the direction of the building, as though trying to tempt us in. I adore her, I realise. The wine hasn't done as much for my chilled-to-the-bone feeling as I'd hoped and I'd kill to go inside. It would be *so* much nicer if there were heaters out here (obviously it's a good thing there aren't – the environment – but also right now it's a bad thing).

'Me too.' I shift around a bit, to try to plant a seed of physical movement in everyone's heads. It's difficult, because my bottom is now practically frozen to the seat. 'Should we...'

I don't finish the sentence because I really don't want to be the person who ruins everyone else's lovely open-air New Year's. I'd be happy for someone else to, though.

'It's quite crowded in there,' Frankie says.

'Crowding's good.' Sulwe half-stands up. 'It's New Year's Eve. We *should* be in the middle of a crowd. And we *should* be warmer.'

'We don't want to lose this table, though.' Frankie gestures around. I waver briefly; she does have a point.

'It isn't like losing this table on a beautiful summer's evening, though, is it?' Sulwe says. 'It's absolutely fucking freezing.'

'I think it'll be too hot inside.' Frankie's standing firm. I know the expression on her face. It says: 'I might look like butter wouldn't melt but no way on this earth will I be giving in on this.'

I look at my watch. It's only half eleven. Thirty more minutes of freezing before midnight strikes and then realistically quite a long time after that, because obviously, once the cheering, hugging and kissing and watching other people's fireworks are out of the way, everyone's going be saying the night's still young and where shall we go next. As long as it's somewhere warm, I don't care.

'I might just pop to the loo,' I say. Similar to the I'm-just-popping-to-the-loo thing when you're at a really boring work event and instead you sneak off home, but this time I'm just going to go inside and get myself as close to that fire as possible.

'Me too,' Sulwe and Nella chorus.

'This is amazing,' I breathe the second we step inside the pub, the lovely, hot, steamy, slightly-sticky-with-beer, slightly-acrid-with-sweat inside air hitting us.

'I know.' Sulwe takes off the beanie she's had covering her entire head and most of her face for the past hour. She'd done her hair in this gorgeous beaded style and had really not wanted to put the hat on, but eventually cold had won out over vanity.

I start to undo my coat as the three of us, as one, edge closer to the fire. I think we all have the same idea: if we're going to get warm, we might as well get *really* warm, to see us happily (or at least without getting borderline hypothermic) through the rest of the night outside.

'Space to push through,' Sulwe hisses in my ear, and gives me a bit of a shove from behind into a little gap between some men, just beyond whom is the fire.

I stumble slightly and next thing I've tripped and landed against a man's very solid chest. I frown. I don't know how I know, but I feel that this is a slightly familiar chest. I look up and, yes, of course, because fate bloody hates me, I see Ben's face.

'Hey,' he says, smiling at me as I take a step back.

I frown again. 'Hey?' How dare he *Hey* me like that so sexily.

Sulwe's right behind me. 'Hello. Where do I know you from?' she asks.

'You rescued us from that hut at the bus terminus,' he tells her.

'Oh *yes*.' I can tell from Sulwe's voice that she's beaming. And of course she is, because he's very charming and good looking.

'You don't have drinks.' Another large man, in a very bold snowman Christmas jumper, just to my right, is looking at us and shaking his head. I'm pretty sure he's seeing at least two of each of us. He leans over to a table between us and the fire, and sloshes red wine into three glasses (which I hope, but am not certain, are clean) and hands one each to Sulwe, Nella and me. He nods, all pleased with himself, and raises his own glass. 'Cheers.'

While Ben raises his glass too, Sulwe and Nella *Cheers* his friend back, so then, call me a sheep, I do too.

'This is Ned.' Ben indicates the large man with his head.

'Ben's best mate,' Ned tells us.

Sulwe introduces the three of us while I decide that freezing outside would be preferable to chatting to the man who's smiling at me with that gorgeous lopsided smile – the smile that, at the bus terminus, made my insides flollop around – but who is completely out of bounds.

'We should get back to the others?' I say.

'We just got wine and it's warm here,' Nella argues.

'Yep, we can't be rude,' Sulwe agrees. 'We have to finish the wine.'

I look at them both. I really don't want to make any kind of scene or put any kind of damper on the night. I just want to finish what's been a lovely evening with my sister, her partner and our best friends.

Fine. I'll drink the wine, I'll chat to Sulwe and Nella next to the fire here, and maybe Ben and Ned too, for as short a time as possible, and then we'll go back outside.

'It actually isn't bad wine.' Ned lifts his glass and downs it like it's water.

'I see you're a connoisseur,' Sulwe says sarcastically.

'Yes I am.' He smiles at her obliviously.

'So you mentioned that you're with friends?' Ben asks. I'm pretty sure he's changing the subject to rescue Ned from Sulwe. Which I can't help thinking is sweet.

There's a short pause during which it's clear that Sulwe and Nella are expecting me to speak, because I'm the one who knows him, and they don't want to talk over me.

'Yes, exactly,' I say when the silence becomes too long. 'We were outside but we got cold.'

'We're on a fake loo trip because we were freezing our tits off,' Sulwe elaborates.

'Then you need to come and stand right next to the fire.' Ned ushers us clumsily through the group so that we're standing with our backs only a couple of feet away from it.

He introduces Sulwe and Nella to a few other people and they all begin to chat, leaving me with Ben. It seems I have no option other than to talk to him.

Well, that or just stand mutely, looking everywhere but at him. I quickly decide that's the better choice and look around the pub in silence. There's one of those glass dome display things on the mantelpiece with a stuffed little bird inside, slightly grim. I switch my eyes from the dead bird to the wallpaper behind it. I quite like its geometric pattern. It's repetitive, though. And I am hot.

I realise I'm going to have to take my coat and scarf off otherwise I might actually faint. I look round for somewhere to put my wine down and Ben holds his hand out for it. Damn him for his instinctive helpfulness.

I look at his hand – his strong, capable-looking hand – and find myself biting my lip.

There's only so much cutting your nose off to spite your face that's sensible to do.

'Thank you.' I hand him my glass and shrug myself out of my coat and then unwind my scarf. I'm wearing a thinnish dressy red top with my jeans, because I'd assumed that we'd be sitting inside this evening, and oh my word it's good to have the coat off and be a normal temperature again.

I stuff my things at the end of the sofa behind me, where a few other people have stashed stuff too, and turn back to Ben to take my glass back.

He's looking at me with a half-smile, which, when I clock it, somehow makes the rest of the pub recede far into the background, so that it's just the two of us. I feel a flush spread over me, and take a large gulp of the wine. And another one. Ned's right actually; this *is* good wine. And drinking it is way less complicated than trying to work out what to say to Ben other than *Stop looking at me like that because I know you have a girlfriend*. So I take another gulp. I'm getting all warm inside now, as well as outside. Physically warm, not emotionally warm. Emotionally, I'm feeling fairly frosty.

Ben takes a long draft of his beer, and then says, 'So how's your French coming on?'

'Not bad, thank you.'

'Good news.' He takes another sip of his beer and I nod.

There's more silence and then I just think sod it. I hate the fact that his stupid smile has just had such an effect on me, and I want to remind him that you really shouldn't look flirty or interested or anything else when you have a partner, and then when I've reminded him of that I want to get even closer to the fire for a minute or two and then go back outside and spend the rest of the evening with my lovely friends – without him.

'Is your girlfriend here this evening?' I ask, looking him right in the eye.

Ben jerks slightly and the beer in his glass sloshes around. 'Um, no.'

'Oh. So what's she up to?' I ask in a very sugary-sweet voice.

Ben hesitates and then says, 'We... split up.'

'Oh, that's a shame,' I say. I wish I didn't want to smile now.

'Yeah, you know, one of those things.' He looks me straight back in the eye, and, honestly, I have no idea what his expression indicates. I do know that I find it very annoying. *Everything* about him is annoying me, from his gorgeously thick, slightly wavy hair all the way down his crookedly handsome face and his nicely solid body to his feet in his Vans. I'm glad he's wearing some very bog-standard shoes because it's literally impossible to find them more attractive than anyone else's. Although saying that, his feet do seem to be exactly the right size to match his body. Oh, for God's sake. I'm an idiot. I'm *such* an idiot because I'm pleased, I'm actually pleased that he split up with his girlfriend, which makes me a terrible person.

'Plenty more fish in the sea, of course,' I say. I feel like I'm trying to imply something, but I don't even know what. That he shouldn't have been so friendly with me when he was going out with her because, stupidly, that made me think he might be interested in me? That he's someone who behaves like he's always got his eye on the next woman? I don't know.

'Yeah, I'm good without any fish at the moment,' he says.

I tilt my head to one side. Is he trying to imply stuff too?

He also tilts his head a little, mirroring me, and I have an urge to get rid of my glass and put my hands on my hips and go all out aggressive-stance.

We stand there, heads tilted, glaring at each other, for a while, definitely approaching at least thirty seconds. Well, maybe not, but it feels like a long time. Too long.

I crack first. 'Great, then,' I say. 'Congratulations.'

He straightens his head and nods, not smiling. 'Thanks.'

I become aware of movement around us and realise that Sulwe and Nella have finished their wine and are on their way back outside. Thank goodness. I pick my coat and scarf up and see Ben's hand outstretched for my glass again.

I give it to him and say, 'Thank you,' and put my coat back on, staying out of arm's reach because I sense that if I get close enough he'll be chivalrous and try to help me into my coat and I don't think I want to feel his hands on any part of me, even through clothes.

I get myself all muffled up, look round for Sulwe and Nella who've been doing the same, and, oh no, a lot of their new friends, literally about half the pub, seem to be coming with us. So I'm guessing that's going to include Ben.

'We're all going outside,' Ned says unnecessarily.

I wiggle myself between a couple of people so that I walk out of the pub flanked by Sulwe and a man I don't know but who is definitely not Ben.

A few minutes later, everyone at our outside table has stood up and there've been a lot of shouted introductions and Ben and Ned's group has merged a little drunkenly with ours.

As people start roaring out the countdown, I realise that I'm standing next to Ben. Of course I bloody am. Fate's been having a chuckle at my expense since the moment the two of us met.

I love a New Year's resolution. I make an extra one as I stand here: next year, as of five seconds from now, I'm banishing fate and Ben from my life. I will *not* bump into him again. He might be single now but I live in Paris and he lives in London and if I misread signs from him last time I could misread them again and I do not want to get hurt.

'Five, four, three, two, one.'

For some reason, I'm still standing here, next to him and facing him. We both mouth, 'Hooray,' and 'Happy New Year,' and then, as everyone around us cheers some more, and lots of people kiss each other – a variety of kisses happening, from big, casual smackers, to serious, tender smooching – we just keep on standing there, both of us quite motionless.

I can hardly breathe. He looks like he's drinking my face in with his eyes, his gaze moving from mine, to my cheeks and then resting on my lips, which I'm fairly sure are parted in a semi-desperate *Kiss me now pleeease* position.

I swallow.

He swallows too.

'Leaf,' he says, gesturing at the trees behind us without looking away from me. His hand comes up and, very gently, he brushes something out of my hair. As he does so, the back of his hand just grazes my cheek. It's only the lightest of touches, but it feels as though he has seared me.

I can't move.

I don't know much about him but I know that he confuses me and that realistically I'd be better off avoiding him. I know that. But as we stand here, I feel that connection again, that feeling of being drawn together by something indefinable, like we were meant to be in some way. I mean, why do we keep bumping into each other?

Ben's lips part too, and he leans a little closer.

It's going to happen.

I feel my heart rate picking up. We're almost sharing the same breath already. We move even closer to each other.

And then someone leaping around behind me leaps *into* me and I tip forward and land against Ben's solid chest for a second time tonight. And as I do so I come to my senses.

I do not want to kiss this man. I have a strong sense that it will not end well for me if I do.

I don't look back up at him; I stare at the white North Face logo on his puffa jacket while I get my breathing back under control.

And then I take a very careful step backwards.

'So.' Ben's voice is a little croaky. 'Happy New Year.'

'Happy New Year.' My voice is way less croaky than his, I'm pleased to say. That's a good start to the new year. I risk a little glance at his face. He looks... shellshocked, I would say.

'Have you...' He pauses. He does a little throat clearing thing that I find unbearably cute. 'Have you made any resolutions? Are you a New Year's resolution maker?'

'Am I a resolution maker? I mean, that's an is-the-pope-Catholic question.' I stop talking because my mind's gone completely blank due to the way his Adam's apple's moving in his throat.

And, good grief, I have an almost-boyfriend. I have Xavier. I wouldn't bet a *huge* sum of money on him not being with another woman right now, because I don't feel like we're exclusive, but from my side, I'm not a woman who dates two people at once. It just isn't for me, even if nominally it *is* okay.

I know that nothing should or will happen between Ben and me, but I don't feel good about finding him this attractive when I'm semi-dating Xavier, and I make an immediate extra New Year's resolution: I need to stop seeing Xavier.

'So I also make resolutions.' Ben's clearly decided that he'd better carry the conversation, such as it is, by himself because I've lost any ability I once had to actually talk. 'The first one is no more binge-watching box sets late at night.'

'What's your latest thing?' I ask. 'No, let me guess.' I know I'm aiming never to bump into him again, but we're already talking, so this doesn't count. I'm never going to speak to him again *after* I stop speaking to him now. '*Peaky Blinders.*'

'I'm actually quite scared by your mind-reading abilities.' Ben pantomime-pats the pockets of his jacket and his jeans and I try not to think about what's inside under those pockets. 'Do I have a TV guide hanging out of my back pocket or something?'

'Nope. I'm just a genius.' I pause. 'Do you actually read physical TV guides?'

'Yep, I'm fully subscribed to the *Radio Times*. I have it delivered every week.' He pauses too. 'No. Not really. It was just for comedic effect.'

'And it was hilarious.' I twinkle at him.

Oh please. I'm flirting. And he's twinkling back now. Flirting too. Though I remind myself I thought that about him in the hut too, and I clearly got that seriously wrong.

'Okay, genius,' he says. 'What's my other resolution?'

'You only have one other?' I'm genuinely surprised. I had him down as more of a three-resolution man.

'Well, my other one is a kind of two-in-one.'

'Glad to hear it,' I say, relieved.

'So come on then, mind-reader, what is it?'

'You need to use your gym membership more and you need to go to bed earlier which kind of goes hand-in-hand with the too much binge-watching.'

'You *are* a mind-reading genius.'

'I know.' I twinkle some more. I suddenly wonder whether Ben does his late-night TV watching *with* anyone, specifically any women, and I stop my twinkling. 'You need to be specific and measurable,' I inform him, as if all people everywhere don't know that. 'Waffly resolutions are no good.'

'Good point. I will go to the gym at least twice a week and I will not allow myself to go to bed later than midnight more than once a week on a night in.'

'Well done.'

'So I'm thinking you have several resolutions,' he says. 'All very specific.'

'Of course.' They've all been shunted down two slots in the priority list now, below not bumping into Ben again and telling Xavier that I don't think we should see each other any more. 'Too many to cover right now but they do include going running a minimum of two miles, twice a week, starting tomorrow.'

'So—' Ben begins.

'We're all going back to Ned's,' Frankie interrupts. 'He lives in one of those flats up there.' She points across to the Kenilworth Court mansion block, a huge Victorian building hugging the corner of the Lower Richmond Road and Putney High Street, diagonally opposite the end of Putney Bridge.

We squint upwards and I imagine us all crowding into Ned's flat. It's likely it'll be cosy up there and I'm aware I'm going back to Paris tomorrow. For a moment I think about going to the flat and maybe getting cosy with Ben just for one night.

No. Bad idea.

I make a big show of pulling my phone out and checking the time and then I say, 'You all go ahead. I really need to go to bed now. It's an hour later than this in Paris.'

'Nooooo,' Sulwe says from behind Frankie's shoulder.

'Yes,' I say. It really is the right decision but it does feel very miserable to be a complete party-pooper. 'You go. Go. Now.'

I want them to go before I change my mind.

'Okay but you can't go home by yourself,' says Frankie, with the faintest of eye swivels in Ben's direction. 'It isn't safe.'

I narrow my eyes. 'It's fine,' I say. She totally had an ulterior motive in saying that. Putney High Street is not exactly the Wild West.

And lo and behold, Ben says, 'I'm pretty tired too. Let me walk with you. If you're walking?' We told each other in the hut where we lived at the time but he doesn't know where I'm staying now.

It feels like everyone is looking at us, and in the end I say, 'Great, thank you.'

It feels like I have no alternative, and going straight up Putney Hill won't be much of a detour for Ben if he's still living up the road beyond the Green Man pub.

We all cross the road together and then after a lot of hugs, the others all bundle inside the main entrance of Ned's block, and Ben and I set off up Putney High Street.

I'm determined not to feel awkward. This is not a walk with a 'shall I invite him in for a coffee or not' dilemma at the end of it. This is just two people going in the same direction and it will finish with a breezy 'Great to see you again, goodbye' outside Frankie's flat, and that will be that and I will move on with my not-seeing-Ben-again resolution and getting on with my life in Paris.

And, actually, it really isn't awkward. There are a lot of very drunk people on Putney High Street spilling out of venues and off the pavement and into the road, and we're kept busy dodging them and laughing about some of the more bizarre mini-conversations that we end up having with revellers.

Things are quieter once we get over the Upper Richmond Road and onto Putney Hill, but the block of flats Frankie lives in isn't that far up, so we manage to fill the rest of the walk with some very mundane chat about sticking to our resolutions and the cute-but-probably-pointless light dumbbells that I'm always tempted to buy myself but never do (and never will).

And then we're outside Frankie's block and, naturally, a small (not that small), stupid part of me feels an urge to invite him in.

But the night is cold and the walk has made me very, very sober and clear-headed – and sensible, it turns out – and so I say, 'Thank you so much for walking me back. Happy New Year again.'

And then I have my key out and am whipping myself inside the building before Ben's even finished his Happy-New-Year reply.

And the fact that I feel very mildly tearful because in another life we might have been so incredibly meant-to-be but actually I'm never going to see him again just underlines that my resolution to stop bumping into him is the right one.

7

LIV

It's nine a.m. on New Year's Day and my Ben-inspired decision to leave early last night is really coming into its own. I'm in Lycra psyching myself up to fulfil resolution number three: running. Frankie and Nella are sitting at the breakfast table – in Nella's case looking like total shit (because she's a normal human being who stayed out until five a.m.) and in Frankie's case very mildly less perfect than usual (because she's super-human and never looks like shit even when she stays out until five a.m.). Frankie's two flatmates haven't emerged from their rooms yet.

'Right, I'm going.' I speak quite loudly because this is the third time I've said it and I'm trying to convince myself.

A small wince passes over Frankie's perfect face while Nella moans, 'Too loud.'

I really am glad that I didn't go to Ned's flat with them last night and am feeling fresh enough for my journey back to Paris today. Another reminder that it was a good idea not to spend any more time with Ben last night.

I'm still thinking about him as I let myself out of the flat and trot down the stairs, out of the main door, out of the drive and left onto Putney Hill (I *hate* running up hills, so I've made a plan to go in a circle that begins with the longest part of the hill because I can't possibly manage a big – medium, anyway – slope at the end), so at first I don't register that it's odd that, as I pass the block of flats two up from Frankie's, Ben emerges from its driveway, also in running kit.

'Morning,' I say, trying not to smile at the sight of his legs in shorts. And then I stop running and turn to look at him. Was he…? Staying with someone there? Another girlfriend?

I start running again, at quite a brisk pace, which, even as I begin, I know is a mistake.

'I live here.' He's jogging along next to me effortlessly.

Oh. I turn my head towards him slightly, managing not to decelerate as I move. 'Really?'

'Yes, really.' He sounds sincere.

I begin to smile, despite myself, despite my don't-bump-into-Ben resolution (maybe next year I should make a resolution only to make resolutions that I have control over). And then I realise that it's weird that when I told him at the beginning of our walk last night where Frankie lived he didn't exclaim that he lives next-door-but-one now and what a coincidence. Or at any point during the walk, in fact. It isn't just weird, it's hurtful. Or disturbing. It's odd for someone to be so… secretive. For no apparent reason.

It also explains why we keep bumping into each other. It isn't fate. It's just being neighbours. I bump into my eighty-four-year-old Paris neighbour Madame Chapron all the time, and I never think that oh my goodness we're meant to be. With Ben, I've just had a classic case of fancying my not-great-boyfriend-material neighbour, that's all.

Fate is not a thing.

'Goodbye,' I say, and make a sharp left into Lytton Grove and sprint off (thankfully it's downhill, although a little too steep for easy running) as fast as I can until I'm round the bend and can bend over out of sight and let my chest heave itself back to comfortable existence.

Totally the right thing to do, I decide when I can breathe again.

And not at all sad. Really. I will not be sad about Ben again. We literally do not know each other. It's a new year and if I do ever bump into him again, I will say 'Hi' and just keep on walking. End of.

8

LIV

Six months later – July 2015

Six months later I'm nearing the end of a very schleppy journey back from Paris and I'm really, really looking forward to getting to Frankie's, even though once I get there there's going to be a lot of hard work to do because she's moving out tomorrow and we have a massive packing fest ahead of us. My Eurostar train was delayed for an hour and a half and the Gare du Nord was heaving. I did have a seat on the platform, but I gave it up to a mother with three very small, screaming children, whose need was clearly greater than mine, and ended up squatting on my suitcase for ages.

And now it's standing room only on this train because I hit the London rush hour, and I have my face pressed into the sweaty armpit of a man holding onto a bar above his head.

The train finally judders to a halt at Putney station and I fight myself through the hordes and onto the platform. I'm immediately filled with relief at the relative *space* around me.

I give my shoulders and neck a little roll and then pick my bag up and set off along the platform and up the steps towards the exit. As I get to around the middle of the flight of steps, I glimpse out of the corner of my eye one of South West London's flocks of parakeets, flying just above the steps on the platform to my right, and look over to see them better.

And below the parakeets, I see a tall, broad, brown-haired man, the sight of whom causes me to gulp uncomfortably.

He seems to sense my eyes on him, because he looks over and his step falters for a moment. Then he lifts his hand and waves. I kind of hover for a second, and then my hand seems to rise of its own volition and I wave back.

I realise that I've been standing stock still and I'm causing a traffic blockage on the steps, so I begin to walk, and Ben gets swept down the steps on his side in a swirl of people hurrying for the train that's just arriving, obscuring my view of the bottom of the steps on his platform.

And that's that.

Maybe – probably – my last ever sighting of Ben, because tomorrow Frankie's moving in with Nella in Clapham, and while I'm sure I'll be back in Putney at some point seeing friends, and might even, one day, when and if I come back from Paris, live here again, this is the last day I'll ever be staying next door but one to Ben.

9

BEN

Nine months later – April 2016

The bar is solid with people, which is always great, because more people means more revenue and I wasn't totally sure about this business when we first invested in it.

It does make it difficult to hear yourself speak though, not to sound too old-before-my-time.

I walk around, checking that everyone, staff and punters alike, seems happy. And, yes, there's a great vibe in here, and from snippets that I overhear, I reckon we have a good mix of pre- and post-cinema viewers, as well as people treating this as a destination bar, which is perfect.

I'm just about to go behind the bar and help out for a while, when I catch sight of two familiar faces. I'm looking at Liv's sister Frankie and her partner Nella.

They're sitting at a small round table, looking into each other's eyes, holding hands with their fingers linked. The very personification of eyes only for each other. The very personification of people who really don't want a relative stranger to bounce up to them and say, 'Hi. How's your sister?'

I should very obviously leave them to it.

I'd love to know how Liv's getting on, though.

The last time I saw her was at Putney train station, in the summer. She was going up the steps in the middle and I was going down the ones to the side. We waved at each other and then she got caught up in the crowd and carried on up the steps. I went back up to try to find her but was held up by the tide of people coming towards me, and by the time I saw her again she was disappearing through the ticket barriers.

Which was obviously for the best, since I know I can't let myself get close to her... But it wouldn't hurt for me to ask Frankie how she is.

Nella says something and Frankie throws her head back and laughs, and the little cocoon they're in seems to expand a bit, so it could definitely incorporate more of the outside world. Me, for example.

'Hey.' I'm over there saying hello before I've had a chance to think any further.

Frankie turns her face up to me, frowns almost imperceptibly, and then says, 'Ben!' She and Liv look very different but there's something in her mannerisms that reminds me of Liv, and I almost sigh out loud, just at the thought of her. Like the way how, when she's amused, her lips first turn down very slightly at the corners, before spreading into the kind of smile that people – me anyway – would walk across burning coals just to see.

'How are you both?' I ask.

'We're good.' Frankie nods and Nella smiles.

I really have nothing to lose by asking the question. 'So how's Liv?'

'Really well.' Frankie nods again, clearly not totally up for conversation with me, either because Liv hates me because she thinks I was chatting her up while I had a girlfriend (possible), or because she just wants to carry on her date night with Nella (probable), or both (also likely).

'We were actually in here with Liv last weekend,' Nella elaborates. 'We watched *London Has Fallen* and then came for a drink.'

Unbelievable. Last weekend was one of the first for a while I haven't been in here. The number of times Liv and I have missed each other. Although, to be fair, some of those misses were purposely assured by me.

'Love that film,' I say. I didn't really like it. 'So was Liv back from Paris for the weekend?' I'm pretty sure I sound over-needy.

'Yep,' Frankie says.

'We're hoping she's going to move back to London soon,' Nella tells me.

'Great,' I say. There's kind of an opportunity for me here to maybe engineer a way of meeting Liv again.

And I am not going to take it.

'Good to see you,' I say, nodding at them both. I resist the urge to ask them to send my love to Liv. 'Enjoy your evening.'

10

LIV

Eighteen months later – October 2017

'Marmalade. It's a no-brainer.' I grin at Mags, the manager of the cinema restaurant round the corner from my flat.

She nods. 'Perfect.'

Perfect, much like this job.

I still can't believe I get to moonlight in recipe – specifically popcorn – development and am *paid* to do it.

'So that's the one to go with *Paddington* sorted,' I say. 'The idea, anyway. Marmalade's quite tricky to work with on popcorn. Too much and it overpowers it and can be slightly bitter, plus you've got to be careful about sogginess.'

'And too little?'

'Just a slightly weird taste and you sit there thinking, "What was that?" I'm pretty much there, though. I think I can have it for you to taste by next week.'

'Excellent. Pricing?'

'We can make a profit at the usual price.'

We charge a pound extra for film-specific popcorn, but cinemagoers in their droves are ready to pay for it.

The cinema is a fancy one in Clapham – velvet chairs, take-your-wine-in-with-you, its own café/restaurant attached – and when I approached them with my flavoured-popcorn-to-match-the-film idea, they were even more open-minded than I hoped they'd be. I'm still working in finance, although I'm back in London and I've switched from a toilet paper and sanitary product company to one that produces regular paper (and cardboard), which, while not hugely more exciting product wise, has a way better boss (and no arsehole colleagues). It's still far from what I want to be doing, though; I want to work in food, but right now (and clearly for the foreseeable future if not forever) I have bills to pay, and I can't afford to follow my dreams completely yet. However, I'm finally being paid (a small amount) for this recipe development job and I love it; the extra money all adds to my saving pot for when I finally dare to try to make the leap into full or at least properly part-time recipe development work, and it's going to look very good on my CV. So I'm extremely grateful to Mags for having given me the opportunity, plus she's actually lovely to work with.

I also get two pairs of free cinema tickets every month, and who doesn't love a freebie, especially one you actually *want*.

'What's on the schedule after *Paddington*?' I ask.

There are several big films coming out, including a blockbustery-sounding one called *The Greatest Showman*.

My mind's immediately buzzing and we bat ideas backwards and forwards between us for another twenty minutes until it's time for Mags to go and check how the restaurant dinner service is going.

* * *

I'm back at the cinema a week later with my marmalade popcorn (I know, but honestly, it genuinely tastes nice, as long as you know what it is you're eating. Sulwe tried some the other day and *hated* it until I told her what it was, and then she *loved* it).

We're debating whether candyfloss flavoured, elephant-shaped popcorn for *The Greatest Showman* is likely to be a) feasible (how am I going to sort the elephant shapes?) and b) at all appealing (do adults like eating animal-shaped food?), when I catch sight of a silhouette passing the opaque-glass door.

The silhouette belongs to a fairly big man, with a strong profile that makes me think – for the first time in a long time, actually – of Ben. I used to see him, or think I'd seen him, really quite often, but now I'm not even sure when the last time I saw him was.

And what is very good is that, even if I *had* just seen him, I really wouldn't mind.

I'm totally over any stupid infatuation I had; I've been in a relationship for five months now, since just after I got back from Paris, with Tommy, an English teacher at a comprehensive in Slough. We met at a mutual friend's barbecue. He's genuinely nice and kind, as well as good company, which is a big first for me after my history of always falling for the treat 'em mean keep 'em keen types.

I glance at the big clock behind the bar. Yes, it's only five p.m. I left work early today for a dentist appointment, which is why I've been able to meet Mags at this time. I don't have Ben down as the most conservative of people, but I do think he'd be a very reliable employee, and I got the impression that he did *have* a job, so he's very unlikely to be in here at five o'clock in the afternoon. I relax and re-focus on the candyfloss-elephant question.

About ten minutes later, we're talking about the upcoming *Star Wars* release and laughing because the only *Star Wars*-related popcorn idea I've come up with is doughnut flavoured ones following on from the famous Princess Leia hairstyle and how it kind of looks a bit like doughnuts splatted against the side of her head. 'It does *not*,' Mags says, hugely indignant, clearly a *Star Wars* fan (I'm not), when the door behind the bar, under the clock, swings open.

And Ben walks through the door.

As Mags says, 'Hi, Ben,' I simultaneously choke extremely impressively on the sip of water I've just taken and up-end the remainder of the bowl of marmalade popcorn next to me.

By the time I've stopped coughing and my eyes have stopped streaming, Mags seems to be introducing me to Ben.

'...popcorn-flavourer extraordinaire,' she finishes, as I give one last hacking cough – ow, burning, how can one little sip of water going down the wrong way cause so much pain – and nod a hi to Ben.

'Hi, Liv.' His voice – gravelly as hell as always – gets me just where it has done each time we've met. 'Good to see you back from Paris.'

'Good to see you too.' I nod, although a part of me is now feeling guilty towards Tommy for the Ben-induced coughing fit. Seeing him shouldn't have had any effect on me.

'Two things.' Ben's staring at the popcorn. 'One, that is exceedingly orange. What *is* it? And two, in case you didn't hear, Mags was just saying that she and I work together.'

'More specifically,' Mags says, 'I work *for* Ben. I didn't realise you two knew each other?'

'Oh, we don't really,' I say, just as Ben says, 'We met one New Year's Eve.'

'Oh.' Mags looks between us as I consciously avoid looking at Ben. 'Did you know that Ben's the owner?'

'The owner?' I parrot, as she picks some more popcorn out of my hair.

'Of this.' She places another piece of popcorn on the olive plate and waves her hand around. 'The cinema and restaurant.'

'Oh. Great.'

What? Ben owns this place? Was he at all involved in me getting this job? I approached forty-four different venues with similar ideas and this was the only one – the *only one* – that got back to me. I very much want to know the answer to my question, and I want to know it now. Mags told me when she hired me that she was new and she wanted to do some innovative stuff and she loved my idea, and I felt at the time that me working with her was kind of meant-to-be for me, career-wise. What if that wasn't true and it was all something to do with Ben?

'Wow. How long have you owned it?'

'Just under five years.' Ben gives me a small smile.

I think back. It's three and a bit years since I moved to Paris and we met in the hut, i.e. less than five years. He didn't mention that he owned this place, even when we talked about my ambition to work with food and my pipedream of opening a café. Well, there you go. It all just goes to show that the connection I genuinely believed we had just did not exist. He didn't just tell me nothing about himself, he actively chose not to share with me even when effectively prompted. And why should he have done? We were strangers, after all.

'Cool job,' I say. 'In answer to your other question, this is marmalade popcorn.'

'*Oh.*' He grins. 'For people watching *Paddington*.'

'Exactly. Or even very discerning people who just appreciate a great, slightly random, popcorn flavour.'

Ben laughs, which pleases me, and then annoys me, because I don't want to be pleased that I've made him laugh. I want to be completely immune to him.

'I've just realised this is why you passed Liv's details on to me,' Mags says suddenly, with a satisfied nod, as if she's solved a little mystery that's been bugging her for ages. 'Because you knew her.'

I have to work particularly hard not to show I'm pissed off, because I do immediately *feel* pissed off. All this time I've genuinely thought that Mags spotted something good in my proposal about the popcorn.

What *is* it with Ben and my imagination? First I thought he and I were meant to be, and then I discovered that, no, he was just my sister's neighbour and that's why we kept bumping into each other. And now I've discovered that, no, Mags's eyes did not meet my CV and covering letter and popcorn idea across a crowded inbox causing her to think 'Oh my goodness that's the catering partner for me', but instead Ben planted my idea right under her nose. In fact, given that he's her boss and she was new, she probably had no choice. Oh my God, I hope she didn't feel like he foisted me on her.

No, it's okay. Even if he did, Mags and I do get on as friends – we went out for pizza last week on one of her two evenings off, and she was the one who suggested it – and the popcorn is selling well and is very popular, so even if she was reluctant at first, she'll definitely be pleased that she went for the idea.

'Yeah,' Ben says, responding to Mags's statement. 'I mean, no.' He's been watching me and maybe I didn't do a good job of hiding my thoughts. 'I mean, only because it really did sound like a great business proposition, as has been proven from the profits we've made from it. And, you know, with

Mags arriving, I'd been thinking it would be good to have a couple of changes. I mean, no nepotism involved.'

He's protesting way too much. But the popcorn *is* popular and personal things can go either way at work – like, I was unlucky with the whole Max thing at my last job, and apparently I've just been lucky with this – and at the end of the day, if you get a job via nepotism and you aren't up to it, it's very obvious.

So I laugh – and I'm pretty sure it's a fairly convincing laugh – and say, 'You know what, if there *was* nepotism involved, then I'm very grateful because I love developing new popcorn flavours.'

Oh my God, what if Mags thinks I slept with him or something, and that's why he recommended me?

'Really. No nepotism.' Ben's voice has suddenly frosted over like the temperature's dropped by about ten degrees; he was clearly just struck by the same thought as me. 'Anyway, good to see you again, Liv. Probably see you around some time. I need to get on.'

And he's out of the door almost before he's finished speaking.

And I'm focusing so hard on looking like an extremely professional business professional that I don't immediately register that Mags is speaking.

'You didn't hear me, did you?' she says. 'I've been thinking about what you said last week when we were out, and I'd love to look at other film-specific snack ideas with you. I love your flavoured chocolate pitch and also the cocktail one.'

'Oh, wow, really?' I would *so* love the opportunity to expand this role. But is she only asking me because of Ben? I decide I don't care as long as it works out.

Later that evening, Tommy insists on nipping out to his local offy for a bottle of their finest Prosecco to toast what he's calling my recipe development promotion. I've come over to his flat in Slough for a planned evening in – he's cooking his special, tagliatelle carbonara followed by Nigella's shortcut key lime pie, both of which are delicious.

I wait for him on his big, squishy sofa – he doesn't have a lot of furniture because he's only just moved in after finally getting the cash together for a deposit for the flat, but what furniture he does have is good – and check my emails, because Mags said she'd put something in writing.

And, yep, she's done it immediately, hooray. I see I have another one from her. It's an invitation to the staff Christmas party, which they're holding next month, a Tuesday in November, to avoid the big rush of Christmas events in December. They're going to close the cinema restaurant for the evening and host it there. I get a little thrill (quite a big one, actually) at the thought that I'm now considered one of their staff. I have a momentary feeling of not wanting to be at the same party as Ben, which is stupid and which I brush away. And then I get a *serious* thrill, because Mags has sent a third email, in which she says would I like to help her cater the party so we can try out some of our experimental flavours on the staff. I fire back an immediate reply: yes, I definitely would.

By the time Tommy gets back with the Prosecco (and some giant chocolate buttons, because I have a bad chocolate habit), I'm in the middle of some solo brainstorming of catering ideas.

'I should have bought *two* celebratory bottles,' he tells me, laughing as I babble away about my initial thoughts. He gets two glasses out and pops the cork and we clink our glasses and beam at each other, before taking big glugs.

As I cough slightly from the bubbles, I realise that I am really, properly happy. Just calmly, nicely content.

Five minutes later, we're in his galley kitchen together, him very gorgeously and seriously chopping herbs while I perch on the one (again very good) stool that he has in there, making notes with a pen and paper.

Pausing the herb chopping so that he can now focus properly on what I'm saying (he isn't the world's best multi-tasker), Tommy says, 'So tell me more about this party and your ideas. If you'd like to?'

So I tell him about the party in more detail than I did before his offy trip, and about what Mags and I discussed – how we might be branching out into chocolate and cocktails and maybe even themed dishes on the restaurant menu on certain evenings. (I don't go into details about specific ideas because I never like to talk about them until I'm sure an idea's a goer.)

'So basically,' I finish, 'it'll be almost like a proper, small part-time food development job, or at least a big project, plus I'm pretty sure I'm going to *love* it.' I realise that, in describing what happened earlier this evening while I was with Mags, I didn't mention anything about Ben.

And for some reason – weirdly, because since the moment Tommy and I met, we've *talked*, and I've told him a lot about Dad dying and Mum struggling since then, and the fact that I didn't totally *choose* to go to Paris, my relationship with Frankie and how much I like Nella, all sorts really – I know that I'm not going to tell him about Ben.

I mean, there's nothing to tell him, really. Not worth talking about. Just a man I bumped into a few times a couple of years ago.

He steps away from his herbs for a second. 'So proud of you.' He drops a kiss on my forehead, and then says, kind of nonchalantly, but also kind of like it's huge, 'I love you.' And it *is* huge, because it's the first time either of us has said it.

I look at his lovely, boyishly handsome face, at the little scar on his left cheek (an incident with his brother and a cricket stump apparently), the kindness shining out of his eyes, the gladness for me that something's gone well in my life, and my heart swells.

'I love you too,' I tell him.

11

LIV

Five weeks later – November 2017

If I say so myself, I've done a good job on the food for this party. Mags and I decided to go for a jungle theme as a practice run for when *Jumanji: Welcome to the Jungle* comes out next month, so we have both jungle décor and a jungle menu that I've had a lot of fun with. We have the obvious exotic fruit options plus some unusual meat canapés, and I've created a Jumanji cocktail involving pomegranates, ginger and a South American liqueur which is a gorgeous pink (*not* disgusting-sea-sick-tablet-coloured, as Sulwe described it), and I'm hoping it will be a big hit.

I'm looking forward to my fellow cinema and café/restaurant employees both seeing and tasting it all (and again I *love* being an employee in a business I actually want to be in). Hopefully they'll be a combination of surprised and impressed. If I'm honest, I'm also slightly looking forward to Ben seeing and tasting it, because I feel like there *was* a bit of nepotism (that I don't really understand) involved in me getting the job, and I want another opportunity to prove that I was worth it.

Mags and I are here early with Samantha, one of the restaurant staff who Mags roped in to help us. I left my actual job half an hour earlier than usual so that I could dash home, change and then get here in time to make sure everything is looking okay.

'You've done an amazing job.' Mags pulls her phone out and starts to take photos of the jungle accoutrements and all the food and drinks laid out along the bar and on a table at one end of the room. 'Liv and Sam, stand in front of the food table' – she snaps a picture of us – 'and now in front of the mantelpiece.'

We've put some Christmas decorations up above the fire because, even though it's November and we have our jungle theme, it *is* a Christmas party. Samantha, Mags and I had a conversation about mistletoe, and I'm suddenly very pleased that we decided not to have any (because no-one appreciates an ill-judged Christmas party snog with a colleague). The way fate's always treated me and Ben, if the opportunity arose, we'd end up in an awkward do-we-don't-we-cheek-peck moment.

'Hey.' Ben's voice booms out behind us, and we turn as one to greet him. 'Wow, this looks amazing. Thank you so much.'

'It was all Liv and Sam,' Mags tells him.

'It was not,' I say. 'Mags has amazing jungle décor vision.'

'You're all fantastic.' Ben moves over to the bar, reaches behind it and pulls out a bag. 'I have little thank yous here for the three of you.' He takes out three gold and scarlet-wrapped presents and hands one to each of us.

'Are we opening now?' Mags says, already ripping hers, which is envelope-shaped, apart. I'm guessing she isn't one of those people who's capable of carefully unwrapping presents and folding the paper to tuck away to re-use it. 'Oh my God, tickets to the David Hockney exhibition at the Tate. Thank you!' Mags loves her art.

She flings her arms round Ben and gives him a big smacker on his left cheek.

'Oh wow. The scarf I saw in Oliver Bonas last week and loved.' Sam gives Ben a slightly more decorous kiss, more of an air one. 'You have some very good spies on the ground. Amazing. Thank you.'

I begin to open my present. Ben's clearly made a big effort to buy things that he knew Mags and Sam would like and I'm wondering what he'll have got for me. If he's put the same level of effort into mine, maybe he'll have asked Mags for hints.

My present box is quite heavy. When I get inside it, I discover it's a pair of cute 1kg dumbbells. To my shame, I remember my past conversations with Ben very well, and I know I told him once that I'd love really light dumbbells but would never buy any for myself because they seem like a ridiculous luxury. And I'm pretty sure I've never had the same conversation with Mags, which means he must remember our chat from years ago. Obviously I remember it too, which I don't want to analyse too much.

'Thank you so much.' I step forward and go for an extremely distant double air kiss to thank him, because it feels too awkward not to do something demonstrative, given that the others did, but also I instinctively feel strange about actually touching him. For a second, as I step in closer, I catch Ben's scent – kind of woody, in a nice way – and I'm transported back to the hut. 'Great present,' I say.

I'm so annoyed that knowing he remembered our conversation makes me want to smile quite as much as it does, and once again I start to feel a little bit guilty towards Tommy.

'Glad you like it.' He gives me this half smile that makes me feel we're in danger of having a holding-each-other's-gazes moment and so I plaster on my most business-like smile and move my eyes firmly away.

Three hours later, I'm taking a breather with Mags and Samantha at a table in the corner of the room, all three of us holding full glasses of my jungle cocktail.

'We did such a good job.' Mags waves her arm around the room at the little groups of people, who are all talking animatedly, laughing, gesturing. The sound of all the different strands of chatter washes over me in the way a very familiar song does when you catch it on the radio. It would be extremely relaxing if it weren't for the fact that every so often my ears pick out the rumble of Ben's voice, definitely the lowest in the room, and it sets me slightly on edge.

'Especially the food,' Samantha says. 'Everyone loved it.'

Mags nods and says, 'Yes, it's perfect, thank you, Liv.' She looks around again. '*Now*, I think we need to get some dancing going.' She reaches behind her, up to the bar, for a speaker she clearly left there earlier, and hooks her phone up, and then presses Play, and the opening bars of *Rockin' Around the Christmas Tree* blast out. 'Come on.' She grabs my left hand and Sam's right hand and pulls us into the middle of the room.

I love dancing and I can't remember ever feeling self-conscious about it, but all of a sudden, as Mags and I do a back-to-back, down-to-the-floor, fake-mic-holding shimmy, I'm wondering whether Ben's watching me. I really hope he isn't, and now I'm really annoyed with myself because I do not want to care about whether he has any thoughts about me at all and what those thoughts might be, beyond obviously wanting him to think I'm doing a good job with the flavours, given that ultimately he's my boss.

'Bennnnnnn,' screeches Mags, very close to my ear, and I look round in alarm, to see her beckoning to him, scarily coyly. She's going to regret that fourth cocktail in the morning.

Ben shakes his head and then rolls his eyes, says something to the two men he's talking to (who both work on the cinema door and are impressively knowledgeable about all things niche cinematic) and they all peel themselves away from the wall and make their way over to us. Mags claps them with huge gusto as they walk over and I clap too – I'd feel I was being rude to her if I didn't – but a lot less enthusiastically.

And now we're all dancing together and lots of people have joined us so we're a really big group. I should certainly not be aware only of Ben, or indeed of Ben at all, because there are so many of us and it's social and uninhibited and it's my first Christmas party of the year and it's all just *fun*, and I should just throw myself into it and not think about Ben (or any one person) at *all*. But the overwhelming sensation I have as I dance is awareness, of Ben, of how his body's moving and whether *he's* watching *me*.

After a *big* internal tussle I manage to focus very firmly on the others and myself and *not* Ben.

About five songs later, I've definitely succeeded in throwing myself into the dancing and I'm out of breath and am at the point where I'm going to have to ditch my orange patent leopard-skin-patterned Jimmy Choo heels – a present to myself for getting the popcorn work and a phenomenal sale bargain – to give my toes and the balls of my feet a rest. Or, I could just sneak away and have a little sit-down in the corner. Mags is really going for it now and I think she might genuinely not notice if every single other person takes a break from the dancing.

I head for the table I was at before, sink onto one of the lovely squishy velvet-covered chairs – the cinema and restaurant are all about comfort, which I very much appreciate at this moment – and pick up the drink that I left here (I know it's mine because I've been using the same green straw all evening, transferring it from drink to drink in an – admittedly pathetic, but every little helps – nod to the environment) and take a lovely long slurp.

'Mind if I join you?' Matteo, the man standing in front of me, does front of house in the restaurant at the weekends.

'Of course not,' I say, wondering whether he just wants a sit down too, or whether he's suggesting *joining* joining me.

'Great evening.' He gets going on some small talk and some very animated anecdotes and I quickly begin to wonder at what point I should make a reference to 'my boyfriend', so that we know that we're on the same page, i.e. we're just having a nice chat rather than anyone chatting anyone *up*. Something, I recall, that Ben did not do back in the hut and which he very much should have done to avoid anyone – me – getting confused and ending up feeling a little – very – embarrassed.

Matteo's just finishing telling me a genuinely very funny story involving a squirrel, a campsite and some strawberries, at which point one of my own stories, which involves Tommy, has popped into my head, so I'm just gearing up for the boyfriend mention, when another man's voice says, 'Mind if I join you?' and *Ben* sits down at our table without waiting even a nanosecond for us to go through the formality of telling him of course we don't mind.

And for some reason I feel a bit weird about telling my Tommy story now. Which means that I should definitely tell it, so I make myself launch into it with great zest, and much dramatic effect, and I do have both Matteo and Ben laughing a lot, and I'm pretty sure that I also have them both registering very firmly that I have a boyfriend.

'So how long have you two been together?' Matteo asks.

I want to punch the air, because now that Ben's back on the edge of my life as my boss's boss, I find myself wanting him to know that I'm not pathetically just gagging for attention from him.

'Over six months now,' I say, doing my best (but possibly failing) to not sound very proud; I didn't have the *best* track record with relationships in my twenties.

'That's nice.' Matteo pushes his stool back and says, 'Looks like you two have stuff to catch up on. I'll leave you to it.' Which does send him down a little in my estimation because it seems like it's the boyfriend mention that's sent him away and that he had zero interest in me as an actual person – only as a potential snogging partner – because he can't possibly really think that Ben and I have anything to catch up on because neither of us said anything to that effect.

And now we're sitting here, me and Ben, just the two of us, and I don't really want to talk to him but I also don't want to walk off because that would seem a little rude.

'I really hope Matteo wasn't bothering you,' Ben says, very seriously, and I nearly choke.

'No, honestly, he was fine. He's lovely,' I say when I can speak again. 'Honestly.'

'You sure? I just, I remember you had... When you went to Paris.' Ben's struggling to get his words out, which, annoyingly, is strangely endearing.

I put him out of his misery. 'Thank you so much for remembering and for your concern, but honestly, Matteo was very respectful. We were just chatting.'

'Although he did walk off as soon as you said you had a boyfriend,' Ben says, his tone a lot more acerbic than usual.

'Yeah, but you know.' I leave it hanging and drink more. Annoyingly, I end up finishing the drink. I liked having it there, for something to do.

Ben looks at my glass and catches someone's eye and within seconds I have another cocktail, and so does he, so now I'm going to have to talk to him for another few minutes.

'I love it when people manage to have insanely good bar presence when they aren't even at a bar,' I tell him. 'Although it's probably a lot easier when you're the boss.'

'Yeah, exactly. That would have been more impressive if none of the bar staff here knew either of us.' He pauses, and then says, 'So how've you been? All good? How's Frankie? And how's your mum doing?' Honestly. He has a very good memory.

I take another few deep sips – I'm loving this cocktail more and more – and tell him how Frankie and Nella are super loved up and discussing marriage and having two babies (one pregnancy each is their plan), and then I move on to talking about my mum.

'She's doing brilliantly,' I tell him. 'On the eighteen-month anniversary of losing my dad, she told Frankie and me that she'd woken up that morning and realised that she'd lost the past eighteen months of her life sitting grieving and not taking a lot of joy in things and that, while she was still grieving and a part of her of course always will be, she owes it to Dad to make the most of the life that she has.'

I stop, to swallow the gigantic lump that's sprung up in my throat, and Ben says, 'It's so hard. My grandmother said a very similar thing although it took her three years after she lost my grandfather.'

'And what did she do then?'

'Took the train to Paris and went to the Folies Bergères because she'd always wanted to. She loved that. Then she took up skiing, aged eighty-two, and immediately broke her leg. She's fine now. And back on the slopes.'

'Oh my goodness, bless her.' I have this image of an elderly lady who looks like Ben and I want to hug her.

'Yeah, she's great. And what about your mum?'

'Well, she took up badminton and also got a part-time teaching job. And now...' I take another big slurp – I *love* this drink – before launching into something I haven't actually talked about with anyone else. Frankie and I haven't discussed it; sometimes you just *can't* say these sorts of things out loud about one of your parents. And I'd feel disloyal if I mentioned it to Sulwe because she knows my mum, and I haven't told Tommy because I think he'd be concerned for me, in a gorgeously loving way, rather than laughing uproariously and slightly gagging which is the only correct response, because on the one hand, gaaaaah, it's my mother, but on the other hand, *go her*. 'So basically, she's started dating. She's been on three dates with a really lovely-sounding man called Simon.'

'Wow. Huge.' Ben takes a big sip of his own drink.

'Yeah. But...'

Ben raises an eyebrow. I nod and then lower my voice. 'She asked us for advice last week.'

'Advice? *Dating* advice?' Ben is slightly round-eyed.

'Yep.'

'And?'

'Yeah. It was bad.'

'*Sex*?' Ben's extremely round-eyed now.

'In a nutshell.' I shake my head at the memory. 'Bearing in mind this is *my mother* we're talking about. She's in her late fifties and she is not someone who talks about these things with her daughters or, I strongly doubt, with *any*one. She said – over a smoked salmon starter at her local gastro pub – did we think she should *dye* her pubic hair.'

'Noooooo.' Ben looks hard at the table and then glances up and gives a huge crack of laughter. 'Sorry. *Sorry*. But oh my God. During the starter as well, so you had the rest of dinner to go.'

Exactly. I beam at him, delighted by his reaction, and drink some more.

'And...?'

I nudge him. 'Are you actually asking if I know whether my mum did the dye and then had sex?'

'I mean, when you hear the start of any good story you always want to hear the end.'

I put my head on one side and consider. 'Fair point. And yet, I very much don't want to know the end of this story. Although I would like her to be happy and Simon does seem nice.' And then I get serious. 'Not as nice as my dad, though.'

Ben immediately gets totally serious too. 'Goes without saying. I'm really sorry.'

We both take very long sips of our drinks.

And then I say, 'Anyway, enough about my mother and her newly brunette pubic hair. How's *your* family?' At which point I realise that he knows a lot about my family and I know nothing about his. I frown and then place my glass very deliberately on the table. Well, I say I place it on the table. The table seems to have shrunk. I get it on there the third time, though. Then I turn to face Ben. 'I don't *know* about your family.' Both my hands are free because I'm no longer holding my drink, so I prod him in the

– nicely solid; no that is *not* a thought I should be having – chest with my right forefinger. 'You are a very secretive person, Ben Jones.'

I prod him again and then he takes hold of my finger and, suddenly, my heart's thudding away like nobody's business and all I can think is that Ben is holding my finger in his very large and capable and nicely tanned hand. And the way he's holding my finger is making me go very, very – I don't know what the word is – *mushy* inside. I don't want to feel mushy. I love Tommy, I do not love Ben... What am I talking about, of course I don't love Ben, I don't even know him really – and this is just not right. I need to push the mushy feeling away.

'Have you been on holiday recently?' I ask. 'Where did you get your tan?'

Oh God, I am definitely drunk.

'The Canaries a couple of weeks ago,' he tells me.

'I see.' I'm not sure *what* I see. I know what I feel though: he's still holding my finger, and all my senses are centred on that. I want to move my hand so that the whole of my hand's in contact with his, link our fingers, feel the pressure of his against mine.

What? What am I thinking? I've gone mad. I peer at my finger and Ben's hand. He should not be holding my finger and I should not be enjoying him holding it. I'm in love with *Tommy*.

I pull my hand away, really suddenly, and Ben says, 'Sorry, sorry, sorry.'

'Nothing to be sorry about,' I say, and stand up, fast. I just want to go home. To Tommy, who is lovely and straightforward and nice, and I love him. 'Goodnight,' I say.

He stands up too, dodges a jungle branch that's come loose from the ceiling, and says, 'Goodnight.' And for some reason, I feel as though my heart's cracking.

I wobble slightly on my feet and look around for my clutch bag. I spot it in a corner on the other side of the room and walk very carefully over in an incredibly straight line (genius) to pick it up.

'Let me see you home.' Ben's materialised at my elbow again.

'No.' I think I might have said that very loudly because he looks slightly alarmed. 'No.' Whoops. Too quiet that time. 'No.' There we go. The perfect loudness. 'No, thank you. I'm good.'

Ben looks round. 'Mags, are you leaving now? Could you drop Liv home on your way if I get a taxi for both of you?'

'Sure.' Mags smiles at both of us.

Neither of us are smiling. I really want to tell Ben that I'm incredibly pissed off with him for making me feel this way again, and I think he might be pissed off with me too, although I'm not sure why.

'Great. I'll call an Uber now then.' He swipes his phone a couple of times and then says, 'Done. Your driver's Ishaan and he's in a Prius. Here in three minutes. Goodnight. Great party; thanks again.' Then he nods at both of us and turns round and heads over to the opposite corner of the room, and I go through the double doors towards the cinema foyer, Mags following me.

12

BEN

What an idiot. What a fucking idiot.

There was no need for any of that. I didn't need to go over and speak to Liv when she was with Matteo because she's obviously completely capable of looking after herself and this party is nothing like the situation she got into with Max.

If I hadn't gone and spoken to her then we wouldn't have ended up talking, and that would have been for the best. She's clearly severely pissed off with me now, and who can blame her? Why the fuck did I take hold of her finger like that? So ridiculously flirtatious, straight after she – obviously purposely – told us she has a boyfriend.

I nod and smile at a couple of the guys who work in the cinema and go to pour myself another drink. They're all great people and deserve to have a fantastic party, and I have a nasty feeling that if I leave now it might ruin the vibe because people often feel like they have to leave if the boss does.

I really do want to leave, though. Actually, I *could* leave – if I head off in the direction of the bathrooms and then just go out the other exit. That's a Liv-style plan if ever there was one. In fact, I'm pretty sure that at one point during that New Year's Eve she did tell me she pulls that trick a lot.

I miss her, I actually miss her, I think as I head out the back of the bar towards the facilities. And I don't even bloody really know her.

Although, I do, I do know her. I feel like I know her right to my core. Like we have this connection.

In another life, I'd have just asked her out years ago. But I don't live another life, I live my life, and Liv lives hers, and I can't ask her out. And I don't think it's doing either of us any favours bumping into each other, or even knowing that there's the possibility that we'll bump into each other.

Actually, I'm probably flattering myself. She's got a boyfriend and is most likely ambivalent about seeing me. But it isn't doing *me* any favours.

I leave the cinema quietly by the back exit and feel cold air hit my throat on my first inhale, and a couple of seconds later I shiver as the chill permeates through my shirt. I should have remembered to pick my coat up from the bar; I'll have to remember to get it tomorrow when I come into work.

As I walk along, the frosty night clears my head, crystallising thoughts that have been swirling around my mind for the past few weeks and gaining in intensity.

I suddenly stop dead in the middle of the pavement. Yes, I've come to a decision. I'm going to take a step back from the restaurant. Mags is doing an amazing job, as are nearly all the rest of the staff. They don't really need my input any more. They can all have a promotion – which hopefully could mean more involvement for Liv too, because I'm pretty sure she'd love that – and I can get out there and look for other business opportunities. It was probably time for that anyway, and there'll be no danger of me bumping into Liv again. Liking her so much but knowing I can't act on my feelings is messing with my head too much.

Decision made, I start walking again.

I'm pleased about my new plan. It's perfect. Not at all depressing. Just... perfect. Time to move on.

13

LIV

Four years later – October 2021

It's four years before I speak to Ben again after that Christmas party. He basically scarpered, or 'withdrew from active management in order to focus on other business interests'. At the time I almost felt as though the scarpering was something to do with me, but in retrospect that seems ridiculously fanciful.

I've seen him four times in those four years. Twice around the cinema: one time inside the restaurant when there was a big event (I stayed resolutely on the opposite side of the room from him and I was pretty sure he was consciously doing the same), and the second time a near miss on my way to work there. I was on my way in and he was walking up the pavement towards me. I was sure he'd been heading there too but decided not to go in when he saw me; he mouthed, 'Hi,' and looked as though he was going to say more, and then instead just raised his hand and gave me a tight little smile, swerved to the other side of the pavement and crossed the road in a scary car-dodging way.

The other two times were when we were both out on Clapham

Common on one of the many walks everyone's done over the past eighteen months. I was with Tommy both times. Ben was with a man and a dog the first time, and the second time he was with a woman. I couldn't help noticing that he was holding hands with her and am ashamed to say that I then found myself gripping Tommy's hand so tightly that he asked me if I was okay.

And now we're both at the same theatre in London's West End – on the Haymarket – watching the same play. I noticed Ben about five minutes in, when his (female) companion pointed at something right at the back of the theatre and he turned round to have a look (and then they very sweetly shared a little chuckle with lots of eye contact which truly pathetically made my heart crack a bit). We're both in the dress circle; he's in the second row and I'm in the seventh. I'm with Sulwe. I don't think the woman Ben's with now is the same one he was with on the common earlier in the year. That woman was very tall, almost as tall as him, and had dark hair, and this one's hair is blonde and curly, and when they're sitting down the top of her head only comes up to about his chin level.

It's weird, because while I have an excellent view of him, he presumably doesn't know, and might never know (unless he can feel my eyes boring into the back of his head), that we're in the same place. And, of course, he might not care, although I did get the impression at that party with the whole finger-holding thing that he *would* care. (I still can't think about the finger-holding without feeling myself flush red, which just makes me feel terribly disloyal to Tommy, even though, as I've told myself each time I've remembered it, it was not my fault.)

I say Ben would care; I think he might have cared *then*, four years ago. There's no reason that he would *now*.

The blonde woman is very touchy-feely. Every time anything remotely shocking or scary happens, she clutches his arm, leans into him, puts her head on his shoulder. If I'm honest, I'm finding it slightly stomach-curdling. I mean, really? Do people need to canoodle at the front of a dress circle? It's distracting for everyone behind them. I can see lots of other couples and they aren't all over each other; they're just sitting watching the play.

As I am doing. I'm very much enjoying it, actually; it's very thought-provoking.

It is *so* long.

Eventually, we get to the interval. It's one of those plays where frankly you can't quite believe that you have to go back in afterwards.

'Drink?' I say to Sulwe as the curtain's still going down. I need a break from the misery of the plot and from looking at the back of Ben's head.

'Mmm?' She's been engrossed in the play. She did English Lit at uni and loves this kind of thing. I'm not so good with dark and heavy (and quite confusing) plots like this.

'Drink?'

'Yes. Great.' She's still in a bit of a glaze about the wonderfulness (really?) of the director's and actors' 'radical new interpretation' as we make our way up the stairs to the top of the dress circle and into the bar.

It's only when we're ordering our Aperol spritzes (Mags got me into them, they're my guilty pleasure, and now I'm taking Sulwe down with me) and I hear a still-so-familiar very deep voice behind me that I realise that I did not think this through. Everyone goes to the bar in the interval. Obviously.

It's fine, though. I don't want to speak to Ben this evening and I won't have to because I won't turn round and he clearly won't know it's me just from the back of my head.

'Ben!' Sulwe *has* turned round and she has evidently recognised him.

'Sulwe!' And he has evidently recognised her. Well, never mind. We'll say hi and then we'll drink our drinks separately on opposite sides of the bar and then I'll watch him canoodling for what will feel like many, many more hours unless the play picks up considerably, and then I will go home to Tommy. Who I love.

I turn round, with slight difficulty, because there's now a huge squeeze in here. I'm pretty sure theatre bars aren't usually this busy. Maybe everyone's in here because they need to drink away their play-induced boredom.

'Hi Ben,' I say.

'Liv. How are you?'

'I'm great, thank you. You?'

'Yeah, really good, thanks.' He moves his shoulders a bit, which creates a bit of space around us. 'Are theatre bars normally this crowded?'

'Exactly what I was thinking,' I say. 'Everyone's obviously very thirsty this evening. The play's quite long.'

'Yes it is.' Ben shuffles himself a bit closer to the bar as he talks. 'You enjoying it?'

'It's great,' I say, very firmly.

'It is, isn't it.' Ben nods.

Sulwe launches into some more superlative-laden analysis of the performance, while I nod a lot. Ben nods a lot too. And then he smirks slightly at me. I narrow my eyes. Does he *know* that I'm being insincere?

'Can you hold my drink?' Sulwe asks me. 'I might pop to the loo before it starts again. I was going to go right at the end of the interval but now I'm thinking the queues might be really long and I don't want to miss any of it. I think they said something about not letting people back in in a lot of parts, because it's so intense.'

I look down at the floor so that she can't see my eyes light up at the idea that maybe I could go for a slow loo break in a few minutes' time and get held in the waiting area for a good portion of the second half. I have a lot of admin I could do on my phone, which would be time much better spent.

As she goes, I say to Ben, 'Lovely to see you. Enjoy the rest of it,' and wonder how I'm going to push my way through the throngs of people without spilling our drinks.

And Ben leans down towards my ear and says very quietly, so that only I can hear, 'So do you really hate the play?'

'Oh my God yes,' I say.

'Me too,' he murmurs. I look up at him and we smile at each other and our eyes catch. For a split second it's like we're suspended in time, and then I remember his companion – who might be right behind me for all I know – and then I think about Tommy, and suddenly I'm furious with myself – and life – all over again.

'Fingers crossed that the second half's shorter. Lovely to see you. Bye,' I say and turn my back and begin the process of pushing through the crowd.

* * *

Ten days later, I'm having dinner with my mother and Frankie. Nella isn't there because she's away for work, but we're discussing their wedding plans anyway, because Frankie is on a mission to have the most perfect wedding of all time.

As we take a breather from some very detailed discussions about wedding dinner napkins and tablecloths, I push dessert menus towards them and say, 'Should we order our puddings? If we're having any.'

'Pudding?' Frankie's staring at me as though I've lost my mind: I've just suggested that a woman with only ten months to go until her wedding should eat a spoonful of ice cream and risk bursting out of her wedding dress. Right.

'Okay, maybe a mint tea for you,' I say. 'I'd like some pudding, though.'

'Me too,' Mum says. I look at her. All evening she's been sounding less, I don't know, buoyant, than she has done recently.

'Are you okay, Mum?'

'Yes, thank you. Totally fine.'

'Okay, what's happened?' Frankie's immediately switched her focus from wedding minutiae to Mum's wellbeing, and I'm pretty sure that if something *is* wrong she'll have all the details out of Mum within minutes.

It's seconds actually. 'I split up with Simon,' Mum says.

'Oh my goodness. What happened?' I say.

'Has Simon cheated on you? I will *kill* him,' Frankie says.

'No, no, entirely my choice,' Mum says. She picks up her napkin and pleats it one way, and then the other. Frankie and I both keep opening our mouths to speak and then one of us kicks the other and we shut up. We know she's going to tell us, because since the pubic-hair-dying conversation she's told us a lot of stuff. Kind of like stuff she would have liked to have told Dad but he isn't here for her to tell him. Weirdly, I think she would have liked to have told him about her dating, because he was her best friend and she told him absolutely everything.

Eventually Mum does begin to elaborate. 'You know what? When I started seeing Simon, I think maybe I was too desperate to get out there, try to start *living* again. I'm very fond of him but I don't love him or fancy him like I loved and fancied your father. I might well never meet another man who I could love like that *and* fancy as much *and* who's a true best friend like he was. But I do need one of those things. Simon's lovely' – she's right, he is; Frankie and I both love him as much as we could love someone who isn't our dad – 'but he isn't enough for me. I felt like I was just settling. And I'm too young to settle. I want someone who's more than just a companion. And Simon deserves more. And maybe I won't meet someone again but this was still the right decision.'

Frankie's nodding as though Mum's talking perfect sense. I'm pretty sure Frankie has all three of the love, fancying and best friend with Nella.

And a tiny voice at the back of my brain that I do not want to listen to is clamouring for attention. Nope. I'm not listening to it. I'm happy. I've been happy for years. I'm contented. Settled. Gaaah, that word: *settled*. No, it can mean two things. I *am* settled *with* Tommy. Not I *have* settled *for* Tommy.

* * *

About a week later, Sulwe and her husband, Lewis (who she married about eighteen months ago), come over to our flat for a takeaway. Tommy and I moved in together a couple of years ago; we live near Twickenham, more or less halfway between our respective workplaces.

Sulwe's brought gallons of wine because she's just had her second miscarriage. I want to hug and hug and hug her; I can't bear the thought of her misery at expecting and then losing a much-longed-for first child; it must be awful. She only accepts one hug though, and then she wants alcohol, goat's cheese and seafood, and as much distraction as we can provide, so that's what we do.

Halfway through the evening, she says something about the play. She and Tommy start talking about late-twentieth-century American playwrights and they're both being *so* earnest. Sulwe always has a slight edge (that I adore) to her, while Tommy's *just* earnest about his analysis (and I adore that too).

But as they're talking, a little memory – of Ben telling me that he didn't like that play either – pops into my head. And I shiver as I remember the way that, as his words were whispered into my ear, his breath whispered across my cheek, and I have to turn away from Tommy for a moment.

* * *

It's two months later and the Saturday before Valentine's when Tommy proposes. We're out for dinner in our favourite restaurant. We've been together for nearly five years now but I did not see this coming.

We go to this restaurant a lot – it's our local Italian and we love it and (we like to think) they love us, and not only because we spend a small fortune in here – and it feels like just another lovely Saturday evening together.

But suddenly, just after we've chosen our desserts, up pops one of the waiters with a bottle of champagne, and behind him two violinists start playing something classic and waltzy. My first instinct – I am so ashamed of myself – is to snigger at the cheesiness of the whole scene.

My second instinct, following hard on the first, is to panic, which does very effectively wipe out any mirth.

And when Tommy places a gorgeous ruby ring on a clean napkin on the table in front of me and says, 'Will you marry me?' I feel... I feel like a rabbit in headlights. I don't know what to say.

Tommy's looking at me with love and anticipation in his eyes, but as I sit staring back at him, the anticipation's falling away and being replaced with a small, puzzled-looking frown, and a bit of lip twisting.

I have to say something. I've been silent for ages.

'I don't know what to say,' I whisper. God. *That* wasn't the right thing. 'I...' I try not to gulp and not to be too hideously aware of all the witnesses we have. I should just say yes. I should shout it from the rooftops. I should be dancing on the table with happiness. But I'm thinking about how Frankie and Nella are when they're together. And I'm thinking about my mum and what she said a few weeks ago, about settling, about the fact that when she was married to my dad she clearly did not ever have feelings of any kind for any other man. And Ben has now popped into my head, and he really, really should not have done.

If my mum's too young to settle, I'm *far* too young, despite the small voice in my head that's pointing out that I'd really, really like to have kids and I'm not as young as I was.

And Tommy doesn't deserve to be settled for.

Oh, my God, the hurt now on Tommy's face.

'Thank you,' I say. No, that was *so* the wrong thing to say. 'I need time to think.'

I want to say yes – I want to so much – but I can't form the word.

Fucking, fucking Ben for popping into my head at that moment.

14

LIV

July 2022

The next time I see Ben, it's a few months later and I'm at a wedding, and it isn't my own, for obvious reasons.

I've actually been finding things a little bit difficult recently. I know that splitting up with Tommy was the right thing to do, for both our sakes, but I miss him, and I know that if he hadn't asked me to marry him, we'd still be happily trundling along together now. I particularly miss him at plus-one-type social occasions, and this year – after having barely been to any weddings ever – I seem to be at them all the time.

Which is totally fine – lovely, in fact – but I'd got used to doing stuff with Tommy, and I liked having him there. 'Like a security blanket,' Sulwe said when I told her this. 'You don't marry your security blanket.' That's true, and it did make me feel better. For a few minutes. The thing is, even if you shouldn't marry your security blanket, you still miss the blanket a lot when you lose it.

Anyway, here I am, in the foyer outside my friend Emmie's wedding. She and her now-husband Lucas only met about eighteen months ago but, as she (very tactfully – we are exactly the same age) told me about one week after I'd split up with Tommy, she isn't a spring chicken any more and she wants three children and she wants to have been married for two years before she has the first one, 'so time is of the essence, Liv, tick tock, tick tock'.

She's also mentioned more than once how I'm her only bridesmaid, because the other three are matrons of honour, being already married. At one point, during a dress fitting, I struggled hugely not to yell, 'Marriage is *really* not the be-all and end-all.' Instead, I just smiled and downed the rest of the champagne the dress designer had given us and then got a bollocking for drinking bubbles too fast and possibly making my stomach bloated.

'This is the stuff that beautiful memories are made of,' Sulwe then said, and Emmie stared at her in such confusion that Sulwe and I both snorted champagne out of our noses.

Right now, I'm just taking a little breather from the reception. We've had dinner and the dancing has started, and it's hot in there and I'm quite tired, and about the seventh person in one hour just asked me about Tommy so I thought I'd come for a little wander outside.

It's quite hot in the foyer. Maybe I'll go properly outside and have a little walk in the hotel grounds. We had photos and drinks out there before dinner and it was lovely.

As I get to the revolving doors at the entrance, I vaguely notice in my peripheral vision a large, kilted man just behind me to my left.

I step into my compartment of the doors at the same time that he says, 'Liv.'

As I revolve with the doors I frown. That's Ben's voice. He's definitely not at Emmie's wedding, though. What's he doing here? We're in Kent. We don't bump into each other outside London.

He emerges from his door compartment and I take a proper look at him. Yep, he's wearing a kilt. That probably means he's Scottish, or his family are, and that's another thing I never knew about him. I don't actually really know anything about him at all. That's quite weird when you think about how much obsessing I've done about him at various points over the years, and absolutely ridiculous when you think that his existence contributed to the demise of my one serious relationship.

'Hi,' I say.

'Hi.' We just look at each other for a moment, and then he says, 'So I'm guessing you're also at a wedding?'

I nod. He was never going to be wrong on that: Emmie went full-on meringue dress for both herself and us. She confidently told us that the whole understated tasteful, sophisticated look is over and it's back to Lady Di-style wedding dresses. I'm not sure she's right and I don't share her taste, but she was the one choosing, so here I am standing in front of Ben in pastel-blue puffs and frills.

'You look lovely,' he says.

'I mean. I do not.' I've seen myself numerous times in a mirror in this dress. I'm at least six inches too short to be able to carry it off. 'I look like one of those toilet roll dollies that elderly ladies used to have.'

Ben's lips twitch but he carries on with the tact. 'You don't. You really do look lovely.'

'Hmm.' That's blatantly untrue and not worth replying to. I gesture at his kilt. 'I didn't know you were Scottish.'

'My mum is. I'm at a family wedding.' As he speaks, he looks over his shoulder. 'Do you...? What are you up to?' he asks. 'Are you...?'

He's being slightly odd. Maybe either the word 'family' or the word 'wedding' has reminded him of the fact that he has a girlfriend, or even wife, inside. Maybe he has married the blonde, curly-haired woman he was at the theatre with. And, wow, I feel a genuine little spike of misery at the thought of Ben being married.

'I'm on my way back inside,' I tell him. I don't need Ben to stir uncomfortable emotions in me again. 'Great to see you.'

There's a bit of a commotion inside the foyer on the other side of the doors, and Ben looks over his shoulder again, quickly, in a very odd way, and says, 'I'd love to go for a quick walk. Join me?' He holds out his arm to me.

I'm kind of intrigued about his odd-seeming behaviour, which I think is why I find myself taking his arm and allowing him to lead me along this little path to the right of the hotel and round the side towards where there's a lovely rose garden, now lit up by a lot of fairy lights strung along the wall of the building plus some moonlight.

'Did you enjoy the rest of that play?' He sounds as if he's asking just for the sake of making conversation. I have no idea why he's brought me into this garden.

'No. I hated it. You?' I withdraw my arm from his because holding it does not feel right (or being honest, it feels *too* right). He lets go immediately.

'Couldn't stand it. The second half was worse than the first, and I would not have believed that possible if you'd told me in the interval.'

'Sulwe loved it.' I want to ask if his girlfriend did.

'Yeah, my... Yeah.' Clearly he doesn't want to mention her to me.

I do not take pity on him. 'I'm guessing your girlfriend did, too? Or you would have left?'

'Yes, she did. Although she isn't my girlfriend. She wasn't really then either. I mean, she was a bit.' He's gone mad. He's turned into the most awkward person I've ever met, and from what I know of him he is not inherently awkward.

I still don't take pity on him. 'Just a fling then?'

'Kind of. Yes, basically.'

'Oh.' I nod. Not much more to say, really.

I'm about to turn to head back when Ben says, 'So whose wedding are you at?' Honestly, *why* is he trying to make pointless conversation with me?

'My friend Emmie. You might remember her from that New Year's Eve.'

'I think I only really spoke to Frankie and Nella and Sulwe. And you, obviously.'

There's a little silence, and then I look up at him, and get massively distracted (aka borderline turned-on) by him swallowing and his whole solid neck and Adam's apple thing, and suddenly I'm just really annoyed with myself, with him, with the fact that I am, utterly, utterly ridiculously, standing in a rose garden in Kent outside Emmie's wedding with a man I used to bump into occasionally, while a lot of my friends, my *proper* friends, are inside.

'I really think I should go back in,' I say.

'Of course. Although should we perhaps just take a stroll all the way round here? The grounds are beautiful.'

'I think I'm good, thank you.'

'I could really do with the company.' He raises his eyebrows and smiles.

I waver. I have nothing to lose, I suppose. And if I'm honest, I wasn't loving that reception. If I had been, I wouldn't have wandered outside in the first place.

'Why not?' I say after another couple of seconds, and we start walking again, further into the rose garden.

It's lovely in the dark, and the darkness reminds me of the first time we met.

'You know they turned the hut at the bus terminus into a kebab van?' I ask.

'I do. It used to make me think of you every time I walked past it, knowing that you had your café plan for it,' he says, and I'm ludicrously delighted that things used to remind him of me. 'You'd have done a better job. Their kebabs were shit.'

'I know. The only one I had gave me food poisoning.' I nearly say that it was the night we bumped into each other outside the pub, the Telegraph, and then I think better of sounding like I've catalogued every meeting we've ever had.

'Was that the night we bumped into each other outside the Telegraph? We went down to the Green Man and I thought I saw you afterwards at the van.' Ben also remembering that evening kind of makes my heart sing.

'Yes. I had the special, which I specifically chose because I thought it would all be fresh and less likely to kill me. And then I spent the entire night vomiting into Frankie's loo.'

'Ever eaten a kebab since?'

'Nope. Never going to for the rest of my life.'

Ben laughs and then we walk along various rose-lined paths in silence for a bit. It isn't a bad silence, actually. I'm mulling the number of times we've bumped into each other one way or another; I start trying to tot them up, but I keep losing count.

'I don't think I've ever bumped into someone I barely know as many times as I've bumped into you,' I say.

'Yeah, I always used to think that too, but then I realised that there are people you do bump into a lot. Like your next-door neighbour, or in my case the man from the drycleaner's down the road. It all depends how much you *register* that you've bumped into someone. Like whether it feels significant or not.'

'True.' I'm surprised I manage to get the word out. The bodice of my dress is suddenly feeling really tight, because Ben essentially just said – unless I am yet again misreading things – that he feels that bumping into me so often is significant.

'So how's your reception going? What was the happy couple's first dance? The groom and bride from my wedding have been taking waltz lessons together. Their first dance was Meatloaf 'I'd Do Anything for Love', and both the song choice and the fact that they were waltzing, counting out loud as they did it, should have made it funny, but actually it was really sweet.'

Ben's abrupt subject change leaves me in no doubt that he did mean the significant thing but instantly regretted it.

I'm very happy to chat about wedding music choices, and wherever else our conversation might wander; I also don't want to talk about significant bumping into people, or fate, as you might call it. It all just feels too difficult.

We carry on walking around the moon- and fairy-lit gardens, chatting about music and food and flowers (neither of us knows anything about plants, it turns out) for a while, and then, prompted by the sounds of chatter in the air, which must be some other wedding guests, I say, 'I guess we should both get back now.'

'*Or* we could just sneak off and go for a drink at that pub down the road. I'm not loving my wedding.' We're standing right under some lights and I can see Ben's face clearly. He looks almost panic-stricken. So weird. About *what*?

I'm tempted but I feel like I shouldn't be.

'I'm dressed like a giant meringue.'

'And I'm wearing a kilt and a velvet jacket. Give the locals something to gossip about.'

I look at him. I *love* talking to him. Pretty much every time I've seen him it's messed with my head, but he's already in there again this evening, so spending more time with him can't make it any worse. Maybe we should finally just spend one whole evening, not in a hut, together, and I'll probably discover he's really boring or he supports fox hunting or is an actual bigamist or something, and then I'll never think about him in that kind of fantasy we're-fated-to-keep-meeting kind of way again.

And I was *not* enjoying the evening before I came out here...

'I'm not loving mine either,' I say. 'You're on.'

15

LIV

As we round the corner of the building, three little boys in satin knickerbockers sprint past us, trailed by two men in morning suits. The men are panting and sweating like they've just run a desert marathon; they boys look like they could run forever, and have more than enough breath left to laugh with delight as they begin to scale the clematis-covered trellis attached to one of the garden walls.

'The pageboys from the wedding I'm at,' I tell Ben. 'And their dads.'

The biggest pageboy is now astride the (at least ten-foot high) wall, waving at his father and chortling so gleefully that I can't help laughing out loud too.

'They are *so* cute,' I say. 'And the one in pale yellow' – Emmie has them dressed in different pastel colours, which they're actually cute enough not just to pull off but to look adorable in – 'has a new baby sister. Who is be-still-my-beating-ovaries level gorgeous. Although...'

'Although?' Ben prompts after a pause during which I wave and grin at the boys and their dads (now at the bottom of the trellis yelling at them to come down), and we carry on walking.

'Well.' I don't feel embarrassed to tell him, because we don't *know* each other; and it's been driving me silently insane for the past few hours and it would be nice just to *say* that to someone. 'Basically, I might have been cooing quite a lot over the various babies at the wedding, and a *lot* of people started asking me about my love life and any baby plans. And the thing is, I'm gathering godchildren like nobody's business, which is lovely, but I'd love to have my *own* baby, but only with the right person, who I have not yet met, and it all just started to grate. A lot. Which is really why I left the reception for a little breather.'

I glance up at Ben and catch another very strange expression on his face.

What?

Oh. Crap. Did I sound as though I was angling in some excruciating way for *him* to father a baby with me? I really wasn't. Really. I wasn't.

Neither of us speaks for a moment – me trying to come up with some kind of joke that makes it *very* clear that I'm obviously not planning to make any demands on his sperm, and him just looking at me weirdly – and then he turns the strange expression off, as though he's flicked a switch.

'Yeah,' he says. 'There's something about weddings and bridesmaids and people's tact. My aunt Flora drank two glasses of champagne in about three minutes this afternoon and immediately asked Anita, one of the bridesmaids, really loudly, if she's going to sleep with yet another best man tonight. And Anita is getting married next month and her fiancé was standing next to her and he has never been a best man.'

'Nooooo.'

'Yep.'

We share a smile-grimace and now it's as though the strange moment never happened, and it's weirdly companionable walking down the hotel drive together, me in my meringue dress and Ben in his Scottish gear. I'm still not quite sure why he's suggested playing hooky from our weddings but the more we walk the more I'm up for it.

It isn't the simplest of walks, though. 'Erm, it's darker than I was expecting,' I say, as I narrowly avoid turning my ankle in a pothole in the road. I say road; it's basically a very rough country lane with no streetlights, and we've walked beyond the reach of the glow from the faux-Victorian lamps outside the hotel's main entrance.

'That's the countryside for you.' Ben pulls his phone out of an inside pocket of his jacket and turns the torch on, which gives me a flashback to us using phone torchlight in that shed together all those years ago.

'I'm disappointed that you don't keep your phone in your sporran,' I say, nodding to the round tassly bag at the front of his kilt to prevent myself from mentioning the flashback.

'There was actually a lot of pre-wedding chat about whether people should or should not keep their phones in there,' Ben says. 'The bride works in fashion journalism and she has a keen eye for detail. She decided in the end that no one should, because apparently your smaller phone is okay but your larger one is too heavy and spoils the sporran's line and she felt that one rule for everyone would be better than discriminating against those with plus size-phones. So we all had to put them in our jacket pockets.'

'Wow. So many decisions in planning weddings. So what *do* you keep in there?' I eye what I can see in the torchlight of bag and then realise what area of his anatomy I am essentially staring at and feel myself colour in the dark. 'And please don't feel that you have to answer that because I've just realised that that's a very intrusive question. Like asking what you keep in your pockets.'

'Sporrans do indeed perform the same function as pockets.'

'So basically you keep marmalade sandwiches in there,' I say in a (very) weak attempt at a joke, while I wonder, quite ridiculously, whether he has *condoms* in there.

Why am I wondering that? What is it to do with me whether Ben carries just-in-case condoms in his sporran when he goes to a wedding, and who he might be using those condoms with? Why am I even thinking about it?

'Paddington and the Queen?' he queries.

'Yep. I love them both and I loved their Jubilee scene.'

'I remember your marmalade popcorn at the cinema.' He directs the torch at another pothole and catches my elbow briefly as I almost trip yet again – these bridesmaid shoes were not built for country walking – and a little shiver of pleasure runs through me; I'm not sure whether it's due to his touch on my arm, his recollection of my popcorn flavouring or both.

I rush into inane speech to cover the shiver. 'I'm still loving coming up with new flavours. There's a romcom with George Clooney and Julia Roberts coming out in the autumn, set in Bali, which is a whole new world of flavour possibilities.'

'I can imagine. Although I don't know much about Indonesian cuisine...'

The light from Ben's torch shows that we've come to the edge of a small village.

'I've been researching it,' I say. 'It varies a lot by region. Balinese dishes involve amazing spice combinations.'

I come to a halt, looking up at the peeling sign above the door of the pub ahead of us – in its heyday it would have said 'The White Lamb' but now it says 'he W ite Lam'.

'So, erm, shall we go in?'

'We've come this far?' Ben has his eyebrows raised in a comical quirk, in recognition, I think, of the fact that the exterior of the building is really not inviting.

'Yes, let's do it,' I say decisively and push the door. Nothing happens, which I'm slightly relieved about. 'Oh, looks like it's closed. Maybe we should find another.'

'Given how small the village is, I don't think there'll be any other pubs in the vicinity, and it's pull.' Ben reaches round me, his arm brushing my shoulder, causing me to jump, and drags the door open.

We walk inside and both stop just over the threshold.

There are only four people in the room, one of them behind the bar, and the other three propping it up. There's no music, and the atmosphere screams that they were talking but have now been disturbed by us and aren't going to re-start their conversation because they're now all busy staring at us instead.

'Evening,' one of the three customers, a man wearing very threadbare actual plus fours, a diamond-patterned jumper and knee-length red socks, says.

'Evening,' Ben and I chorus, very rabbit-in-headlights-like, the pair of us.

'We'd love a drink,' Ben says into the silence that follows.

'Of course.' The barman spreads his hands in the direction of all the glasses on the shelf above him. 'That's what I'm here for. What can I get you? I'm Logan by the way.'

'Hi Logan,' we both say.

Ben looks at me and I say, 'I'm actually really thirsty. I might just get a lime and soda for now.'

'And I'll have a pint of Kentish ale.' Ben goes over to the bar and pays with his phone, so to my disappointment there's no sporran action.

'Make yourselves comfortable and I'll bring them over,' Logan tells us.

We thank him and then head over to two armchairs next to the fireplace. Making ourselves comfortable is not entirely possible because the four of them are still staring at us plus the chairs are stunningly *un*comfortable, with a spring actually sticking right out of the one I try to settle on.

'On second thoughts, maybe the wooden chairs in the corner,' I whisper to Ben, and stand up.

We move over to the corner and sit ourselves down. The table in front of us is visibly sticky and the pinky-red swirly wallpaper at my eye level has a large brown damp patch on it. When Ben suggested a drink at the pub I was expecting more of a cute, chocolate-box, roaring-fire (although it's been a hot day), busy-but-not-too-busy-with-pleasant-regulars, classic English country pub experience.

'So are you escapees from a fancy dress party or a wedding?' asks the plus four man, sitting himself down at the table right next to us and angling his chair so that we are essentially now a little group of three.

I wasn't just expecting a more attractive pub, I was also expecting more of a one-on-one experience with Ben.

'Wedding,' Ben says.

'Bridesmaid and best man?' asks one of the two other customers, a man wearing a slightly grubby navy suit and a large beard. He makes his way over to us too.

'Kind of,' I say, as Ben says, 'Sort of.' We smile at each other briefly and then we have to shift our chairs around so the bearded suited man and the third customer, a man in unremarkable jeans and a Gap T-shirt, can join us.

'Did you know each other before the wedding or have you just hooked up this evening?' the suited man asks and then they all stare at us.

'We've known each other for a while,' I say, as Ben says, 'Not really hooking up.'

'Exactly,' I say, quickly, in case it sounded to Ben as though I thought we *were* hooking up. 'We aren't hooking up. We're old friends and we thought we'd pop out for a drink.' Why are we even answering these questions?

They all sit and nod, and I realise that they *could* ask us now why we didn't just stay at the wedding and have a drink there.

'Long story, really,' I say. 'So this is a lovely village.'

Ben nods vigorously. 'It's great.'

'We like it,' the plus-fours man says. 'Do you play darts?'

'Not regularly,' I say.

'Me neither,' Ben says.

'Then it's time you started.' The plus-fours man stands up, opens a small cupboard in the wall and pulls out little pots of darts, which he hands to us, while Logan, with a bit of a flourish, does something with the wall and suddenly a darts board appears from nowhere.

We both gape slightly at them, raise our eyebrows a little at each other, and then simultaneously say, 'Great.'

Within no time at all, the plus-fours man has asked our names, told us their names and organised us, with Logan, into three teams of two. I'm paired with him (Harry) and Ben's paired with Fitz (the suited man), leaving Logan and Jake (the Gap T-shirt man) as the third pair. I'm really very surprised that my evening has panned out like this but actually quite happy. I mean, who doesn't love playing darts in a bordering-on-scummy pub with complete strangers while wearing a ridiculous dress?

The dress is particularly ridiculous, and it's quite hard to get a good throwing action because of the tight bodice and cap-sleeves, so my first dart goes seriously off-target and hits the bar.

Over the ensuing tutting, Ben says, 'I think Liv's hampered by her dress. Those sleeves look quite restrictive. I think we should allow her a few practice throws.'

Everyone agrees, Fitz a bit reluctantly (he's already looking like he has a *very* competitive personality), and I stand behind the line (which Logan informs us is called the oche) and get throwing. After I've discreetly unzipped my dress a tiny bit and have had a bit of a warm-up, I get into my stride and am regularly hitting the board.

'I know what would help you more.' Logan disappears behind the bar and returns with a tray, six full glasses and some matches. 'Some flaming sambucas.'

We all stare as he lights the first sambuca, counts to eight and then covers the glass with his hand, which puts the flame out, before inhaling the air underneath his hand and downing the shot.

'I am not doing that,' I say. 'I don't want to get burnt. Also, at the risk of sounding like a total party pooper, I'm kind of good with my lime and soda.' I have a very strong sense that getting drunk around Ben might cause me to say all sorts of stupid things.

'Just one,' wheedles Logan.

'Fine,' I say, extremely weak-mindedly. 'But only one and I'm not doing the fire bit.'

Logan lights mine and then puts the flame out with his hand, which I can't help thinking is quite unhygienic (he has his palm firmly over the whole of the rim of the glass for *seconds* and his hand does not look that clean) but I decide not to mention this. I down half of it and then shake my head.

'I don't want to be rude,' I tell him, 'but that is *grim*.'

'I think they taste a lot better if you're already drunk when you start on them,' Ben says.

Within about fifteen minutes, I've still only had half of one sambuca, Ben's had two, and the others have all had about five. We're all getting very competitive with the darts (I'm hitting the board on every go now) and the others are noticeably improving the more they drink, so I decide that I'll have a glass of white.

Ben looks at me suspiciously. 'Have you asked for the wine because you actually want to drink it or because you think it'll improve your play?'

'That's for me to know and you to worry about,' I say, taking a big slurp before aiming very carefully and, oh my *goodness*, hitting the bullseye. 'Yesssss. I'm a *genius*.'

Harry raises his hand and we perform an enthusiastic high five, before I practically down the rest of my wine in one, because clearly alcohol does indeed improve darts performance.

Another couple of sambucas in, resulting in a bit of a diminution in the standard of Harry's darts play – it seems that there is an optimal amount of alcohol and he has now gone beyond that – he confides that he was the Kent over-fifty-five darts champion three years ago, which makes Ben narrow his eyes even more and focus even harder.

I'm *really* enjoying watching Ben play darts. I like his look of concentration, I love his competitiveness and I *love* how his biceps flex as he throws and the fact that I have full licence to stand behind him and watch (ogle) his broad shoulders and narrow hips as he takes aim. Really, the only thing that I could fault about this evening is that it involves Harry, Fitz, Jake and Logan. They're all nice and actually quite good company, but I would, I realise, very much like to be alone with Ben. Still playing darts though. This is *fun*.

'Would you like any help?' I ask in my best innocent manner, when he misses the twenty by a whisker and hits the treble one instead. 'Maybe if you aimed just a tiny bit to the left.'

'That's very kind, thank you,' Ben says, 'but I think I'm absolutely fine.' He fake-glares at me and then the glare morphs into a grin, and, honestly, I nearly melt inside.

'Another glass of wine?' Logan suggests.

'Lime and soda again, actually, thank you,' I say. I feel as though one glass of wine on top of the two glasses I'd already had at the reception was enough because I definitely need to keep my wits about me this evening. I still don't know why Ben was so keen to come for a drink and I can feel myself falling right back into infatuation with him, and based on the past eight years or so since we first met, and the number of times my heart's felt a little bruised by him, even though we really barely know each other at all, I feel like I need to be careful.

Eventually, Harry and I win the game (an ex-over-fifty-five-Kent-champion is a force to be reckoned with) and Logan looks at the clock, exclaims and dashes over to the door to lock it.

'Bloody police'll have me otherwise,' he explains.

'Local copper doesn't have enough to do,' Jake confirms.

'Is that clock right?' I ask, squinting up behind the bar. It says it's half past midnight. 'We should maybe get back.'

I don't mind about the late night – you don't expect an early one when you're going to a wedding – but while darts was fun, now it's over I'm a bit tired and I don't really fancy returning to being interrogated by our new friends, and I have a nasty feeling that they now feel they know us well enough to ask *any*thing; and I did kind of want to talk to Ben alone at some point this evening.

'Definitely,' Ben agrees, taking his jacket off the coat stand next to the door and shrugging it on. 'Nice to meet you guys. Thanks so much for the game.'

The temperature's dropped quite markedly over the time we've been in the pub and I find myself shivering a little when we get outside. Ben notices immediately and within a couple of seconds has his jacket off and is holding it up for me to put my arms inside.

'But won't *you* get cold?' I ask. 'I mean, you're wearing a skirt too.' And based on how he reacted to some very persistent questioning on the subject from Fitz, I think there's a good chance he's underwear-free beneath the kilt.

'Tartan's thick and I have long socks and my shirt has long sleeves,' Ben says, cleverly manoeuvring the jacket so that somehow I already have my right arm inside and am putting my left one in without even really realising I've moved.

'Well, thank you,' I say, deciding to give in with a good grace because he's right; his clothes definitely are thicker than mine and being cold is not fun. The jacket's a lovely deep velvet and already slightly warm from the few moments Ben wore it before he gave it to me, and there's something very intimate about wearing something straight from someone else's back. I also think I catch the hint of his masculine scent on the fabric. Basically, if I'm honest, I'm *loving* wearing it.

Ben switches his phone torch on again and waves it around a little.

'Erm, is that another pub?' I say. 'Over there.'

He aims the torchlight where I'm pointing and as one we take a few steps towards it to get a better view. And, yes, it looks like the gorgeous, olde worlde, chintzy, ivy-and-flower clad, stone-built English pub that I was expecting.

'Ha,' Ben says. 'Sorry about that.'

'No.' I shake my head. 'No sorries. I really enjoyed our darts match.'

'Me too actually.'

'Are you sure?' I ask very seriously. 'Given that you lost *big*? Because we were much better than you.'

'Carry on like that and I'll be challenging you to a one-on-one match. Then you won't be able to hide behind any ex Kent champions.'

I laugh and then Ben holds his arm out. I take it, and we set off back to the hotel, arms linked.

'So you haven't left London for a while, you said?' Ben asks. 'Where do you usually go on holiday when you go away?'

'It varies.' I tell him how I still go back to Paris for the weekend sometimes to visit friends but that I don't take that much holiday the rest of the time because I left my job and am still working hard to build up my new recipe development business and am also ploughing as much cash as I can into it so I don't have much spare for holidays. And then I find myself telling him how I did do a couple of beach holidays with Tommy and somehow I move on to explaining that we broke up a few months ago, and, as I'm speaking, my mind's going in parallel wondering whether I'm telling him this on purpose, and what my motive is in doing that. I mean, at the beginning of our walk, I mentioned not having found the future father of my kids, but I didn't feel the urge to state explicitly that Tommy and I split up, but now I feel like I'm almost telling him on purpose. But what is that purpose?

'Yeah, I'm also solo this weekend,' Ben says. 'Well, I mean, generally solo also.'

I want to look up at him because I want to see the look on his face right now, but I don't want him to see mine, because I think I might be smiling in a cat-got-the-cream way, just at the thought that *finally* I get to talk to him at a time when we're both definitely single, and then I realise that this is *exactly* what always happens to me. I start weaving small (quite big actually) fantasies around how our (actually non-existent) relationship might pan out from wherever we are at that moment and then I get disappointed (that's an understatement).

The hotel lights are showing pale shimmery yellow not too far ahead of us now. Our little trip to the village has been a total fail from my perspective, in that the whole point of it in my mind was for me to get over Ben once and for all, but in fact I'm right back at the weaving-fantasy stage. I mean, right now I feel like I'm going to miss him when we go our separate ways in a minute. I feel cheated, robbed; I was supposed to get to spend an entire evening alone with him, and that hasn't happened.

Without thinking any further, I blurt out, 'Fancy a coffee when we get inside? I have a lovely room on the top floor under the eaves. It's very nice. They've done it in a Farrow & Ball kind of greige – Badger's Foot, something like that – with geometric velvet curtains and upholstery.'

Yes, Liv, everyone bases coffee decisions on paint colours and fabric choices. What is *wrong* with me?

I know what's wrong with me: I've flipped straight back into fancying the pants off Ben. I should not have flipped straight back here. I *know* that it never ends well for me.

'How can I say no to coffee in a Badger's Foot and geometric velvet room?' Ben's voice contains the beginning of the deep rumble of his laugh and the effect it has on me causes me to do almost a full physical squirm.

'Great. You'll be pleased to hear that the tiles in the bathroom continue the geometric effect,' I say, and he gratifies me with another rumbly laugh (generous, because I'm not making great jokes here).

And then we descend into an awkward silence. I don't know why Ben isn't speaking. *I'm* not speaking because I'm worrying that he thinks he's coming in for *coffee*-coffee, and I don't want *coffee*-coffee, I just want to talk and to find out that actually he isn't remotely my perfect man after all, and then say goodnight and goodbye and finish the weekend with my heart and sanity intact. And I'm also worrying that if I'm honest with myself I do slightly want him to come in for *coffee*-coffee. But I don't *want* to want him to come in for *coffee*-coffee.

'Nice Farrow & Ball on these walls here too,' I say, as, having collected keys from behind the reception desk, we go up the swish staircase that leads from the ground floor to the first floor.

'Indeed. And lovely curtains too,' Ben says. 'And carpet.'

I decide to stop talking. This is not taking away from the awkwardness. I kind of want to just say that maybe we should actually go our separate ways right now and goodnight. But also I do not want to say that.

I lead him to the end of the long first floor landing and up some winding stairs (still nicely Farrow-&-Ball-ed and with lovely carpet) to the second floor and right to the end of the landing, where my room is.

And then I open the door and we go in together.

16

BEN

I walk into the middle of Liv's room with her and say, 'Loving the Badger's Foot,' while I continue to ask myself *what* I think I'm doing.

We're adults. Usually, in this scenario, coffee is a euphemism. All adults know that.

But I should not be here in the expectation, or hope, or plan, that our coffee will be accompanied by anything more than a pleasant chat to round off a pleasant evening with an old kind-of-friend. Liv's comments earlier only underlined that. And I should not lead her – should she be expecting, hoping or planning any such thing – to think that I am up for anything more than a pleasant chat.

Because I cannot allow anything to happen between us. I don't want to let Liv down and I don't want either of us to get hurt.

'So. Coffee.' Liv's kicked off her heels, displaying her beautiful, delicately-boned, sparkly-green-toenail-topped feet – yes, that's right, I'm actually finding her *feet* turn-me-on attractive – and is on her way across the room to where there's a tea tray on top of a chest of drawers.

There's a king-sized bed symmetrically placed under the eaves in the middle of the wall, and there's one armchair, angled in one of the corners opposite the bed. I'm not going to stand up the whole time I'm in here; that would be weird. And I'm not going to sit on the bed; that would be weirder.

But I don't want to look rude and go straight to the chair either, so I carry on hovering in the middle of the room.

'Why don't you sit down?' Liv disappears into the bathroom with the kettle and I hear the sound of a running tap.

'Great, thanks,' I say, very over-heartily, and sit down in the armchair, because clearly that's where she must have been intending me to sit, rather than on her bed. I press my knees together, as you do when you're sitting down wearing a kilt – every time I wear this thing I wonder if women find skirt-wearing as annoying as I do – and decide that I need to say something that subtly demonstrates that I'm here just for a quick post-pub chat and nothing else.

Unfortunately, my mind's gone blank. I spent a lot of my childhood using chat to get myself out of trouble and for most of my adult life I've been in jobs where my ability to stream inane small talk has been one of the key reasons I've been successful, yet here I am completely dumbstruck.

Eventually, I fall back on the other favourite British conversational topic beyond the weather: travel.

'So did you get here by car or train?' I ask. I suppose the great thing about me being so boring right now is that if Liv *was* harbouring any desire to do what adults often do in this situation, she's probably now thinking better of it.

'Train.' She's busy rifling through the selection of infusions next to the kettle, picking each one up and checking it out. I love the way that whenever she's doing something, big or small, she really focuses on it. She does it with pretty much everything I've ever seen her do: rescuing that cat, organising the food for a party, developing crazy popcorn flavours. And of course in conversation; when you're with her she makes you feel like you're the only person in the world she wants to be talking to. I've seen her do that with her friends too. It has the effect of making you want to be in her world, always. 'What would you like? I can offer you a whole variety of herbal teas and some novelty coffees.'

She sounds as though she's very firmly keeping us both away from the minibar, which is definitely a good thing. She looks up at me with her gorgeous smile and my lips curve in response.

'Novelty coffee?'

'They're described as "instant flavoured coffee". We have chocolate-flavoured, peanut-butter, sherbet-lemon and rum.'

'Any regular coffee?'

'Nope.'

'Hmm. I know this is unfashionable but I'm not a big herbal tea drinker. I think I'm going to have to go rum coffee because it's the least-disgusting-sounding option.'

'Rum coffee it is. And I think I'll join you. It must be a kind of pre-mixed Irish coffee. I'd go so far as to say it actually sounds quite nice.' She looks around the room for a moment.

'Searching for your phone so you can make a note of coffee flavour ideas?' I ask.

'Exactly.' She beams at me, then locates her phone on a little table just inside the door and reaches for it. I exert extreme willpower and look away from the excellent view of her cleavage that she's inadvertently given me.

When she's finished a quick bit of tapping into her phone, apologising to me the whole time for what she says is her rudeness, while I assure her that it isn't at all rude, she hands me my espresso-sized coffee and takes her own, before sitting cross-legged under her dress in the middle of the bed.

'That's actually not bad at all,' I say after my first sip.

Liv sips hers and gasps. 'That's coffee-flavoured rum, not the other way round.'

And then we smile at each other and both pretty much down our drinks, even though they're quite hot.

'Another?' she asks.

'I think I will.'

Halfway through our fourth coffee-rums, Liv leans forward and says, 'So I have a question for you.'

'Yes?' I'm pretty sure there's no question that she would preface like that that I want to answer.

'Why were you so keen to go for a walk round the garden with me and then to the pub?'

'Um,' I say. That is a question I am *not* going to answer. I just can't.

Although... I waver for a moment. Maybe it would be easier just to tell her once and for all, so that nothing like this will ever happen again.

But no. I don't want to upset her and I also don't want her to think badly of me, even though that shouldn't really matter since we obviously can't see each other again after tonight.

'Was it...' She leans forward and bites her bottom lip for a moment and I find myself staring at her mouth, mesmerised. I want to climb onto the bed next to her and trace the line of her lips with my finger, and... No, I do not want to go there. 'Was it for the same reason that I wanted to go to the pub with you?'

I blink, trying to focus on her words and not on the way she's moistening her lips now and how gorgeous she looks shifting around on the bed and tucking her feet more firmly under her.

She's waiting for my reply. I think hard and manage to remember what she just asked.

'No.' I shake my head. 'Definitely not.'

'How do you know?' she asks, frowning a little. God, even her frown is turning me on.

I know because there's one main reason I wanted to take her for that walk and I know that there's no way hers was the same, but I'm not going to tell her that. I should have just said *Yes*.

'Why did *you* want to go to the pub?' I ask, turning the conversation on her before realising that that's a stupid question because she's already told me this. 'Hated your wedding that much?'

'No.' She shakes her head hard and her curls jiggle against her shoulders. 'I mean, yes, I wasn't loving it. But that isn't the main reason I wanted to go.'

'So what was the reason?' It's stupid of me to repeat the question, because I'm not going to tell her *my* reason, and I'm pretty sure now that it won't help either of us if she tells me *hers*, but apparently I can't stop myself.

'I wanted to find out that I don't like you,' she says, very seriously. 'You've been in my head on and off for over eight years now and I don't want you there any more. So I thought I'd spend a whole evening with you and basically get you out of my system.'

I nod, wondering what she means by 'spend a whole evening'. Like, does that involve, for example, well not for example, just, does it involve sex?

'Do you support fox hunting?' she asks.

'What?' I'm a little befuddled by the abrupt subject change.

'Do you support fox hunting?'

I shake my head. 'No. I mean, yes I'm sorry for anyone who loses their job as a result of the banning of blood sports, but no, it's barbaric and I do not support anyone hunting animals for fun.'

'Dammit,' she says. 'Are you a bigamist?'

I shake my head again and say nothing. There's really no explanation necessary there.

'Dammit,' she repeats.

I look at her beautiful face, so familiar to me as though it's drawn on my heart, her mad toenails, the way she's rocking the ridiculous toilet-roll-holder bridesmaid's dress, and I know that I care *so much* about her happiness, and I feel that I need to be honest.

I say honest, not fully honest. I don't think I can do that. But as honest as I can manage.

'I have no idea how you feel or how you think about anything,' I begin. 'By "anything" I mean, in fact' – I clear my throat – 'me.' I put my cup down on the floor to the right of the chair while I try to organise my words. 'I like you, a lot, but... for various reasons, I cannot have a long-term relationship. Or mid-term.'

I realise, suddenly, that having come this far, one night only couldn't hurt. As long as we agree in advance that it would be one night only. If that's what Liv wants, if she would like one night, knowing that we won't, can't, continue into an actual relationship. And she did just say she wanted to spend an entire evening with me and get me out of her system. Maybe that could be a mutual thing.

'I could only ever do' – I clear my throat yet again – 'just one night.'

'Just one night,' Liv repeats.

17

LIV

I stare at Ben.

I'm very confused.

I just asked him why he was so keen to go for a walk with me and somehow that ended up in him telling me, I think, that he'd be totally up for a one-night-stand but absolutely not for anything more than that (which actually, when I think about it, still does not tell me his reason for wanting to go for the walk). I'm pretty sure that is *not* flattering. And it isn't what I was expecting. I also get the impression that Ben's actually surprised himself; I really don't think that his intention in asking me to go for the walk was to get me into bed.

So that's the first thing I'm confused about.

The second thing I'm confused about is what I want. I *wanted* to get Ben out of my system, fast. That hasn't gone well so far this evening. Right now, as I reflect, I'm staring, gazing at him, and part of me is cataloguing the sheer perfection of him. He seems kind, decent, funny and chivalrous. I love talking to him; we have an amazing connection. And he's very handsome and I'm pretty sure that a very nice body lies under his shirt and kilt. The only thing wrong with him from an 'allow myself to think of him as the potential love-of-my-life' perspective is that we don't *really* have an amazing connection. It's more like a series of missed connections. And after eight years of nearly but not quite spending time together, he's just told me that all he has to offer me is 'just one night'. Not just one night and then we'll see. Just one night, full stop.

I'm still staring. He's still gazing back. I *love* his eyes. They're quite wide apart and are greeny-grey, with brown flecks around the outside of the iris; and his mid-brown eyelashes are so thick I'm almost jealous. He must be mid-to-late-thirties now and he has little creases at the corner of his eyes, which, of course, just serve to make him even more attractive.

I want to have the right to touch his face, trace his cheekbones, run my fingers across the roughness of his end-of-day stubble.

'Just one night,' I say again, very slowly. Not as a statement, or as a question. More as an idea, to be explored. I would, obviously, *love* one night with him. But I would probably, obviously, be very sad to say goodbye to him afterwards.

But am I not going to be sad anyway?

Ben still says nothing.

I look around the room. Maybe all those rum coffees were not a good idea. Maybe they've affected our thinking.

We need to work the alcohol off somehow. I don't want Ben to have any regrets about whatever does or does not happen tonight, and I'd clearly be keen not to have any regrets myself either.

'We should dance,' I say.

'Dance?'

'Yes. We need to work the rum off. And also' – I'm warming very quickly to my theme – 'I missed out on a lot of the dancing at Emmie's wedding. I *love* dancing.'

'I'm not surprised.' Ben smiles at me as I hoik myself off the bed and take his hands, giving them a little pull to encourage him to his feet. He stands up and smiles more as I lead him into the only proper dancing space in the room, between the side of the bed and the bathroom door. I'm shorter without my heels on. Ben's very tall. But not too tall. Just... perfectly tall. 'Are we dancing to music?'

'Yes we are. And happily, I have the playlist that Emmie sent us all – her bridesmaids.' I let go of one of his hands to reach for my phone. A few swipes and taps later, and I have the playlist going.

The first song up is "Unchained Melody".

Ben raises an eyebrow.

'Yes,' I confirm. 'Emmie likes old, cheesy love songs.'

Oh, okay. I've basically just forced him into dancing to old, cheesy love songs with me.

'Well, who doesn't?' he says politely.

And then we stand there, still holding hands, neither of us really moving. And then I start to sway a little as the intro builds, and then Ben does, and then, somehow, we move our hands so that we're palm to palm, at about my shoulder level, and then we link fingers and then, just as I think Ben's going to put our linked hands behind my back, so that I fall against his chest, which I'd be very happy about, he lets go of my left hand and twirls me round and round by my right until I'm breathless and laughing. And then he catches me in a waltz hold and I can barely breathe from the sheer pleasure of it. His left hand is lightly against the small of my back and it feels like it's almost burning me there. My left hand is in his other large, firm hand, and he's definitely the one leading this dance, moving us gently around our little dance space.

Our bodies are as close as they could be without touching and I'm barely able to think about anything other than the warmth I feel from his body so near to mine, and whether we'll actually brush against each other. *This* is why all those Bridgerton-era heroines got so het up over waltzing, I think, a little desperately trying to cling on to any thought other than, just... *Ben*.

As the music finishes, he dips me right back over his arm, and then sweeps me up into a quick hug, before releasing me so that we're just holding hands again, our hands between our bodies, but otherwise not touching.

I fight for some coherent thought and manage to say, 'You're *good*. Did you learn all that from *Strictly* or have you had lessons?'

'Lessons. A work thing once.'

I can't believe the amount of emotion I felt there during those few words: misery at the thought of him taking lessons with a partner followed by relief that it was a work thing.

'Well, they were good lessons,' I say, hoping that he hasn't noticed how heightened all my reactions seem to be.

And then the Black Eyed Peas start belting out 'I Gotta Feeling' and we're off again, this time shimmying and clapping and jigging, facing each other and close to each other but not touching.

I *love* it when we do an imaginary mic thing together. We really go for it on the *woo-hoos* and then there's a big bang on the wall opposite the bathroom and someone shouts, 'Keep it down,' which makes us both laugh a lot more than it should.

Next up we have Justin Timberlake and 'Can't Stop the Feeling!' and we turn the volume down a little on my phone and dance in an exaggerated tiptoe way, pointing at the angry-neighbour-wall, which makes us both snigger like we're the funniest people who ever walked the planet.

Whitney Houston and 'I Wanna Dance with Somebody' comes next.

'I'm not ashamed to say,' I tell Ben during some serious swaying and (I *am* ashamed to say) some imitation horse-geeing (I'm really not sure why I'm doing that), 'that this is one of my favourite songs of all time.'

'Rightly so,' he agrees. 'Whitney was a goddess.'

It's on the first iteration of wanting to feel heat with someone in the second round of the chorus that Ben and I match palms and then link fingers again. We remain like that, gazing into each other's eyes, for I don't know how long, and then he gently pulls my hands down so that now our linked hands are either side of us and we're very close together. He lets go of my hands and slides his round my waist, and I find myself placing my hands on his perfectly, gorgeously, solid chest. I can feel his heart thudding, and I'm pretty sure that it isn't just from the dancing.

I only barely register Whitney switching it up into 'Higher Love'. All I can think about is Ben and the fact that this is *real*. He is here with me, in the flesh, and he's holding me and I'm touching him. That little bit of awareness sparks a tiny bit of awkwardness – a *like whaaaat* feeling – in me, and my brain goes into self-preservation mode, taking me out of the moment a little, and I wonder if I'm about to find out whether he is or is not wearing anything under his kilt. I snigger slightly.

'What's funny?' He smiles at me, a soppy kind of smile, and my heart lurches.

And suddenly nothing at all is funny.

'I was just thinking about your kilt,' I manage to say, but I'm not focusing on what I'm saying and I don't think he even really hears me.

Instead, he moves one hand up to tug my hair, just very, very lightly, so that my head's tilted back, and then he lowers his head, and, very gently, brushes his lips against mine.

We take our time. The kiss becomes urgent, passionate, demanding, on both sides, but we don't hurry. At the back of my mind is the 'just one night' thing, and maybe it's there for Ben too; I don't want this to be over sooner than it has to be, and maybe he feels the same way.

Eventually, somehow, we're on the bed and we're making each other laugh because the zip on my dress is difficult to undo, and the sporran that Ben is *still* wearing is very much in the way now.

It turns out he *does* have trunks on under the kilt. 'Yeah, not a true grandson of Scotland,' he says as he pulls the neckline of my dress low and kisses and nips me with his teeth, while reaching his hand up under the skirts of my dress. I shudder with pleasure and have no further ability to talk about Scottish men's underwear habits.

We don't talk at all for a long time, until I discover that the sporran does *not* contain any condoms, which on the one hand pleases me hugely – Ben was clearly not planning to have sex tonight, or if he was, he's an idiot, which I don't think he is – but on the other hand is *really* inconvenient, because I also did not come equipped with safe sex measures.

'We can... improvise,' Ben tells me and I begin to gasp at some of his improvisation.

Later on, after a lot of *amazing* improvisation, we discover that the hotel was a lot more forward-thinking about its guests' possible sexual needs than either of us, and that whoever equipped my en suite with a *lot* of condoms was determined that their guests wouldn't be restricted to just your bog-standard Durex. I mean, there are a *lot* of options.

And so we stay up all night, having a lot of sex. The best sex of my entire life.

I think we eventually go to sleep around seven in the morning, spooning with Ben hugging me into him, our legs entwined, the sheets from the very-trashed bed only approximately across our nakedness, our heads on the same pillow.

It's been, hands-down, the best night of my life.

I'm woken from a sleep that's taken me a long way away by what, after some time, I work out is knocking on the door.

I take a few moments to gather myself, and then I remember. I feel a big smile beginning on my face and turn my – quite fuzzy actually – head to look at Ben.

Ben is not there.

I frown and raise myself on my right elbow and look around the room.

Ben's clothes aren't here either.

The only sign of him in the entire room is a message in biro on a postcard of the hotel, placed on top of my phone. The message reads:

Best night of my life. Goodbye. Bx

18

LIV

An hour and a quarter later, I'm sprinting into the train station three miles from the hotel. A hard bit of my bag bangs against my right ankle every time I step with that foot, my cross-body handbag's threatening to garotte me and my lungs are on fire. I haven't run this fast since school, and I'm not enjoying it.

As I hurtle inside and then come to a stop under a noticeboard, to try to work out where to go, I register vaguely that it's one of those places that are strong candidates for 'prettiest station in Britain'. The station building's olde worlde, there are window boxes containing perky-looking flowers, and it's all very *clean*.

It looks like there are two platforms and the London-bound train goes from Platform 2. I'm standing next to Platform 1; Platform 2 is over a footbridge, and there are quite a lot of people standing there, some of whom I recognise as wedding guests. I'm pretty sure that I have *no* time left before the train arrives, so I ignore my loudly protesting lungs and thigh muscles, heft my bag up again and go for one last Usain Bolt-level push.

The train comes in as I hit the second step on the way up to the bridge.

And it goes out as I hit the third step from the bottom on the way down to the platform.

'Nooooo, waiiiiit,' I scream, as if it's going to make any difference.

I really wanted to get on that train. It was one of those non-refundable special deals *and* I paid £5 extra to book a seat so that I wouldn't have to stand after what I thought might be a big night, not realising *how* big it would be or *how* shit I'd be feeling right now. Plus I'm pretty sure I remember from when I booked that there aren't a lot of trains stopping at this station, which is why most people wisely drove.

I refused offers of lifts from several people who I knew would capitalise on having me trapped in an enclosed place and spend the entire journey instructing me to start a family as soon as humanly possible, and instead came with Sulwe and Lewis. Unfortunately, they're driving straight to a family barbecue in North London now and I decided – incorrectly – that getting the train straight back to London from here would be easier than them dropping me off at a different station.

I am so desperate to get home.

I need to have a massive cry in the privacy of my own flat before picking myself up and reminding myself that Ben and I *agreed* that last night was a one night only thing and that I should therefore have nothing to be sad about. After all, my aim (I think) in doing what we did was to get Ben out of my system.

I already know, though, that I just succeeded in doing the exact opposite of that.

If I'm honest, it wasn't my aim anyway by the time we started the dancing. Maybe the whole thing was just down to fancying the pants of him and having no willpower. Plus those rum coffees.

Anyway, I'm not going to think about him now and possibly (probably) end up crying on this platform. I'm going to find out when the next train is and make a plan.

I put my overnight bag down and squint up at the noticeboard. The writing's really small and I don't have my contacts in because my eyes were too sore from lack of sleep and crying. I squint harder. Nope, still can't read it.

'The next one's in two hours' time.' Ben's voice comes from behind me.

I stand there motionless with my back to him for a long moment. My first reaction is: thank *goodness* I spent several minutes applying a *lot* of eye make-up and foundation to disguise my tear stains and red eyes. My second reaction is: what an idiot to have spent all that time on make-up. If I'd spent less time sorting my face, I'd either have made the train or been able to have a longer shower and maybe feel less crap right now.

I'm going to have to speak to Ben.

I turn round, slowly, and say, 'Thanks. The writing's very small.'

'Yeah.'

We exchange half-smiles and neither of us says anything for a few beats, and then I say, 'Bye, then,' and pick up my bag and begin to trudge past him and back towards the steps.

19

BEN

I shouldn't call after her. I shouldn't walk after her. I shouldn't do anything other than just stand and watch her go.

Except.

I'm wondering. Maybe it wasn't bad luck that our two weddings were at the same time in the same place; maybe it was *good* luck. Fate.

Ever since we first met in that hut, I've felt like in a parallel life we would have been completely meant-to-be. Maybe, somehow, we're a little bit meant-to-be in *this* life. Just for a while, anyway. We're both single, both living in London. Maybe something between us could work for a while.

Or maybe it couldn't. Maybe I'm just engaging in a case of extreme wishful thinking.

Yep, it is wishful thinking. Of course it couldn't work. It wouldn't be right for me to imply that I can give more than I can. But I can't see that spending an extra few hours together now, waiting for the train and then travelling back together, can make a lot of difference to how either of us is going to feel after a night like last night.

'Liv.' My voice rings out a little too loudly.

'Yes?' Her voice, by contrast, sounds very small. She half-turns and looks at me over her shoulder. I find myself taking a sharp breath. She looks like she has bags under her eyes and she's wearing a lot of eye make-up, way more than I think she normally wears, which I'm guessing might be to cover up tiredness, and her hair's up on top of her head in a messy bun, and her clothes are quite haphazardly thrown-on, as if she got dressed in the dark. And she's just... *beautiful.*

'Do you want to get a coffee?' I hear myself ask.

She hesitates. 'I'm not sure.' And then she hesitates some more, while I just wait. And then it's like she gathers herself somehow. 'Also, are there even any coffee places here? I mean, talk about arse end of nowhere. Picturesque, obviously, but I'm not seeing a lot of amenities.'

I smile, because it sounds like she's decided she *would* get a coffee with me if we could.

'There's got to be coffee somewhere.' I walk forwards and hold my hand out for her bag, and she shakes her head. 'You sure? It looks quite heavy and I feel like I should put my gym-going to actual use. And, you know, impress the laydeez with my guns.'

'Well, if you put it like that. I'm not *loving* carrying it.' She passes it to me.

'Woah, that's heavy. What's *in* there?'

'Hairdryer, shoes, bridesmaid's dress, a lot of hair and make-up products. You name it.'

I nod. 'Fair enough. Right. Let's go and hunt down the coffee. Or at least some water. Or a bench to sit on.'

We exit the station and bump straight into a man and woman in their thirties like us.

The woman throws her arms round Liv and says, 'Liv! Where did you go last night? And we missed you at breakfast.'

The woman lets go of her, takes a step back and looks at me and then down at my hands, noting that I'm carrying two overnight bags and Liv's carrying none. Then she raises her eyebrows and sticks her hand out in my direction. I put down one of the bags to free my right hand and shake hers.

'I'm Sarah. I don't think we've met?'

'This is an old friend, Ben.' Liv has an I'd-rather-stick-pins-in-my-eyes-than-perform-this-introduction demeanour. 'We just bumped into each other so we thought we'd go and grab a coffee while we wait for a train.' Sarah's mouth opens, and Liv says, very fast, 'So I'll see you at Sulwe's at the weekend,' and gives them both a quick hug before turning to her right and beginning a fast walk.

'Great to meet you,' I tell them before taking the few long strides necessary to catch her up.

'Sarah was *so* on the brink of suggesting that we double-date coffee,' she says. 'I could see it in her eye. I'm not keen to go back in case we bump into them again but I think I started us walking in the wrong direction.'

'I think you did too,' I agree. There were a few houses on the road on the other side of the station and I think I glimpsed the top of a church spire that way. This way is just fields and trees on both sides of the road. Very pleasant but not looking like somewhere where we can have coffee. 'It's nice, though. Scenic.' I'm also not keen right now for us to go back to the station and possibly bump into people it would be awkward to see. 'Walk?'

'The bags, though.' She puts her hand out. 'Let me take my own one now?'

I shake my head. 'Honestly, it isn't a problem.'

'Sure?'

'Yes. Look.' I lift my normal-weight bag and her ridiculously heavy one up to shoulder height as though they weigh nothing, and stagger slightly, which makes Liv laugh a lot. I feel ridiculously proud of myself for inducing her laughter, and I feel my mouth spread into a broad smile.

'There's a picnic table through there.' Liv points to a little clearing about fifty metres from the road. 'Shall we sit down?'

'Good idea.'

Is it, though? I'm beginning to worry that she might want to talk about last night. I have nothing to say beyond what I told her at the time, about it being one night only, and I don't think talking about it now would be a comfortable conversation for either of us. I should have thought of this when I called out to her in the station.

I put the bags down next to the table and we sit – a little awkwardly – on opposite benches.

'So are you hungover?' Liv pulls a small bottle of water out of her handbag, takes a drink, wipes the neck and offers it to me.

'Thank you.' I take the bottle. It would be ridiculous not to share it after all the bodily fluids we shared last night. God. 'No. I'm lucky hangover-wise. Rarely get them.'

And also we did a lot of exercise during the night and probably worked off all the alcohol.

'That *is* lucky. I get really bad ones. Worse with red wine and certain spirits. And I'm not great with mixing.'

She twists the lid back on the bottle and I find myself mesmerised by her slim, lightly-tanned hands. She has her nails painted a delicate pink, a very bridesmaidy-colour when I think about it. I noticed them last night too, when she was throwing darts. And later, in the bedroom. I think Liv normally has her nails painted stronger, more in-your-face colours, like the green on her toenails. Turns out all colours look gorgeous on her.

'Look.' She lowers her voice and indicates with one of her pink-tipped fingers. 'Rabbits. They're so cute.'

When we finish admiring the cute rabbits (if I'm honest I'm admiring Liv's cuteness more than the rabbits' cuteness; I love the curve of her cheek, the concentration in her eyes and the small smile on her face as she looks at them), Liv steers the conversation in the direction of some birds in the branches above us and how they remind her of a couple of male wedding guests peacocking on the dance floor yesterday evening. And then we're sharing wedding anecdotes and then we begin to talk about films, and soon I'm pretty sure that she has as little wish as I do to talk about last night, and I relax.

'We should keep an eye on the time,' Liv says some time later, during a lull in the conversation in which she's been yawning a little and I've been fighting the impulse to walk round the table and gather her into my arms and either kiss her silly or maybe just carry her over to a patch of grass and have a little snooze together. We *really* did not get a lot of sleep last night, which is clearly why we both missed our train. She pulls out her phone. 'Wow, we've been sitting here for well over an hour. The train's due in about twenty minutes.'

'Better start wandering back, then?' I suggest and she nods.

We carry on our easy conversation as we meander along the road. It's nice. It's also heart-breaking, because I feel like I could happily talk to Liv every day of the rest of my life, but I know I'm not going to.

Sarah and her companion are of course there on the platform when we arrive.

'So how do you two know each other?' is Sarah's predictable opener after we've re-helloed.

'We met through mutual friends one New Year's Eve,' Liv says, without looking at me.

'And you—' Sarah is clearly keen to delve into what we're doing together now and whether there's anything between us.

'Yes,' Liv continues. 'It was lovely to bump into each other again on the platform here, so we thought we'd catch up while we were waiting for the train.'

'And what do you do, Ben?' Sarah is a determined woman it seems.

'I work in the hospitality industry.'

'I always wonder what that means,' she persists. 'Barman or owner of the Ritz?'

'Somewhere in between,' I say, 'but I do enjoy working behind a bar when the opportunity arises.' It really pisses me off when people are snobby about bar – or any other – work.

'Sorry,' she says. 'Just looking out for Liv.'

My feeling of hostility towards her softens a little.

'I hope the train's going to be on time.' Liv looks slightly pained.

We immediately hear it rumble in the distance.

Fortunately, the train's quite busy and there are no four-person tables free. Sarah and her still un-named companion apologise profusely about taking the first free double seat that we all come across, and then pretty much leap into it, and Liv and I continue down the train. We pass a lot of single seats but both keep on moving until we find a double one, and then we kind of look at each other and nod; Liv slides in first and I sit down next to her.

The journey to London is over two hours. There's a man on the seat across the aisle who first eats a very smelly, entirely brown-coloured meal out of a Tupperware container and then farts several times even more smellily. Also, the leg room is not generous, it's very hot because the air-con isn't working and the windows don't seem to open.

It's no question the best train journey of my life.

We snigger about the farting. We carry on making animated conversation out of almost anything. In the net pocket in the back of the seat in front of Liv we find a Sunday newspaper open on its puzzle page and discover that I'm way better than her at crosswords (the easy one; neither of us can do the cryptic one) and she's way better at sudoku than me. I notice that I love the way she writes her capitals and numbers firmly and evenly (she's the one with the pen). We bicker about whether Coca-Cola or Pepsi has a better flavour (obviously it's Pepsi) and we have a heated argument about the merits of open-air versus indoor swimming pools versus swimming in the sea (obviously sea-swimming is the best).

And I spend a lot of the time battling with myself (and succeeding I'm proud to say) not to touch her in any way. When she leans forward over the newspaper, some tendrils of hair fall forward across her cheek, and I'm desperate to brush them back and allow my finger to trace down her neck and across her delicate collar bone. I also, most of the time, want to put my arm around her shoulders and pull her into me and just feel her against my side. Obviously there's other stuff I'd like to do too, most of which would probably be illegal in public.

I don't do any of it and it requires serious willpower.

I'm still loving just sitting next to her, though.

I'm beyond disappointed when our train pulls into London Victoria. I just want to keep on talking to Liv. Every time I make her laugh, I feel like I've won a prize. Every time she smiles at me, I just want her to keep on smiling. And I love hearing everything she says. I don't want it to stop.

It's going to take me a little time to recover from this.

As the passengers around us begin to stand up and gather their belongings, I think about how, if we were to spend the rest of today together, it really wouldn't make the whole thing any bigger than last night and today have already been; it wouldn't make it any more of a thing to get over. And if it's that way for me, it must be that way for Liv – assuming she feels similarly about me, which is of course a big assumption – so I'm not being selfish.

'Are you free this evening?' I ask. 'Would you like to come over? To mine?'

Liv looks at me, her mouth formed into an O shape, her eyes wide, and says… nothing.

And Smelly Man farts again, really loudly.

Liv does that laughing through a closed mouth thing that people do when they're trying to be polite and not laugh, and I'm pretty sure I'm doing the same thing.

And damn Smelly Man and his ridiculous flatulence, because maybe now she won't answer my question, and I can hardly ask again.

And then… she says, 'I'd like that,' and I feel as though my heart misses a beat.

20

LIV

Was that the most stupid snap decision I've ever made?

I'm staring blankly into the aisle beyond Ben, trying to work out whether I'm ecstatic that it isn't goodbye yet, terrified that when it *is* goodbye it's going to be *bad*, or able just to go with it and enjoy the moment, when I notice that the smelly farting man is about to put his Tupperware into his suitcase and it's leaking.

'Excuse me.' I lean across Ben to attract the man's attention, enjoying the fact that my shoulder's against Ben's arm for a totally valid reason (i.e. neither having-sex-that-we-shouldn't-have-been-having nor unable-to-resist-the-temptation-to-get-a-bit-too-close). 'Hi. I just noticed that your box is leaking and I thought you might like to know so that it doesn't go on all your stuff.'

'Thanks but I don't mind a few stains.' Unbelievably, the man leers at me and says, 'Know what I mean?'

I giggle, which is a thing I do when I'm shocked, and I *am* a bit shocked. However, I don't feel at *all* threatened; we're surrounded by a *lot* of other people and I'm next to Ben who is very large and bristling angrily, and the smelly man is surprisingly small now that he's on his feet (clearly a long body, short legs person, because he looked quite tall when he was sitting down). Now, he's just kind of laughably grim.

Ben does not giggle and says, 'Sorry, what?' Without looking at him, I know that he's properly angry, because his voice is strange and hard and I can feel that his entire body's gone tense.

'Nothing, mate, just a joke.'

'Not funny, though. Maybe think harder about how the recipient of your supposed jokes might feel?'

The man zips his suitcase up hard, but not quite fully, and, leaving a trail of brown sauce behind him, pushes past some other passengers, muttering 'Fuck you' as he passes.

Ben goes all inarticulate and says, 'Er,' a lot and then finally says, 'I hope that didn't bring back any difficult memories for you.' And my heart melts even more than it already had; he clearly remembers what I told him about my work issues with Max from all those years ago, and is clearly concerned that I might be upset.

'Thank you,' I say, and smile. I think it's a wide, foolish, wearing-my-heart-on-my-face kind of smile, but right now I really don't care.

We remain suspended in the moment for quite a long time, I think, until someone bumps their bag against Ben's shoulder and he looks round. Then he unfolds himself from the seat and I follow him.

I realise as I scramble down the steps and onto the platform that I don't know whether Ben was suggesting that I go straight back with him now or whether he thought I'd go home and then go over later. I'd kind of like to go home and get changed, although that would be awkward because I wouldn't like to look as though I'd made a huge effort to look nice, plus what if he then changed his mind? And also, now I think about it, if we're only going to have this one day together, I don't want to waste time.

'The quickest way's the Victoria line,' he says, obviously expecting me to go with him, and I smile.

It's a busy day on the Tube, one of those London summer Sundays where everyone's out to enjoy the weather but for some reason they cannot enjoy it anywhere they can get to on foot so millions of people have piled onto public transport, so they end up enjoying the beautiful weather in a Tube carriage rammed with sweaty bodies. The upside for me is that the body I'm most closely jammed up against is Ben's, and he isn't sweaty (he just smells of pine and lovely muskiness) and he's hard in all the right places. Also, he's too tall to be able to see my face when we're shoved this close together, so I really am enjoying myself a lot and I can smile as lustfully as I like without him knowing.

I'm disappointed when the crowd in our carriage thins out at Euston and then King's Cross and if I don't want to look scarily crazy-stalker-like I have to take a step away from him. And then I feel really self-conscious because it occurs to me that going on the Tube with someone back to their flat is quite an intimate kind of thing to do.

Ben screws his face up a bit and says, 'You know what I'm thinking now?'

'No?' I ask, alarmed. Is he going to tell me that this is a bad idea? It probably *is* a bad idea, but I discover that I'm very desperate, firstly to have a few more hours with Ben and secondly not to be blown off by him a good fifty-minute journey from home.

'I'm really wondering what state I left the flat in. I mean, I'm quite a tidy person, honestly. And clean. I'd go so far as to say very tidy. But also I did leave in a bit of a rush yesterday morning, and I wasn't expecting anyone to come over this evening. So just to warn you, I could be presenting myself as a bit of a slob.'

'Well, I'm shocked,' I say, extremely relieved that he isn't binning me right now (and also delighted that he wasn't expecting anyone else to go over today). 'And yes I will very much judge you if there are stray undergarments or coffee mugs strewn around. And if the bathroom floor isn't clean enough to eat your dinner off, I mean, I'll be *appalled*.'

He wrinkles his nose at me and laughs, and this is the moment where I wonder for the first time whether I'm falling in actual love with him, before shoving the thought out of my mind very hard.

'My mother's never once arrived at my flat and immediately pulled a pair of marigolds on,' I continue, to distract myself from his gorgeous, lovely, wonderful smile and the way my heart's lolloping around inside my chest. And there it is again: the word *love* is popping into my head once more.

Ben laughs again and oh my goodness, yes I do, I know I do, it's insane and it's ridiculous and I'm an idiot but I love him, I do.

And oh my goodness, *shut up*, I tell my stupid mind. I don't even really *know* him. Except I do, my traitorous mind tells me. I know him in my bones. Sometimes you don't have to spend huge amounts of time with people to *know* them, the extra time is just for gathering facts about them.

Ben's flat is very... Ben, I think, as he opens the door and then ushers me in, saying in an excellent parody of a polished estate agent, 'Just focus on the *potential* that the flat has to be well-presented.' And then he zooms very fast around the open-plan kitchen sitting room, gathering up bits of crockery and a couple of magazines and some hoodies and shoes, stuffs them all into a large cupboard to the right of the front door, and says, 'Well, there you go, it was perfectly tidy all along. Don't know why I was worrying.'

I laugh and say, 'It's lovely.'

And it is. It's on the first floor of a lovely Georgian terrace and the large windows opposite me overlook a communal square garden at the back. The room's painted a striking greeny-blue which looks amazing against its pale cream woodwork and the big windows. There are a couple of big, squishy-looking sofas that immediately make me think about curling up and having a little snooze.

'Cup of tea? Glass of water?' Ben asks, moving over to the kitchen area that's round the corner from the rest of the room.

'Water would be great, thank you.' It's thirsty work travelling across London on a hot day. First, though, I *really* need the loo.

The bathroom's greige tiled, and has a huge shower and big, thick bottle-green towels. The effect all this has on me (i.e. the start of some very enticing Ben-related fantasies) makes me think that my mind's becoming very one-track (focusing very specifically on sex with Ben).

When I get back into the living room, Ben's just closing another cupboard door.

'Just taking advantage of your bathroom break to finish my tidying,' he says. Which is extremely, entirely, completely plausible – after all, he did his speed-tidy-up when he opened the front door – except there's something about his body language that has me confused. He's meeting my eye too much, spreading his shoulders too widely – all very nothing-to-see-here – exactly how someone behaves when they're consciously trying to look unshifty. What could it be, though? I really don't think he's hiding evidence of a wife, for example.

Maybe he just has a very embarrassing hobby. I think that *must* be it. I really don't believe he'd cheat on someone.

'Fancy a walk around the local park?' he asks. 'And then maybe a takeaway?'

I feel as though he's trying to distract me from whatever he's trying to hide. I hesitate for a moment, and then shrug internally. I do not think he has a secret wife or a dead body in his freezer. And if he's embarrassed about his crochet or train spotting or insect taxidermy hobby, then I should respect that.

'I'd love that,' I tell him.

I'm not going to let myself think about what might happen after the takeaway and how (and when) we'll say goodbye. Just. Not. Going. To. Think. About. It. I'm not. I'd love to stay the night, though; I'm going to be gutted when this very surprising weekend is over so I might as well make the most of it before that happens.

As we leave his flat and laugh our way down the stairs to the front door, he seems completely back to his usual self and now I'm half wondering what his unusual hobby must be and half wondering whether I was imagining things back there.

Ben leads me to a lovely park a couple of roads away and we amble around for a while and then sit on some grass surrounded by trees and flower beds full of riotously coloured blossoms, soaking up the sun and each other's company.

He's just telling me some *excellent* gossip (involving a Britney outfit and three avocados) about someone who used to work at the cinema in Clapham when we hear the tinkle of an ice cream van.

'I could murder a Mr Whippy,' Ben says. 'You?'

'Yes,' I confirm. I'm almost salivating just at the thought. It's a very hot day.

We make our way down to where a queue's already forming next to the van.

'Oh my goodness.' I'm delighted. 'It's proper, creamy ice cream.'

'I know.' Ben nods. 'I'm going triple scoop.'

'Which flavours?'

'Cherry, coconut and peanut butter.'

I stare at him. 'Are you joking?'

'No?'

I shake my head. 'That's a bad flavour clash. I'm going for the classic triple.'

'And what is that?'

'Salted caramel, vanilla, chocolate. *Obviously*.'

'Too conservative,' Ben informs me. 'I thought a woman who loved to experiment with flavours would be less boring with her ice cream choices.'

'Not boring.' I nudge him, hard. 'Just wise.'

'Yeah, whatever.'

We take our ice creams, still arguing about flavours, back to the grass.

They're big scoops. Ben manages to scarf all of his before any melting happens, but I still have nearly half of mine left when it reaches the dripping stage.

'Honestly, can't take you anywhere.' Ben wipes a bit of runny salted caramel off my chin with his finger and then, very slowly, bends his head towards mine. We hover for a few long seconds with our lips millimetres apart, our breath mingling, our eyes open, just looking at each other. The anticipation is gloriously agonising. I love his eyes. He has *great* eyelashes, very dark and thick. I catch myself thinking that if he had a daughter and she inherited those eyelashes she'd never need to worry about mascara.

And then his eyes crinkle at the side and I know that he's smiling. We both move in just a tiny bit closer, and then we're kissing.

He tastes of, well, yes, cherry, coconut and peanut butter, and he tastes *gorgeous*. I'm not thinking that straight because of the kiss but a small part of me is definitely wondering whether he's right with his weird ice cream combo. The rest of me is just sinking into the kiss and wondering whether there's anywhere to hide so that we can have sex right now without anyone seeing us.

And then I stop thinking completely, and just sink fully into the moment.

We kiss for a long time, until we're disturbed by something odd-feeling banging against us. I swallow a scream, open my eyes and see that there's a dog licking up the remains of my ice cream and that at some point I moved onto Ben's lap, and that, while we're still fully dressed, I'm not sure that we look totally PG-rated because I'm kind of straddling him and, yep, I don't even want to think how this could have looked to other people.

'We're in *public*,' I squeak, and slide off his lap.

Ben's eyes – his whole face – look glazed and he just nods.

'I'm thinking we should carry on with our walk.' I stand up and give myself a bit of a shake to make sure my clothes really are all where they should be.

'Ben.' His name is called by a cheery male voice behind me. 'How've you been?'

Ben blinks, does a definite eye swivel between me and the man, and then sticks a big smile on his face and says, 'Yeah, good, thanks. Been busy; I was away at the weekend at a family wedding. What have you been up to?'

They have a quick chat about the wedding and cricket – I didn't know Ben was a cricket fan but he seems to know a lot about it; clearly I have plenty to find out about him and I know that I'd like the opportunity to learn more but realistically I won't – and then Ben, who is still looking quite eye swivelly and is moving from one foot to another a bit too much, says, 'Anyway, we'd better go. Sorry, I realise I didn't introduce you. Liv. Warren. Old friends, both of you.'

'Surprised we haven't met before, then.' Warren raises his eyebrows.

'Yeah. Well. You know. Busy lives.' Ben starts to edge away. 'Catch you during the week maybe.'

'You going to Wednesday beers?' Warren calls after us.

'Definitely,' Ben says over his shoulder, as he basically shepherds me away.

Again, there's something a bit weird about his demeanour, something slightly constrained and evasive. To be fair, though, if I'd bumped into a friend, I'd have been quite keen to get away too. No one wants to introduce their one-night stands to their friends, however lengthy and weirdly mini-relationship-like the one-night stand might be. In fact, I'm probably the one who's being weird, constantly reading things into the way he's behaving.

We don't hold hands on the way back to his flat but we do walk in an arm-brushing, closer way than you would with someone there was no change of snogging again later, and we talk about whatever our eyes fall on: London buses, pigeons and a pile of vomit round the side of a pub that's a strange thing to see at this time of day.

When we get back to the flat, I stand just inside the doorway wondering *what now*. Should I maybe just say, 'Goodbye then, thanks for a lovely afternoon and, er, last night.' It's Sunday, it's a school night, maybe he's one of those people who never goes out on Sunday evenings because he's in bed at nine p.m. ready for a crack-of-dawn start on Monday. We can't just start snogging again; what happened in the park was very in the moment and now we are very much not in that moment.

'So what takeaway do you fancy?' Ben's swiping his phone, and music starts from one of those round portable loudspeakers. He looks up. 'If you still want to eat here?'

Do I want to? We did not have a lot of sleep last night and it's work tomorrow. And this – whatever this weekend has been – is going nowhere, as stated explicitly by Ben, and as agreed with by me.

I should definitely go. I just *feel* that he isn't in any kind of commitment mode and I do not like getting hurt.

But...

'I'd love to,' I say, beaming. 'As long as you don't try to talk me into any cherry-coconut-peanut-butter meals.'

It turns out that our takeaway and Netflix tastes are a lot more aligned than our ice cream ones. Also, so are our drinking ones; I'm planning not to get even mildly tipsy, and it seems that Ben feels that way too. He opens a bottle of red but we both end up drinking a lot more water than wine and there's more than half a bottle left when we've finished our crispy duck rolls.

It's nice. It's friendly. We're having a lovely evening.

I genuinely don't think I'm *expecting* to have sex with him again or stay the night, until, halfway through our takeaway, Ben puts his glass down and leans forward across the dining table and very gently kisses me.

And then – I'm not sure who moves first; maybe it's completely simultaneous – we stand up and walk along our sides of the table until we get to the end and suddenly it isn't gentle at all, it's urgent and passionate and really very soon we're on the sofa *doing stuff*. Completely sober.

It's gorgeous. It's amazing. It's *so* good that when Ben scoops me up in his arms and carries me to his bedroom and turns the light out and we get into bed together and he says, 'Stay just for tonight?' I don't think about the really important Zoom meeting I have at nine in the morning and was planning to prepare for this evening or the fact that I have no spare pants or the fact that at this rate my heart's going to shatter into a million pieces when we *do* say goodbye.

I just sigh and smile and kiss him back and say, 'I'd like that.'

21

LIV

By some amazing miracle, at about five in the morning I notice the time and remember my meeting and have the gumption to set the alarm on my phone for seven.

When the alarm goes off two hours later, though, it takes me several minutes to peel my eyes open and another several minutes to have the willpower to drag myself away from Ben's warmth and kisses and get out of bed.

I pick up my phone to check the exact time and give a little scream. It didn't take just several minutes for me to get out of bed after my alarm went off; it took thirty-seven minutes. Actually now thirty-eight.

'Shit, shit, *shit*,' I screech.

'What?'

'I have a *big* meeting in one hour and twenty-two minutes and I need to prepare for it *and* look presentable.'

'Where's the meeting?'

'It's a Zoom. So at my flat.'

'Er.' Ben scrunches his face and raises his eyebrows like you do when you're about to impart bad news. And then imparts bad news. 'You do know there's a combined train and Tube strike today?'

'*What*? No!' I'm already frantically Googling. 'Oh, fuck.'

The meeting's a pitch for a big new client and I just needed to do a couple of hours' more preparation. I thought I had a really good shot at getting it, and I *really* wanted it.

'I do have a possible solution for you.' Ben swings himself out of bed and I'm momentarily distracted from my work nightmare by the sight of him. Nakedness *really* suits him.

Then I remember my predicament. 'Time travel?' I ask. 'Because there's no other solution.' There's no way there'll be any Ubers available on a strike day, the buses will be completely full and the roads will be jammed anyway, and I need to get ready and prepare and *gaaaaaaaaah*.

'I have a home office,' he tells me, disappointingly pulling some pyjama bottoms on. 'And a spare laptop. So you could do your meeting here? And then you'd have over an hour to prepare?'

Hmm. I do have toiletries and full make-up with me because of the wedding, so I could definitely put enough slap on to ensure that no-one can notice over a screen that I've barely slept for the past two nights (was the lack of sleep worth it? *Yes*, it was worth it).

'I don't have any clean pants with me, though,' I say. 'And do you not want to work from home today?'

'I mean you *could* do a meeting in yesterday's pants?' He pauses and swallows. I'm pretty sure he's thinking about when he tore them off me last night. I swallow too; that was *good*. 'Or I could go and buy some more from the Asda down the road? Or obviously you could go but then would you be wasting preparation time... And I'm cool to work from the kitchen table.'

'Erm.' I *really* want to win this client. And I really don't think I can make it home in time to start the meeting and I'm not great with working in a cab and I need to get ready. 'Are you sure about the pants purchasing?'

I do not function well if I'm not wearing clean underwear.

'Totally.'

'Well, in that case, thank you. I'd be incredibly grateful.'

By the time I'm out of the bathroom after a very speedy shower and make-up session, Ben's in the kitchen with a five-pack of very sensible black bikini-style pants and croissants and orange juice (freshly squeezed, with bits in, hooray). I apply incredible willpower and do not react in any way to the look in his eyes when he sees me still slightly damp wrapped in the large fluffy towel he gave me, and seize the pants and go off to get dressed.

When I make it back into the kitchen, he says, 'Okay, I'm going to set the laptop up for you now and then I'll leave you to it so you can prep while you eat,' and he takes himself out of the room.

While I'm prepping in his kitchen and then in his office, I actually miss him. I mean, I'm still in the same flat and I'm missing him. I am going to feel *terrible* when we finally say goodbye later this morning.

Unless this is actually the start of something. But realistically, I don't think it is. Because has anything changed in Ben's mind since he said he could only do a one-night stand? I know we're on two nights now, but the principle is presumably still there. Like this was just a very long (and perfect) one-off.

When I emerge from the longer-than-expected meeting, Ben is indeed at his kitchen table working. He's head down, fully focused on the screen.

I turn to tiptoe back out but he looks up and says, 'So how did it go?'

'Really well, thank you. I'm so grateful to you for suggesting that I do it here. That last hour of prep made all the difference.'

I feel like I'm bubbling over with delight at just *how* well it went; the prospective client told me at the end that she was definitely going to give me the project and within seconds of the end of the meeting she'd sent me an excited Yes-we're-going-to-do-this email.

I look at Ben's laptop and notebook. 'I shouldn't disturb you. I'm just going to gather up my stuff and get going.' Despite my work happiness, crushing, genuinely *crushing* misery fills me as I say that because I think there's a good chance that we aren't ever going to see each other again, unless we have another chance meeting.

'Coffee first?' he asks.

I leap pathetically at the offer of a few more minutes with him. 'That would be lovely,' I say.

We take our coffees out to the communal garden and sit on a bench and watch some small birds eating seeds from a wooden feeder on a pole that one of Ben's neighbours has put out.

One of them's really pecking with its head backwards and forwards.

'Do you think that's a woodpecker?' I'm frowning, trying to remember *any*thing about birds.

'I want to say yes, because, you know, it's pecking wood, but then I have this vague memory from my grandmother that they're green.'

'Is she still...?' I realise that his grandmother is the only member of his family he's ever mentioned to me, thinking back to when he told me about her skiing after she lost her husband.

'Still with us? Yes, very much so, thank goodness. Still skiing' – he smiles and I *love* that he clearly remembers that conversation as well as I do – 'and still extremely opinionated and a fantastic cook and rummy player *and* knowledgeable about birds and plants and stuff.'

'She sounds great.'

'Yeah, we've always had a lot of fun with her.' And then his smile drops a little and his face closes off and I realise that he's thinking about something I'm not privy to, and as I'm about to ask, as delicately as I can, if he's okay, he diverts the question with a clearly intentional subject change. 'So if it isn't an if-I-tell-you-I'll-have-to-kill-you thing, tell me about the client you just won?'

I laugh and say that I would actually have to kill him, but accept his cementing of the conversation firmly away from his grandmother, and after a few more minutes I've pushed his slightly weird don't-want-to-talk-about-my-family thing out of my mind. I mean, actually, it probably isn't weird. *Loads* of people don't like talking about their families. It's probably weird that I *am* happy to talk about mine.

As always, we find our chat meandering in many different directions, and I know that I could stay here all day, but my phone's buzzing away with messages and emails and eventually I say, with extreme reluctance, 'I should go. I have work to do.'

'You're welcome to work in my office for the rest of the day?' he says immediately. 'Travel's going to be difficult today. Sushi for lunch?'

'I *love* sushi,' I say.

I love you, I think, and then I slap that thought away. The lack of sleep's getting to me; I'm being ridiculous.

We wander back up to the flat, and as we walk we don't actually hold hands but our arms and sides brush a lot, in a way that you'd never do with someone you weren't either sleeping with or hoping to sleep with.

I settle down to work in Ben's office at his insistence, and despite my tiredness and, just, Ben, I have a very productive hour and a half writing up some more detailed ideas for my new client (and again *squeeeee*) until we have our sushi break, because I love my business almost as much as I love Ben. And, *no*, I have to stop this. I don't love Ben. I'm just infatuated. How do you love someone on so little acquaintance? You don't. I clearly don't. Oh, who am I kidding. I'm very much on my way to loving him a lot.

It's a good lunch. The sushi's delicious and the company is Ben and the more I talk to him the more I like him. I'm enjoying myself very much.

And then midway through a mouthful of salmon and avocado maki, I look at his gorgeous, kind, and also extremely crooked-handsome face and I realise that I'm in danger of messing up my career because of him. I have to go. I have a business and a life and when he's broken my heart, whenever that is – be it in about five minutes' or five days' time – I will need my job and my life to keep me going until I'm over the broken heart, so I do not want to mess up my work. I *could* take some time off this week around meetings and a couple of deadlines, but not completely, and right now I really need to go home and spend some time in my own kitchen on recipe development for my new client so that I can fire off some more ideas later on. I also need to check a couple of other recipe points for other clients. And I need clean clothes.

Appetite suddenly gone, I place my chopsticks very carefully and very neatly in the middle of my plate and say, 'I'm actually going to have to brave the Tube strike experience now. I have some work that I really need to do at home.'

'Of course.' Ben puts his own chopsticks down and gives me a straight-mouthed smile.

We just look at each other for a very long time, definitely several seconds, and then I think: actually, why am I trying to precipitate the end of this thing with Ben – I'm pretty sure that stopping now will not make me feel any better than stopping tomorrow – and I suddenly blurt out, 'Would you like to come over? Now? I don't have much work to do, just a couple of things. I could cook dinner for you?'

He doesn't hesitate. 'I'd like that.'

'Cool!' I squeak.

I open my mouth to tell him to bring pants, and then think better of it. I mean, if I'm being honest, I know that I want him to stay, but I don't want to admit that.

So I just beam and say, 'Cool,' again.

We go on the bus because I'm being frugal at the moment. It's very hot again and we have to take three separate ones and they're all very crowded. Without Ben, it would have been a really annoying schlepp, but with him it's like a fun adventure.

'Eek,' I suddenly say, as we're walking up to the front door of my lower ground floor flat. 'I did pack in a hurry and I did not leave it that tidy. Okay, you sit and read your emails or do a work call or something in the kitchen while I sprint round everywhere else.'

I know for a fact the kitchen at least is tidy; I cook all the time and I always clean up. Which is a lot more than can be said for my bedroom because I packed in a big rush.

I have the flat tidy quite quickly in fact and when I go back into the kitchen Ben looks so *right* sitting there at my table tapping away on his laptop that my heart lurches yet again.

If it's possible to be companionable with someone you've known vaguely for eight years and then had amazing sex with on and off for forty-eight hours, then we have a gorgeously companionable afternoon. Just like it always has done, it feels meant to be between us. It isn't, though, I keep having to remind myself. Is it?

I work manically and finish all the non-cooking work I need to do by early evening. I've actually been so focused on my laptop for the past hour that I've genuinely stopped taking little peeks at Ben (followed by serious internal smiling), so I'm surprised when I look round at him and discover that he's moved from the table to the sofa and is sound asleep.

There's something about seeing people asleep. Even people you can't stand look quite endearing when they're that vulnerable. And when it's someone you *do* like... My heart's melting and I just sit and drink in the way he looks, reminding myself of how my friend Ankita told me how when she had her baby she would waste hours every day just *staring* at her gorgeousness.

I'm still looking at him when he opens his eyes slowly. A smile works its way across his face.

'You tired me out last night,' he tells me.

I gasp because I didn't think we were referring to that stuff out loud, and then I laugh, and say, 'I think you'll find it takes two to tango.'

'Fancy another tango?' He squeezes his face into a big, saucy wink and holds his arms out towards me, and, obviously, because willpower is definitely not my middle name when it comes to Ben, I walk straight over.

And then, yes, we're *tangoing* again pretty soon.

Some time later, when we've tired each other out a lot further, I tell Ben that I need to have a shower and then get cooking, because I have a few recipes I need to try.

'I'd love to taste your recipes,' he tells me. I squeak because all I can think about is the way he's tasting *me* right now.

Obviously, he joins me in the shower. And obviously, it takes longer than your average shower does. But eventually, we're out and dressed and I'm cooking and talking Ben through the ideas I'm working on. I don't normally like talking about my ideas at *all*, but this evening I don't mind telling him. In fact, I actively like telling him. That's weird, I register, because in all the five years I was with Tommy I never wanted to discuss my ideas with him at this stage of recipe development.

'So do you want some help?' Ben pulls one of my aprons on over his head and I smile, firstly because it's cute that he wants to help and secondly because the apron he's taken is the gigantic boobs one that Sulwe gave me for Christmas.

And soon we're working away together and again, it's just *comfortable*.

And also very, very erotic, basically, like when a tiny bit of butternut squash and cumin cake mixture (genuinely delicious) splatters onto my cheek and Ben decides to lick and kiss it off. Normally I'm very anal about keeping my kitchen spotless but all I can do is shiver with delight as he daubs more mixture onto me and then I'm daubing too and suddenly yet again we're having sex but this time in my *kitchen* and involving *cake mixture*.

It's amazing.

I don't get a lot of work done for quite a while.

And then, as we're lying there, *naked on my kitchen floor*, which is not something that has ever in my life happened to me before, and, what's more, I'm *happy* about it, I ask Ben if I can cook dinner for him.

He trails a finger down my stomach and I shiver some more and he kisses me and through his kisses he tells me he'd very much like that.

And then, suddenly just wanting to *know*, just a bit, about whether maybe this could begin to go somewhere (if I even want that, which I'm still not sure about because I do not want to get hurt, although, really, I'm going to be hurt no matter what now and of *course* I want it), I say, 'And then you could stay tonight?'

Ben lifts his head and looks at me for a long moment, and my stomach drops in fear that he's going to say no.

22

BEN

Liv's looking at me with scary hope in her eyes, like she *really* wants me to stay.

I really want to stay too. But is it stupid?

This is a decision, now. Before this, for the past forty-eight hours, we've just been working off instinct. But right now I could – *should*? – just walk away. I could tell her that I'm so sorry but I have to go and it's been a great weekend and goodbye, and hopefully prevent her being hurt more further down the line.

And then she drops her eyes and I realise that she's already going to be hurt. And I know I'm going to be gutted when I do leave. So, really, what difference is an extra night going to make? In for a penny, in for a pound. Or something.

I bend my head and kiss her full on the lips as I run my hand up her side from her hip to the underside of her breast.

'I'd love to stay,' I say.

Her eyes open wide and I can feel her smile into our kiss.

Maybe half an hour, an hour, I don't know, later, I cradle Liv against my chest and kiss the top of her hair.

'Oh my God,' I say, looking around her kitchen. 'We've trashed this room.'

'I know.' She sounds pretty happy about it. 'And I have to say it's weird that I really don't care.'

I nod. It was sparkling when we got back and she didn't know anyone was coming, so she must actually keep it like that the whole time.

'Okay,' I say. 'You get in the shower, and I'm going to clean it up.'

'That is very, very kind,' Liv says, 'but at the risk of sounding like Monica from *Friends*, I'm not one hundred per cent sure that you can *totally* clean it to my standards, so I might just do it myself.'

'Well.' I aim for a Chandler-from-*Friends* pose (difficult while lying down on a kitchen floor with a woman half on top of you). 'Could I *be* more offended?'

'*Are* you offended?' She sits up and as her hair covers my face for a moment, I breathe the scent of her shampoo in, hard.

'No of course not. In fact, could I *be* more relieved? I hate cleaning. *However*,' I add hastily, 'I would be very, very happy to help on this occasion because if I remember rightly I did start the whole cake mixture mess situation.'

'You did,' she confirms. 'Although if *I* remember rightly I did join in.'

I nod. She did. Very enthusiastically.

'Okay,' she decides. 'We're both going to clean, but I'm going to be in charge.'

And, honestly, even cleaning is fun when it's with Liv.

When we're finished and showered and cleaned up and sitting like civilised people on the sofa in Liv's sitting room, I say, 'Is there a shop nearby that sells underwear?'

'What, after all that, you didn't bring pants?'

'Yep, only the pair I was wearing, and they got cake mixture on them.'

Even as I was making the decision not to pack them, I still didn't know why I wasn't: was it because I knew I shouldn't stay and didn't want to tempt myself more, or was it because I was scared that Liv wouldn't ask me?

Liv makes delicious Mexican food while I buy pants and – I think because both of us are extremely tired – we actually make it all the way through the meal before we're kissing again. And then we fall into her bed and, contrary to my initial expectation, both go to sleep pretty quickly. My younger self would be ashamed of me but that's what two nights of close-to-zero sleep does to you once you're in your thirties. Plus, just cuddling Liv is very, very nice.

I wake up first in the morning. We slept with me spooned around Liv and she's still curled there in my arms. *God,* I wish we could wake up like this every morning for the rest of our lives. Her mad hair's spread over the pillow and my arms, and I can only see a small bit of her face peeking out from under it. I can't help myself moving some away from her cheek gently and dropping a very light kiss there. She stirs, smiling in her sleep, and in that moment I know that I'm in love with her.

Well, of course I am. If I'm truthful with myself, I'd say I have been in some form since almost the moment I met her.

I also know that if she's up for it I'm going to stay around today. Because, as I thought last night, what difference can one more day make now?

23

LIV

I'm pulled out of a very deep slumber by clattering sounds from the kitchen. For a nanosecond I'm panic-stricken and my sleep-dulled brain's desperately trying to remember where I put the hockey stick I borrowed from Nella a few years ago for an ill-fated 'let's do team sports and get fit' resolution, so that I can defend myself against the burglar I think I can hear.

And then I remember... And I'm not sure whether I'm about to be happy or sad. Clearly, it's Ben. But what's he doing? Is he whipping up a delicious first-of-many breakfasts together? Or even a today-only breakfast? Or is he packing up his laptop and cake-mixture-stained trunks before he heads out of my life forever?

Okay. I need to find out. I'm going for the sticking plaster approach.

When I'm out of bed I pull pyjamas on immediately, because I'm terrible at being naked other than in the heat of the moment or for showering, and head straight out of the bedroom and into the kitchen.

Instantly, I see and smell that the clattering was breakfast related.

Ben's gone for almost silver-service levels of presentation: napkins folded on plates, cutlery carefully laid, a jam spoon... I smell what I think are scrambled eggs and smoked salmon, and I see a plate laden with French pastries and a big bowl of strawberries, raspberries and blueberries.

Well. I don't know what's going to happen next between us – if anything – but right now I'm impressed.

'Wow. You're a breakfast god.'

I wish I'd put a bra on under these pyjamas given that it looks like I'm about to eat a lengthy breakfast. I'm really bad at being naked even *under* clothes. I might just go back to the bedroom and get slightly more dressed.

'Yes, I've actually impressed my*self*.' His mock-smug smile is *very* endearing.

'I'm going to be back in two seconds.' I scoot off to the bedroom to get a bra on.

By the time I'm back, Ben's making hot chocolate.

'Honestly, be still my beating heart,' I say. 'I *love* hot chocolate. You're an extremely gifted breakfast chef.'

'Yep, I have a special talent for getting things out of packets and plating up.' He puts a plate of perfectly scrambled eggs and smoked salmon garnished with some sliced tomatoes and parsley in front of me.

'Oh my goodness,' I say. 'This is amazing. You're welcome to make me breakfast *any* time.' Oh. Awkward silence. That is *not* the kind of thing you should say in this very specific how-long-are-we-going-to-be-doing-this-for-maybe-only-today situation. 'So, thank you.'

I smile as un-awkwardly as I can, pick up my knife and fork and dig in. And soon, things feel better, because the food's delicious. I gush about it and then talk very earnestly about salmon farming and provenance until we're very safely away from foot-in-mouth territory.

We head back to awkward silence at the end of breakfast though. I have a strongly niggling feeling that this isn't going to end well for me but at the moment I'm having the most amazing time and I don't want it to stop.

Dishwasher loaded, I decide again to go down the sticking plaster ripping route.

As I press the On button, I say, 'So I have an in-person lunch meeting but other than that I'm working from home today.'

I think about this evening. I'm supposed to be meeting my mum and Frankie (Nella's babysitting their three little girls) and my mum's new partner, Declan. We're getting together today – Tuesday – because Mum's been very into experiences and seizing the moment since she began to date again, and she and Declan are just back from a cruise round the Balkans and are away again this weekend bungee jumping in Wales. I haven't seen them since before the cruise and would obviously love to hear how it went (Declan sent photos to us of Mum on stage doing Tina Turner karaoke plus apparently they did a lot of amazing sightseeing).

However, I'll be able to catch up with Mum and Declan next week when they're back from Wales, whereas I don't feel that confident that Ben will still be in my life then. And with her whole seizing-the-moment ethos, I think – know – that Mum would understand that I'd like to make the most out of this.

Whether or not I would actually tell her or Frankie about it is another thing, and it's not something I want to think about now. I would normally tell them about anything, but Ben... No, not going to think about it.

Because while this, whatever this is, between Ben and me, has morphed from an agreed one-night stand into a three-night one bearing all the hallmarks of the start of an actual relationship, every so often I recall his words on Saturday evening. He was very clear that he couldn't offer more than one night and he must have had a good reason for saying that.

Okay, apparently I *am* thinking about it.

I've been wiping the table while I've been thinking.

I decided on a sticking plaster approach. I should do it.

I turn to Ben and say, 'Have your...' And then I bite back the rest of my question. I just don't have the courage to ask him if his feelings about the possibility of a relationship have changed.

'Have my...?' he asks.

I rush out the words, 'I'm free this evening, so you'd be very welcome to stay if you'd like to.' I'm not going to ask about his feelings and I *am* going to take as much time with him as he's willing to offer. In essence, I am burying my head in the sand.

I busy myself giving a final, gratuitous, wipe to the table, because I don't want to look Ben in the eye in case he can tell how much I'd like him to stay despite worrying he's going to say no.

'I'd love to,' he says, with no hesitation whatsoever, and I feel my shoulders lighten. It does still feel as though I might be living on borrowed Ben-time, but while I have him, I'm going to make the most of it.

He smiles at me in a very goofy fashion, and I'm pretty sure my smile mirrors his.

'My meetings are this morning. What time are you back from your lunch?' he asks. And then immediately says, 'No, no, sorry, forget I asked that. I don't want to hurry you. Just text me when you're done and back home. I'll grab a coffee while I'm waiting.'

'No, that's silly.' I open the drawer where I keep my two remaining spare keys (the other three are with Mum, Frankie and Sulwe; since the shed incident I've always liked to be belt and braces about not getting locked in or out) and take one out. I offer it to him. 'Why don't you take this and let yourself in whenever you get back?'

He looks at my hand holding the key and I look at my hand holding the key, and no, no, no, this is not good. I should really have thought about what it might imply before I offered him a *key to my flat*.

'I mean, just for today,' I say, cringing internally as I say it. Ground, please do just swallow me up right now.

Ben stares at my hand for a *long* second longer and then says, 'Great. Thanks. Better remind me to give it back later.'

'Absolutely.' I nod at least three times, I'm not sure why, and then, thank *goodness*, he ends the awkwardness by putting the key in his pocket and turning to gather up his stuff.

When I finish my lunch, I find a message from Ben on my phone saying that he won't actually be back for a while.

I hear him letting himself into the flat about four p.m., and I realise that, despite the fact that the report I've been writing is genuinely engrossing, I've had half an ear out for him the whole time since I got back. I'm beaming internally and I feel like it's probably all over my face as well.

'Afternoon.' He drops a kiss on my lips and says, 'Cup of tea? I'm parched,' before heading for the kettle.

I beam even more, because it's truly lovely. And it isn't just lovely, it feels comfortable, a bit relationshippy.

He's changed into a shirt and chinos, I note, as I watch him make the tea. I wonder if he's brought a spare pair of pants with him this time.

When I ask him if he'd like roast chicken for dinner – I just happened to slide into Tesco on my way home at lunchtime and buy the chicken and five different types of vegetable – I'm not even that nervous about his response.

And I'm proved right; he just smiles and says, 'I'd love to. Can't beat a roast.'

The evening's amazing. We have great conversation and lots of gasps from me (luckily I have Ben to cling to in the opening scene) as we marvel at the latest James Bond, *No Time to Die*, on Netflix (both of us have been meaning to see it but hadn't got round to it), and finish the night with *great* sex. When I look at my messages in the morning and see that I have one from Frankie telling me that I missed a fantastic evening and that Declan's truly lovely and she thinks he could be Mum's next One, I do wish that the timing had been different, because I would have loved to have been there, but I do not regret for one moment blowing them off or my tiny white lie (I said I had a work thing). I don't even feel guilty about the fact that Frankie says she hoped the work thing went well.

In the morning… Well. In the morning, after a bit of a mad rush, Ben puts on clean pants and a clean shirt, which he apparently just *happened* to have in the backpack he had with him, along with his toothbrush, and *then*… he sets off for a meeting, still in the possession of *my key*. Without really mentioning it. He just still has it. And when he leaves, he says, 'See you later,' and I feel as though I might explode with happiness.

He texts me mid-morning and asks if I am home at lunchtime and do I fancy sushi because he's visiting a Japanese restaurant that he might invest in and they're trying to give him a *lot* of free sushi.

Oh yes please I do fancy sushi.

I text back.

I fancy Ben too. So. Bloody. Much.

And I'm starting to feel as though I might actually be the luckiest woman in the world and that maybe I might have gorgeous, wonderful Ben for a little bit longer than just-for-now.

24

BEN

I'm supposed to be going for beers this evening with some friends. I've just had a reminder text from my mate Omar.

Our university friend Ned's been living in Tokyo for the past couple of years and he's going to be there and I'd really like to see him, plus the rest of us normally catch up at least once a week and I haven't seen any of the guys for two or three weeks, other than bumping into Warren at the weekend with Liv and being keen to get away because he knows me too well.

I should really go and see them. You shouldn't abandon your friends. And once this interlude with Liv is finished I'll need them. I'm not sure I'll find the words to tell them much about her beyond that I'm gutted about a woman, but I know I won't want to deal with the end of this by myself. So, yes, I shouldn't bin them this evening.

However, since this thing with Liv *is* going to finish, I find myself desperate to make as much of it as I can.

So I send another message to her asking if she'll be free this evening because I've been given really a *huge* amount of free sushi and I'm not sure if I want that large a lunch on top of the (amazing) waffles she made us for breakfast.

Liv confirms twenty minutes later that she is indeed free and that she is also still quite full.

So I'm pulling a sickie for this evening.

I text Omar back and tell him:

I'm really sorry mate but I've got some kind of weird summer virus and need to stay home, but definitely next time.

And then off I go back to Liv's, via a sushi place to top up the free stuff I got, to back up my little story, and when I get there I let myself in with her key, and wish that I could keep the key forever.

I can't, though, I remind myself, as Liv greets me with a 'Hey' and a naughty half-smile, which makes me kiss her hard on the lips.

For now, though...

25

LIV

By Thursday, as I whip eggs and caster sugar together for a passionfruit pavlova, while Ben's out for an early evening run, having been staying with me the whole time since Monday afternoon, I know that this has been the best week of my life.

I mean, it's been amazing. So much fun. So much banter. So much sex. *So* much making me hope that actually this could be going somewhere after all.

I smile at the peaks of meringue mixture in my mixing bowl. It *would* be really soon for us to get together properly, except, also, arguably it wouldn't, because we've been in and out of each other's lives for eight years now. And at our ages – I'm thirty-four and he's thirty-seven – not everyone hangs around.

I know that I love him, I think, as I spoon quenelles of the meringue mixture into a circle on a paper-lined baking tray. Maybe this could really be it now. Maybe those eight years were just fate's way of making sure we didn't meet properly until we were really ready. Maybe that's what all those missed connections were about.

This week has felt *so* meant to be. The fact that it happened at all. The fact that we were both able to spend most of the week working from home, with only a few Zooms to get in the way, and, if I'm honest, fairly minimal work done on both our parts. The fact that even the *weather*'s been perfect, like we've been on the most magical staycation in my flat.

Later, as we finish the separate, individual pavlovas that I made for our pudding, Ben's making me laugh telling me about his five- and three-year-old nieces. His eyes light up as he talks about them and my heart expands even further than I thought possible.

Bruno Mars's 'Marry Me' starts on the radio and oh my goodness it really is like it's meant to be. As the chorus starts, I have to struggle to stop myself nodding and pointing at the radio and saying 'Exactly'. Because I *do* want to marry him. I mean, it doesn't have to be actual marriage, but I *do* – I want to be with Ben forever.

'Do you have any pictures of the girls?' I ask, to stop myself blurting out *Will you marry me* (I'm not joking, I'm almost there). And also, obviously, I'd like to see pictures.

'I have a *lot* of pictures.' He picks up his phone and starts to flick through. A few seconds into his flicking, he definitely comes across a photo that he doesn't want me to see, because he suddenly angles his phone differently, into his chest, like he's worried that I might be able to see the screen. I glance at his face and there's the tiniest of frowns. My happiest-week-ever bubble doesn't exactly burst but it definitely deflates slightly. He's probably just flicked to a photo of an ex or something, and no-one shows photos of exes to the person they've been shagging for five days, and of *course* he has exes, so there's no reason that I *should* feel a bit flat. Maybe it's just that I don't want any reminders that there's a world outside just the two of us this week.

'Here we go.' He's holding his phone out to me now and the frown's gone.

'Aww, they're *so* cute!' I exclaim. They both have dark curls and they're holding hands and clearly dancing and, just, be still my beating heart. *I want one.* I want a gorgeous little baby girl of my own and I want Ben to be the father. 'Your brother and his wife are very lucky.' I look again at the photo. 'If you and I had a little girl maybe she'd have blonde curls.'

And *gaaaaah* what what *what* did I just say?

I risk a glance up at Ben and he's just *staring* at me, with a really weird look on his face. Not good. Really not good.

I shake my head very hard. 'I don't mean you and *me* having a baby, I didn't mean to imply anything ridiculous like that, it was a figure of speech. I used the same figure of speech with Sulwe last week.' Oh yes, *so* convincing. I'm just digging an even deeper hole with everything I say. What is *wrong* with me? I know what's wrong with me. I've fallen completely and besottedly in love with Ben and I'm making stupid plans for the future in my head and I'm suffering from lack of sleep and so I'm saying things out loud that no sane person would normally say in this situation.

Ben's completely silent, so I rush into a subject change, the first thing that comes into my head.

'You know Frankie had twins? She and Nella only planned for two children but Nella really wanted to be pregnant with her own biological child, so she had one too, with a sperm donor. Luckily not also twins.' He's still silent so I keep on talking. 'And the great thing about sperm donation now is that children have the automatic right to get details of their father if they like, so you don't have that detective-work nightmare that a lot of adopted people experience looking for their biological parents. Sulwe's been looking for hers ever since she started trying to conceive at the beginning of last year, and it's made an already stressful time more stressful, and so far she's got nowhere.'

I can't believe I haven't told him about this before, actually, but there's been so much to talk about. And there's still so much to say. I feel like I could talk to Ben for ever. Assuming he doesn't run for the hills after my *what would our baby look like* faux pas.

I would love *so so much* to have children with him. No, this is *ridiculous*. Except it isn't. We've known each other for a long time and lots of people at our age get together very quickly. They do.

I look back at the gorgeous picture of his nieces.

'They're beautiful,' I repeat.

I look up at Ben and he isn't looking at the screen; he's looking at me, with the strangest, twisted near-grimace on his face. Oh God, he's obviously still thinking about my baby comment and not liking it.

And then his expression morphs into a normal one and he says, 'Okay, I'm going to load the dishwasher and make you coffee while you put your feet up because that was a lot of cooking.'

'I like cooking and it was my pleasure,' I tell him after a beat during which I'm wondering if I imagined his grimace, 'but thank you, I would *love* to put my feet up and watch you work hard for a few minutes.'

He grins at me, and I push away the thought that his grin seems slightly forced. I sit back in my chair and watch his arm muscles flex as he clears up.

He makes me laugh dancing in time to the music on the radio, brandishing utensils and crockery like he's a particularly flamboyant pole dancer and they're his stage props, and by the time the dishwasher's ready to go on, my sides are aching and everything between us feels back to normal (as far as there's a normal after such a short time together). He was obviously just a little bit taken aback before by my baby-related verbal diarrhoea, but I'm pretty sure he's recovered now from his momentary surprise. I briefly consider having another go at explaining it away and then decide to let sleeping conversational dogs lie and just be very, very careful not to say anything stupid like that again. Until, hopefully, our relationship is more established...

We take our coffees over to the sofa and manage to drink at least half a cup each before we're kissing again.

'Did we agree that we were going to watch that Nureyev film this evening? *The White Crow*?' I say (well, pant) between kisses. Ben made me watch one of the *Star Wars* films yesterday and I remained totally unconverted, although if I'm honest I'd watch anything with him.

'Yes, we did.' Ben slides his hand up a little and I give a very pleasurable shudder, before very, very strong-mindedly reaching over for the remote. Serious relationships are not all about sex and we are watching this film.

We actually do watch most of it, although we do also distract ourselves quite a lot.

As the credits roll, Ben says, 'Nice evening for a stroll?'

I nod. I *love* that it feels like we've reached a relationshippy stage. You don't go for an evening stroll with a one (or five) night stand, do you?

It's a clear night and, unusually for London, there are a fair few stars visible.

We wander down to Clapham Common and then just stand, with Ben's arm round my shoulders and mine round his waist, enjoying the warm evening and the night sky.

And then Ben turns to face me, and he says, 'I love you, Liv,' and it's like I've waited my whole life to hear those words from his lips.

'I love you too,' I say, and then I reach up on my tiptoes to kiss him, and then we enjoy a long, definitely bordering-on-inappropriate al fresco snog.

We make wonderful, languorous love that night and, if having sex with Ben all week has been amazing, making actual love, and knowing that it's mutual love, is a whole world better.

It's perfect.

26

LIV

When my alarm goes off in the morning and I battle through the haze of only-just-awareness following a very deep sleep before flailing my arms around to find my phone and hit the snooze button, I realise that Ben's got up before me. I wriggle in happiness, wondering whether he'll have gone full mega breakfast or just got us croissants. I decide to allow myself a few more minutes in bed before getting up, and close my eyes fully again. We did not get a lot of sleep last night. Maybe we can have a little siesta this afternoon.

As I drift back to sleep, I'm smiling, re-living Ben's *I love you*, and all that that implied. Like... we're together. Properly together.

I smash the snooze button several times and when I finally wake up properly it's nearly ten. On a Friday, a *work* day. It's sweet that Ben's left me to sleep but I need to get up *now*.

I pull on pyjama shorts (very short ones, which Ben very much likes) and a T-shirt (I'm still just not good at walking around naked, however much of me Ben might already have seen) and wander out of my bedroom.

There's no sign of him in the sitting room, and he isn't in the bathroom or the spare room. Maybe he's gone for a run.

Although...

Something big is niggling at me.

Oh.

There is also no sign of any of Ben's stuff.

Oh.

Well, maybe he's gone home to do some laundry. Or maybe he has *actual* work today.

Also, he's placed my key in the middle of the table.

Again, oh.

But, actually, that doesn't mean anything other than he isn't planning to come back in the next few hours. And obviously if he *has* gone home to do laundry or work or both, it would have been very presumptuous of him to have kept the key. It really doesn't mean anything.

I go back into the bedroom to where my phone's charging. He's probably texted me to tell me what he's up to. Which – obviously – is totally fine; I would never expect to live in someone's pocket or vice versa.

He hasn't left me a text.

I immediately have an urge to phone him just to see what he's up to. It's actually good that he isn't here, I tell myself, because I really should focus hard on work today given that it's Friday and I haven't done *that* much work this week; I need to pick up on some loose ends and leave myself in a good position for getting back on top of things next week. So, yes, it isn't like I want him to come back right now (I do want him to come back right now), it's just that I'd love to plan my day. And the weekend. I mean, it isn't like we're going to spend the entire time together – we do both have the rest of our very busy lives to lead – but also I'd love to see him a *little* over the weekend. Or at least at the beginning of next week. If he's free.

I shouldn't hassle him, though. Except, it isn't hassling if I'm just saying *Hi* and asking if he'd like to meet up at some point over the weekend. He loves me. I love him. It isn't hassling to text. Or maybe call.

I call him. His phone doesn't seem to be working because there's just one of those long single beeps.

Okay, well, I'll send him a WhatsApp and then I'll get into the shower and then I'll eat my breakfast (Weetabix because, as it turns out, Ben did not buy me a croissant or any other kind of breakfast this morning, which is clearly totally fine because actually why should he) and then I will very single-mindedly and focusedly and professionally work very hard and catch up on all my work.

When I get out of the shower, I check my phone immediately. There's still only one single grey tick so my message can't have gone through.

The single grey tick does not turn double all day.

Late afternoon I crack and call again (obviously he'll be able to see if there are several missed calls from me and I do not want to look like a stalker but apparently I'm just going to *be* a stalker). It still sounds like the phone isn't working or it's off or something.

Okay. Never mind. I still have a lot of work to finish today. I'm working and I am not thinking about when exactly Ben will call me. Obviously he'll call me soon.

Except, oh God, what if he's had an accident? What if that's why his phone doesn't seem to be working and he hasn't called me?

My heart's beating very fast and my hands are clammy and I slightly wonder if I'm going to have a panic attack.

I focus very hard on breathing normally for a few moments and then open all my social media and hunt for Transport for London and then the Metropolitan Police. There don't seem to be any posts about dead or horrifically injured unidentified men in their thirties.

I can't exactly go round calling local hospitals given that I'm not his next of kin and he obviously does have an actual next of kin because he has his family. So, really, there's nothing I can do except carry on working and assume that if anything bad has happened to him someone else will find him and sort him out.

As I open a long email from the (lovely) client I won at the beginning of the week, some logic percolates through to my brain. Ben took all his stuff with him and left my key. So he intended to go home. So he has probably not had an accident.

So actually maybe his phone is just not working. Or he's lost it somewhere where he doesn't get a signal. Maybe he dropped it on the Tube or something. Having got up a lot earlier than me today he must be shattered after last night. Tired people are definitely clumsy.

Okay. So. I'm going to send him an email just saying: *Hello, just me – not sure your phone's working – here's my email address – speak soon, Liv xxx.*

It's easy to find his work email address because even though his surname's Jones, there aren't that many Ben Joneses working in his very specific sector, and I do know the names of some of the businesses he's involved in, including the cinema.

The server bounces the email back. Is that because his phone isn't working? Is that how it works?

I'm not sure. Something icy is beginning to form round my heart and I really want to know, so I message Sulwe, because her brother works in something indescribable in IT and always knows these sorts of things, and ask her to ask him.

I don't refer to Ben, because I haven't told Sulwe about bumping into him outside the wedding and how our week then panned out. I pulled a headache excuse when she asked where I went mid-evening at the wedding, and have been evasive all week about what I've been up to, telling her I'm busy with work.

Sulwe gets back to me quickly with Yemi's answer, which is: Nope, that is not how it works. Your emails are not affected by your phone not working; you can obviously just access them via a different device.

Yep, that's obvious.

So Ben's phone is not working and has not been working all day. And his email address has perhaps been changed.

I don't want to jump to horrible, miserable conclusions, but also I have to accept reality when it's basically slapping me around the face. It feels to me as though Ben has quite possibly just disappeared – from my life anyway – and has changed his phone number and also his email address.

I stare at the backsplash of my hob as a montage of images and conversations from the past few days work their way across my mind.

Why would he have just disappeared? After telling me in such a sincere-seeming manner that he *loved me.*

I mean, there was my comment about our baby having blonde curls. But he told me he loved me *after* that, and then we made love almost all night. That can't have been it.

I can't really think of any plausible reason other than that he has a wife or serious girlfriend. Maybe she's been away this week and that's why she wasn't at the wedding with him. And it was evidence of *her*, not a hobby, that he was hiding in his flat.

I realise that a not-ideal sizzling sound and a burning smell are coming from below me and look down. I've burnt the halved plums I was cooking in butter and cinnamon.

I turn the hob off and sit down at the table and put my head in my hands.

This does not feel good.

I realise that I'm gulping out big, hiccuppy, snotty tears and I can't do anything about them.

I remember how there was definitely something on his phone that he didn't want me to see when he was looking for photos of his nieces. So that will have been a photo of his girlfriend I presume. And he was very weird when we first bumped into each other at the wedding. Like he really wanted me to go for a walk with him but he also clearly really wanted to steer me away from the venue. That was probably so that none of his friends or family in there would see him with another woman.

There have been other odd things too – really, a lot, now I think about it – but right now my eyes and head and everything feel too swollen with tears and misery to be able to sift through the memories properly.

I don't know how long I'm sitting there for before my phone pings and I seize it. Maybe it's Ben and there's a perfectly sensible explanation for his uncontactability today and everything's ok and I've been catastrophising *ridiculously*.

No. Nothing new on my chat with Ben.

I swipe back and find that the ping was a message from my old colleague Dee. We're supposed to be going to the cinema this evening.

I can't go, I just can't.

I put my forehead on the table and really sob for a moment.

And then I sit up. While I don't feel like I can bear to go out, I also cannot sit here in my flat and give in to the extreme, incredible emptiness that I'm feeling right now – emptiness at the thought that Ben has spent five days having sex and fun and chat with me (and Scrabble, we even played Scrabble – who *does* that with someone they don't properly *like*?) culminating in him telling me he loved me and now he's just buggered off and is actually ghosting me. If I give in to it too much, I feel like I'll be in a trough so deep that I'll struggle ever to climb out.

Oh God, though.

I'm going to miss him *so much*. I loved being with him. I love – loved – *him*.

Past tense, though; I already know that. He just isn't going to call me back. All the niggles I felt about odd things he said or did are solidifying into certainty that this is it: he's gone.

Oh God, the emptiness.

No.

I am not going to let this ruin my life for the next however long. I'm going to the cinema.

I tell Dee that I'm manic with work and can't manage a drink beforehand but will see her in the foyer, and then I time it so that I make it there just as the ads are starting, so we need to get our skates on if we're going to get inside the auditorium at the end-of-the-ads-beginning-of-the-trailers sweet spot.

There *is* time, however, after we arrive for Dee to peer into my face and say, 'Are you okay? Do you have hay fever?'

That'll be because my face is all puffy and red from crying. I put quite a lot of foundation, concealer and blusher on but apparently not enough.

'Yep,' I lie, 'but I should be okay soon. I've taken antihistamines.'

Dee nods, apparently satisfied, and then we're inside the auditorium and it's dark and obviously we shouldn't talk because that's rude to the other cinemagoers. I do, despite my best intentions, end up constantly checking for messages on my phone plus having a little sniffle under cover of the darkness, so thank goodness for the fake hay fever excuse.

I decline the suggestion of an after-film drink, blaming my hay fever (I'm loving that lie now) and take myself off home.

I know that I'm not going to get to sleep easily, so I busy myself dragging all the bed clothes off the bed and sticking them in the washing machine along with the towel Ben was using because I am not going to allow myself to sniff in his scent from the sheets and then wallow in further misery.

When I've made the bed I take a long, very hot shower, and then I crawl under my duvet with *The Silver Spoon*, a thick cookery book of classic

Italian recipes. Call me odd (Frankie always has and Tommy used to, in a nice way) but I've always loved reading recipe books in bed. I can't imagine being able to get to sleep quickly tonight, so I'm probably going to have a lot of reading time.

I do actually nod off quite quickly – probably the result of having had very little sleep last night plus crying a lot is tiring – but then I wake up at the crack of dawn (literally five a.m.) and cannot get back to sleep. I try to read but can't concentrate because I keep on trying (truly pathetically) to stalk Ben on social media. The stalking doesn't work because he doesn't seem to *be* on social media, which I did already suspect because over the years I have to my shame already made the occasional unsuccessful attempt to find him on various platforms, and he is nowhere to be found beyond a photo and his email address in the 'About us' section of one of his businesses, the one I found earlier.

In the end, I pull on some (rarely worn) Lycra and take myself for a run, and that's a good thing, because I'm not a natural runner and physical misery is a lot less depressing than mental misery. As a result, all I can think about for the next half hour is my burning thighs and lungs.

And then I'm back home to my empty, empty flat. A week ago it was lovely and just the right size for me. Now it feels too big for one.

After a shower, I sit at my kitchen table and stare at my phone.

My urge to call Ben is pathetically strong. I'm not going to; it's one thing stalking someone and another being obvious about it, and I don't want him to see a billion missed calls from me.

I could phone him from my landline, though. There's no way he'll know the number's mine. Yep, I'm doing it. It's only eight a.m. and Saturday but I think he's a fairly early riser on days where he hasn't been up half the night having sex.

As I look at his number on my mobile and punch the numbers into the landline handset, I'm already feeling hopeful and happier. He'll pick up, he'll be hugely relieved that I've called him because he lost all his contacts somehow and couldn't call me, and we'll make a plan for seeing each other very soon.

There's the long, single beep.

Okay, not to panic, it's still early and maybe he's asleep and that's the sound you get when someone's turned their phone off overnight.

I busy myself for the next two and a half hours with housework and admin in the hope that when I try again Ben will pick up and give me the perfectly rational explanation for his incommunicado-ness over the past twenty-four hours and everything will be okay.

At ten-thirty I call his number again. He'll definitely be up now and his phone will definitely be on. I know from this week that he naturally wakes up by nine at the latest, however little sleep he's had, and that one of the first things he does is check his messages, so his phone will be off airplane mode, if that's what the problem's been.

My heart's beating faster as I tap the digits in.

And then… it's still a long, single beep.

And just like that all my hope goes and all the weirdnesses in Ben's interactions with me over the years and the past week flood into my mind in a big whoosh and that's that, I just *know*.

For whatever reason, he has seemed drawn to me ever since we met – I really don't think I've imagined our connection – and we spent six amazing nights together but now he's walked away and I'm certain he won't be coming back.

I mean, after a few conversations and some finger-related flirting at the cinema, he seemed to change his entire job just to avoid me. And the finger thing was not up there with six nights (and days) of sex. So it's entirely plausible, based on what he did then, that he would change his phone number and email address to avoid talking to me.

So I need to pull myself together, fast, and *cope*.

Work will be okay. You can always immerse yourself in work. I'm feeling pretty strong grief right now, almost like I've been bereaved, and work was really helpful for me after my dad died.

The weekends, though, the weekends are shit, and this one's going to be particularly shitty. The loss of my dad was a greater loss than this, of course it was, but this feels lonelier. Then, I kept myself busy trying to distract and help Mum; and Frankie was going through exactly the same as me at the same time, so we fully understood each other's feelings. Now, though, there is no-one who knows how I feel because, for a start, no-one knows what I've been doing all week. And no-one exactly knows about the way Ben and I have been kind of in and out of each other's lives for the eight years before that, because it's always felt almost fanciful telling anyone about it.

Thinking about my dad, I remember how on the one-year anniversary of his death I was also feeling a little wistful about Ben, and I *really* despise myself.

What an *idiot*.

For ages, I sit and shake my head at myself and my gullible stupidity and cry and wander round the flat and then cry again and at one point even kick a leg of my bed (stupid – it really hurts my toe and does not make me feel remotely better).

And then my phone pings and I leap on it and then feel deeply disappointed when I see that it's a message from Sulwe.

And then I despise myself, *really* despise myself, and suddenly decide that I am not going to be an idiot any more. I'm going to go for a walk now and do my grocery shopping in person instead of online to get some fresh air, and then this afternoon I'm going to catch up on some of the work I did not do this week because I was busy shagging the ghosting arse that is Ben, and then I'm going to go to Sulwe's party this evening even though I am very much not feeling at all like a sparkling party guest.

I manage to immerse myself in my work, and if I'm honest, it was slightly stressing me out around all the sex and the fun that I did so little this week, because I *love* my new business and I'm incredibly lucky to be able to make a (moderate) living out of doing something I love and be my own boss, so I'm actually really pleased to get a solid six hours in and feel almost back on top of things. And it's lovely not to think about Ben (much, anyway).

The party is not so good.

As I walk in the door, the first two people I see are Sulwe and Sarah.

Sulwe says, 'What've you been up to this week? You've been very quiet on WhatsApp.'

And simultaneously, Sarah says, in a particularly penetrating voice, 'Who was that gorgeous man at the station?'

'Ooh, what gorgeous man?' Sulwe asks, as several people turn round.

My mind whirrs very fast for a moment and then I remember that my dad – who was full of excellent actual real-world advice – always used to say don't lie but, if you do have to, make it a good one and make it as close to the truth as possible so that you don't tie yourself in knots. I do want to lie in that I do not want to announce my heartbreak to everyone, but, yes, I'm going to go close to the truth.

'Just Ben from the hut and that New Year's Eve,' I say.

'Oh yes.' Sulwe nods. 'He *is* gorgeous. How come you were with him?'

'I bumped into him at the train station in Kent,' I tell her. 'He was at a wedding in the venue right next to ours, would you believe it.'

'Emmie said when she booked it that there was a special offer if you booked your wedding and a certain number of rooms that weekend; that must be why his wedding was there too,' Sulwe says sagely and completely illogically. I nod, happy with her response. Hopefully we can move off the Ben topic now.

'So what did you get up to with him on Sunday?' Sarah asks.

I have a difficult time not rolling my eyes; she's clearly been bursting to ask since she saw us get on the train together, but *honestly*.

'Just coffee.' I raise my eyebrows slightly, hoping that that will imply that surely this conversation should be over because this really is not anything that anyone would bother to talk about.

'You went in the opposite direction from the village, though? So no coffee shops?'

Honestly, *why* is Sulwe friends with Sarah?

'Well, yes, figure of speech,' I say. 'We went for a short walk and sat on a bench and both drank water from water bottles we had with us. It was nice to catch up.'

Sulwe clearly thinks that Sarah's gone slightly mad, because she smiles at her and then pulls me by the hand away from her towards the middle of the room and whispers, 'Weird interrogation.'

I nod and say, 'Yeah, but you know Sarah,' and then change the subject to the exciting pregnancy news Sulwe announced widely last week – she's now reached fourteen weeks pregnant (her first three pregnancies very sadly ended in first trimester miscarriages) – and fortunately that's it, we're done with the Ben topic.

I avoid Sarah for the rest of the evening, and drink three glasses of white wine and eat a lot of Doritos, gossip a bit about things I'm struggling to be interested in and do some dancing. At half eleven, I leave, pleading tiredness after a very busy work week.

And there you go, I think, as I Uber it home. I can do this. I can continue with my life without Ben in it. This week was just a weird interlude. I will be perfectly happy again extremely soon.

On Sunday I work hard and make one of my very-expensive-per-visit once-monthly visits to the gym *and* go swimming and then in the evening tackle some admin, and then on Monday I go to the gym again and work very hard too. I also message a couple of friends to get more things in my diary so that I'm just *busy*. I do the same on Tuesday.

By Wednesday lunchtime, home from the gym, I feel like – as long as I continue to keep myself extremely busy – I'll soon be back on an even, if slightly dull, keel. I'm proud of myself and I'm not, I decide as I peel potatoes manically, going to think about how I'm going to manage emotionally without putting in the daily hours of a turbo-charged workaholic followed by the training regime of an Olympic wannabe (at least I'm finally making the most of my gym membership). Hopefully I'll just gradually wean myself back to normal life and in the meantime I'm going to be *very* on top of my business, the queen of all things admin and the most toned I've ever been.

And hopefully at some point Ben won't be very frequently (okay pretty constantly) on the edge of my thoughts, pushing his way into everything.

On my way back from the loo after getting the potatoes on to boil (I'm making a parmentier), I see that I have some post lying on the doormat. I pick the three envelopes up *and*, in my new admin-queen persona, open them immediately. I have a bank statement. I file it, congratulating myself the whole time. Maybe I'll actually be *grateful* to Ben for precipitating the new Organised Admin Woman that I have become. I also have a pension statement. I file that too.

The other envelope is handwritten. It contains a postcard.

The postcard is a picture of the cinema that Ben part-owns and where I still work on a consultancy basis. It's a very historic art deco building. I think maybe it's some kind of invitation or something.

But then my eyes and brain register the handwriting and the signature and the word *love* and my heart begins to tip-tap away in my chest. Maybe...

And then I begin to read, and no.

27

LIV

Liv,

I'm not sure whether I'm doing the right thing in writing to you but I find that I can't help myself.

You're amazing. I love you.

But we can't be together.

I suppose that I just wanted to write to say that it's all me and not you. You're wonderful and I cannot believe that anyone wouldn't love you and want to be with you.

If I could change things, I would in a heartbeat. But I can't.

And so that's that.

But please don't ever believe that it was anything to do with you that I had to leave. It isn't.

I really do love you with all my heart. Thank you for a wonderful week.

Ben

On my first read-through, I can barely keep going to the end. I'm just staring and blinking and shaking my head. By the end of my third time through it, I'm crying.

I don't know how many times I read it in the end, but I do know that my emotions change as I fully take in what he's written.

By the end, I think I'd punch him if he were in the room.

I'm amazing. He loves me. Why, thank you Ben, so bloody kind. *It isn't me, it's him.* I mean, why would anyone bother to write a whole little letter just to trot out a stupid tired cliché? Of course it's partly me. Unless he's going to be single for life.

I punch a cushion viciously into shape, and then another one.

I'm so beside myself with conflicting emotions that I literally cannot physically sit down.

I pick up two letters I have to post, stick flip flops on and march up to the post box on the corner of the road, nearly taking my toes off several times in the process, stabbing uneven bits of the pavement too hard with my feet.

Then I march back to the flat.

This is actually not fair, I think. He gets to write a letter to me saying... well, nothing... but it was clearly what he wanted to say, and he was able to say it.

I have things I want to say. I mean, I don't right now because I just don't really *understand*, but I *would* have things to say if I did.

I want closure. I want to know whether it's true that it's him and not me. If it's me, like I'm just not the right person for him, I want him to have the honesty to tell me that. And if it's him, like he has a partner, or there's some other reason that I can't think of right now, I want him to have the honesty to tell me *that*.

I need to speak to him.

I'm going to go to his flat. I grab my handbag and some Adidas shoes (my toes are *sore* now) and then I march myself back out of the front door and off in the direction of Clapham Junction train station.

I get to the station very quickly because I'm properly angry now and the anger is lending me wings. As I round the corner into the station, I nearly take out an elderly couple holding hands as they stroll along the pavement. I swerve to avoid them and get my feet tangled up in the wheels of one of those foldable bikes, which a slightly tetchy looking woman in a smart navy trouser suit and Nike Air Forces is trying to unfold right where I wasn't until I made my weird sideways move.

When I've finished apologising profusely, I take a deep breath and...

carry on hurtling straight into the station. I really don't want to miss the train because I really want to get there and speak to Ben. What if he's going out this evening?

I actually get a train immediately, only trampling a few dozen people in my stampede to get through the carriage doors as they close, and sit down and try to catch my breath.

It takes me a while to notice the woman opposite me staring pointedly at my hand and I realise that I'm drumming my fingers on the table surprisingly loudly.

'Sorry,' I mouth, and take my phone out to try to distract myself. I can't be bothered to read my emails or reply to any messages or look at the news or even play Candy Crush, which I've recently got addicted to a decade later than everyone else. My impatience to arrive and speak to Ben is on a level with that Christmas-present-opening impatience you feel as a child when your parents decide they'd like to make a cup of tea first, except this is infinitely worse, because the feeling's interlaced with anger and dread and worry.

As I walk up the path to Ben's front door, I realise that I don't know what I *am* expecting but I do know that I'm not expecting what happens when I ring his doorbell.

There's an intercom thing and it's answered by a man who is not Ben.

'Oh, hi,' I say, too fired up to wait until this person – I'm guessing a friend – has gone. I want at least to tell Ben that I'm here. 'It's Liv. I wondered if you could let Ben know that I'm here.'

'Ben Jones?' That's a strange question, surely, given that the man is Ben's friend and in his flat. Unless there's more than one Ben there, I suppose.

'Yes. Thank you.'

'Ben's moved out,' the voice tells me.

'Moved *out*?' I parrot.

'Yes. I'm the lettings agent. I'm just showing a viewer round.'

He left my flat on Friday. It is now Wednesday. Five days. In that time he has moved out and has a lettings agent showing viewers round? What?

Okay. I've come this far. I'm not going to shy away from a bit of humiliation.

'Could I possibly get Ben's contact details?'

'I'm really sorry but I can't give out a client's details without permission.'

Fair enough but *bugger*.

'I'm happy to call him now to confirm if you like?' the man offers.

'That would be great, thank you.'

'Okay, hang on.' Over the intercom there's a bit of static and a bit of silence and then I hear him say distantly, clearly away from the intercom speaker, 'Hi, Ben, it's Josh from Bentley & White. I have someone here, oh, hold on a moment.' He then comes back to the intercom and says, 'Sorry, could I get your name again?'

'Liv Murphy.'

'I have Liv Murphy here,' I hear him telling Ben. 'Could you just confirm that you're happy for me to give her your contact details.' There's a short silence where he's obviously listening, and then he says, 'No problem. And I'll be in touch later about the tenancy.'

I pull my phone out, ready to take down Ben's number or forwarding address, when the man says, 'Liv, hi, apologies but Ben thinks you have the wrong person, so unfortunately I can't give you his details. Sorry. Although sounds like it's the wrong Ben Jones anyway. Good luck finding the right one and have a great evening.'

'Thanks,' I manage to say, before I begin my great evening by crying big, choking, snot-tears back down the path.

I walk around the streets for a few minutes until I have my stupid crying under control, and then I make my way back to the Tube station.

I stand on the platform thinking what kind of tosser tells you in such a sincere way that he loves you *and* writes you a note saying that, and then tells his estate agent that he doesn't know you? Who. Bloody. Does. That?

I'm furious, I'm hurt, I'm confused, and apparently I've now flipped into full-on online stalker mode. He must be on social media somewhere. When I looked for him online before, I didn't actually want to be a stalker, so I didn't really, really go for it. Now I do not care at all if I'm at borderline arrest-me-now stalker levels. I just want to *know*. What actually happened? Why did he leave?

I really don't think he's on social media. After fifteen minutes of assiduous searching, I manage to find a photo of him on a night out with Mags and some others from the cinema from before I worked there, and the others are tagged and he is not.

I sit back and stare at the dirty train window above me. I feel kind of dirty myself now, if I'm honest. I don't like cyber stalking.

I feel a tiny bit as though I'm losing my mind.

I need to talk to someone.

Sulwe or Frankie.

Except talking to anyone is tricky because I've never actually really told anyone about me and Ben. Insofar as Ben and I have never been any kind of a thing in their eyes.

A memory surfaces in my mind from when I was in Year Twelve and I started seeing Ned Morgan (the tosser): Mum got worried and told me that it wasn't a good relationship if your partner caused any kind of rift between you and your friends, and if someone was a keeper they'd be friends with your friends.

Hmm. I've always kept the Ben thing a secret from everyone.

Although to be fair, it wasn't like there was anything to say really.

But even so.

Okay, I'm calling Sulwe and Frankie. I need to talk.

We begin our summit at nine forty-five that evening because Sulwe has a work dinner that she can't get away from and when I said (disappointed but trying not to be too needy) no worries we could do it another time she insisted we should do it this evening, and I caved very fast because I am in fact extremely needy.

Frankie arrives wearing what she says is 'leisure wear' but what I think are her pyjamas (she likes an early night), carrying a bottle of red. She tells me she's very happy to stay overnight if I like because Nella has the kids fully under control.

Sulwe arrives in a very impressive tangerine-coloured power suit and mega heels despite her pregnancy (she doesn't do trainers with work clothes because she says this 'modern' principle of comfort over style is bullshit), carrying two bottles of Prosecco, some alcohol-free wine and a packet of cigarettes.

'None of us smoke and you're pregnant,' I point out.

'I thought you might need to start.'

'No. I've already become a cyber stalker. I don't need a nicotine addiction too.' I also don't need an entire bottle of Prosecco to myself. My head's developed a permanent ache over the past few days and what I need is water.

I do accept one glass though.

'So what's been happening?' Sulwe's straight in there.

'Well, in summary,' I begin.

'No.' Sulwe's shaking her head and Frankie is wagging her finger at me. As one, they tell me that they don't want a summary, they want full details.

'It's going to take a long time,' I warn.

'Then it takes a long time,' Frankie says.

'Exactly,' Sulwe agrees.

'Okay, then.' I take a deep breath and then launch into the whole story, from the shed up. I go into full details, and it's punctuated first by Sulwe halting me so that she can get paper and pen to go full private eye and make a list of clues, and then by the two of them at different points stating with satisfaction that they *knew* there was something. Just telling the story takes a good hour and a half. And then they need to exclaim a lot over Ben's bastardry in the past week.

'There's definitely something fishy.' They've finished their immediate exclamations and Sulwe's looking at her list. She wrote it in green biro and she's now circling things with a red pen. 'His change of mood in the shed. Him not telling you that he lived close to Frankie. Avoiding you at the cinema. Being weird outside the wedding. Buggering off now. I mean, when you add it all up, it does sound like he has another woman. But also when you add it all up it does sound like he really cares about you.'

'But not as much as he cares about the other woman,' I say glumly.

'She must have been away for a week,' Frankie says. 'The weekend of the wedding and then all last week.'

'I'm confused, though.' Sulwe completes an intricate red flower doodle and admires her handiwork for a second. 'Why has he moved out?'

'Well, maybe he was already moving out?' Frankie stretches at her end of the sofa. 'And that's why he left when he did? Or because the other woman got back?'

I shake my head. 'I really don't think so. I was there at the beginning of the week and his flat was not at all like your flat would be if you were moving out – and on Monday he got a big Sainsbury's delivery with several bags of pasta and rice, which you wouldn't do if you knew you were moving out at the weekend – and the only reason we came here was that I wanted to. *And* I don't think there was any evidence of another woman there.'

'What was he doing while you were in the bathroom though?' Frankie asks.

'I don't know.' I'm thinking hard. 'Definitely something surreptitious. But the bathroom didn't have a woman's stuff in it. And I feel like there couldn't have been much around because he wouldn't have been able to clear all of it away. I would have noticed.'

'What if the other woman didn't live there and didn't visit him there because her house is much nicer and he has now moved in with her? What if it's somewhere outside London? What if they have *kids* together?' I hate Frankie's suggestions. Because they really make me wonder if they're true. Oh God. Maybe the little girls in the photo are actually his daughters rather than his nieces.

'But' – Sulwe points the red pen at each of us in turn – 'it wasn't the same other woman throughout the whole time you've known him, was it? *And*' – she points the pen again – 'the first time, in the shed, when, if he was a total arse he could have done what he liked with you and got away with it, he completely owned up about his girlfriend. Which suggests that he really liked you and maybe got into some flirting which he should not have done but ultimately chose not to do anything two-timey.' I like Sulwe's thoughts a lot more than Frankie's.

'It's genuinely weird.' Frankie's perfect brow is perfectly furrowed. I don't know how she does that. I'd look like a gargoyle if I tried to copy her expression. 'All the signs point to him having another woman but also all the signs point to him not having another woman.' She's right and the not knowing is a killer.

'So what should we do next?' Sulwe shares the last third of the first bottle of Prosecco between my glass and Frankie's while I realise that my mum was very right about talking to your friends about things because I feel a lot better that Sulwe's talking about what *we* should do rather than what *I* should do. I very much like the group support thing. 'Should you just ignore him, leave it and get on with having an amazing life without him, which you are totally going to do? Or not?'

'I think from everything you've said that you need closure,' Frankie says.

I nod. 'I don't think I want to spend years constantly looking over my shoulder worried that I'll bump into him somewhere, not knowing how things will pan out.'

'So then you need to find him and speak to him,' Sulwe states. 'And your question will be *what the actual fuck*.'

'Yes.' I nod. 'I do. Thank you. I feel better knowing what I definitely need to do.'

'Okay then, let's do it. How hard can it be to find someone?' Frankie picks her phone up and starts tapping, and then says, 'Oh.'

'Very difficult when he's called Ben Jones and your only tool is Google?' Sulwe asks.

'Very hard,' Frankie confirms.

I nod.

'Fortunately' – Sulwe points the neck of the empty bottle at us in turn for emphasis – 'we have additional tools at our disposal.' She puts the bottle down and points at her head. '*Knowledge*.'

'I've said it before and I'll say it again.' I smile at her. 'I would hire you to do *any* job.' (Except cooking.) She can talk total obvious crap *so* convincingly.

'Yes, I am good,' she says and picks up the second bottle of Prosecco. Apparently if she can't get drunk herself she's going to make sure we do it for her.

'So back to the knowledge,' Frankie says. 'You need to write it all down, Liv, and then just work through it all, checking mutual friends and places he's worked and so on.'

After a sofa-viewing of *Ocean's 8* (during which Sulwe actually sobs, for no good reason; her nail-hard exterior hides a very soft interior), they both stay over. Frankie and I sleep in my bed (thank goodness I changed the bedclothes after Ben) and Sulwe takes the sofa bed (all three of us trap our fingers in it hard when we're putting it up and wonder whether we'll have to go to A&E).

Over an early and speedy toast-and-butter breakfast washed down with orange juice and paracetamol (my initial instinct that Prosecco would not be the way forward was completely right; Frankie and I are *so* hungover), we agree that I'm still going to try to find Ben. Sulwe and Frankie are still very fired up and very keen to help me.

In Sulwe's words: 'The Ben Jones hunt is *on*.'

28

BEN

I'm glad of the unseasonal rain biting against my forehead and cheeks; I miss Liv so much it's almost physically painful and the rain's slightly distracting.

I'm pleased about the lactic acid pounding through my leg muscles as well, as I push myself just a little more to reach the top of the next small mountain.

When I reach the summit, I bend over for a moment to catch my breath, and then look around. Objectively speaking, the view's amazing. There's a good reason that tourists come from far and wide to the Lake District.

I am very much not in the mood, however, for appreciating views.

I'm not in the mood for appreciating anything if I'm honest.

God, I need to shake this off. I cannot be with Liv. I am not with Liv. I have moved away for a while so there's no danger of her being able to contact me. I need to move on. Maybe work hard. Look for new business opportunities. Get myself down to the pub in the evening, reconnect with old friends and make new ones. Anything.

Liv's both an old and a new friend, my mind tells me. For fuck's sake.

I set off downwards, fast, so I'm too busy making sure I don't break my ankle on the scree to think.

But when I pause for breath and some water, she's still at the top of my thoughts. Should I have sent that letter, told her I loved her? I don't know. I wanted her to know that she's perfect, she's wonderful, I adore her, and my leaving was nothing to do with her; there's nothing about her that would make any sane person leave her. But maybe she'd have been better off if I'd just said nothing.

I spot a hawk in the sky, hovering in awe-inspiring majesty. That has to be a good life, nothing to think about except where your next meal's coming from. It suddenly swoops, almost faster than my eye can register, and within hardly any time has returned to the sky, holding a small animal in its beak. And that, by contrast, is a tragic life, and oh my God, I'm losing my mind; I'm deeply sad suddenly for the family of the creature that's just been caught. I'm sure a psychoanalyst would suggest that I'm projecting my own grief over Liv onto a mouse family.

I want her to be here so that we can laugh – or maybe just smile – together about the fact that right now my sentimentality has me wanting to say a silent prayer for the mouse's soul.

I want her to be here so that I can hug her, hear her voice, watch her face, just... *love* her.

Fucking hell. I'm a joke.

I'm going to finish this walk, I'm going to go back to the house, have a shower and go to the pub for a steak and kidney pie and a good pint – or five – and I am going to stop thinking about her and be happy.

29

LIV

I have a lot of work on and I'm determined not to let my business suffer, so I don't actually have time to start looking for Ben until the evening.

The first thing I do is reply to Sulwe's sixteen messages on the WhatsApp group she's set up (I know; if I didn't already know what she was like and wasn't extremely pleased that she's helping with so much enthusiasm I'd be very freaked out). She's pointed out that, while we did record everything that I can remember that's ever happened between Ben and me, we all forgot to record extra facts I know about him, and says that she needs *all* details (other than intimate unless he has any particularly unusual sexual inclinations that might help us in tracing him).

I reassure her (or disappoint her; I'm not quite sure) that Ben did not exhibit any sexual habits that would allow us to trace him (what, no sadism at all? she asks) and we move on to everything I know about his home town (London), shoe size (unknown but his shoes are quite big), university (Bristol), university subject (I don't know but I think he once mentioned something about essays), godchildren (yes I think he has some), siblings (he has at least one brother – the father of his nieces – assuming they are indeed his nieces and not daughters) and recent holidays (I think he said he'd been on a city break to Lisbon in May with a couple of friends).

'It's like he's the most generic person ever,' Frankie writes.

I bristle because he is not generic, he's pretty close to perfect. Until I remember that he dumped me pretty spectacularly.

'Suspiciously generic,' Sulwe replies. She'd make such a good detective.

The second thing I do is call Mags. I've kind of known for days that it might be a good idea to call her, but I was too upset to do it. Now, after the catharsis of telling Sulwe and Frankie everything in excruciating detail, I have myself under much better control. I'm just going to ask her if she has Ben's number. Simple.

'Hey, Liv, how are you?'

'Good, thank you. How are you?' We haven't actually spoken for a few months other than by the occasional message. I still do some work for the cinema but Mags left to work in a Michelin-starred restaurant in a very fancy front of house role, and our schedules have meant that it's hard for us to meet.

After I've politely asked about her work, girlfriend and dog and all the mutual acquaintances (other than Ben) that I can think of, I say, 'So I have a favour to ask.'

And as I say it I suddenly realise that I can *totally* ask her – why did I not think of this before? – whether Ben has a serious partner that she knows of.

'Anything,' Mags says.

'I wondered whether you had Ben Jones's contact details. And also, well, um, this is a weird one, but...' Yes, I *can* totally ask whether he has a partner, obviously, but how am I actually going to phrase it? *Does Ben have a girlfriend or a wife?* That isn't a normal question is it, really, about someone?

'Yes, I've got his number. I'll forward it to you. And what's the weird one?' Mags sounds agog.

'Well.' Oh, fuck it. Why, actually, not just be open with her? I know she knew him first but she and I worked closely together for several years and became very good friends and still are, even though we haven't been able to see each other much recently. 'So, basically...' Yes, easier said than done. I still can't get the words out. And then suddenly they pour out of me. 'Basically, we hooked up at a wedding in Kent ten days ago and spent nearly a week having sex and then on Friday he disappeared. Completely. Like he's changed his phone number and moved out of his flat and everything. And then he sent me a letter telling me that he loves me but that he couldn't be with me so he's gone. And a part of me is wondering whether he has a *wife* or something, in which case I suppose he's just a total arse and it is what it is and I need to lick my wounds and move on, and part of me wants some closure and wants to know what's wrong with me, but most of me's worried about him and wants to know that he's okay.'

Woah. That was... a lot. I feel quite good, though. Very good, actually, that I can say it. Because it's been huge in my life and it's really hard pretending that nothing enormous has happened to me recently. I want to acknowledge it out loud.

Not to *everyone*, obviously, I'm not going to tell the lady in the greengrocer's when I pop out later to buy oranges, or announce it to the bus driver, or to my elderly neighbour when I go round this evening to pick up my Amazon delivery. But to friends, yes, why not.

Mags has been silent for ages. Finally, she speaks. It isn't profound. 'Wow,' she says.

I wait.

'I'm sorry,' she says after a couple more seconds. 'That sounds huge. Would you like to meet?'

'Yes please. When's good for you? I can do pretty much any time,' I say, not at all desperately.

'Tomorrow evening?'

I'm actually supposed to be going to the cinema with Sulwe and Frankie then, but I know they'll understand, especially since I think Frankie's main motive in suggesting it was to cheer me up. Sulwe will be particularly pleased if we postpone because she's gone very dog-with-bone over the Ben hunt, and when she isn't asleep (she's finding pregnancy very tiring) she wants us all to hunt at all times. She's added about fifteen messages to the 'Find Ben' chat in the last hour alone.

'Perfect.'

The number that Mags sends through to me a minute or two later is the same as Ben's old one that no longer works, so even if he now has a new number, he obviously hasn't shared it widely.

Another minute after that she sends me a message saying, 'Oh okay, that number doesn't work any more.' Clearly she's tried to text him.

And then a couple of minutes later she sends me another message saying, 'Literally this evening just got a new email address from him. I sent him an email and got a reply saying out of office for the foreseeable.'

She doesn't forward his new email address to me and I don't ask for it. I don't want to put her in an awkward position and there's no point anyway; it's quite clear that he wouldn't reply to anything I might write. In fact, I realise, I don't *want* to write anything to him. I want to speak to him and find out the truth and react to that. He obviously doesn't want to hear from me and it will not help me to compose and send a garbled *maybe this has happened and if so here's my reaction, but alternatively if it's actually this, then* here's *my reaction*.

We meet at a wine bar in Shoreditch near Mags's restaurant, and I make myself act like a nice person who's actually interested in other people rather than the self-obsessed misery I've become this week, and do ask properly about her life again, before she says, 'So tell me everything.'

So I do.

The conversation (essentially a monologue I have to admit) goes quite differently from how it went with Sulwe and Frankie last night. Mags *knows* Ben, and she knows him quite well. She has a number of interesting points to make at different junctures, including:

'For all the time I've known him I'm sure he's never had a serious girlfriend.'

That one pleases me but also makes me worry that there's some weird issue going on.

'I knew there was something between you the first time I saw you together. If I'm honest, I thought he'd asked me to hire you because you'd slept together.'

That one makes me squirm.

'I've always, *always* thought he had a thing for you. Something in the way he used to look at you. Especially at that jungle party.'

That one makes me nearly smile and nearly cry.

'He's such a good friend. When my mum died, he came round with some really fancy frozen ready meals and a bottle of red and just *listened*. And then he kept on checking in on me, just the right amount.'

That one makes me sniff.

'He adores his nieces.'

That one makes me sniff too. Sentimental sniffing because he was gorgeous about them and relieved sniffing because *yesssss* they *are* his nieces and not his daughters.

Basically, Mags does believe everything I say but she does not believe that Ben is an arse.

'It's odd,' she says when I've finished telling her what happened. 'I'm worried about him. I can't understand why he would feel that he had to leave. I'd be *astonished* if he's done something bad. I mean, apart from anything else it's so unlikely that he would have been hiding a partner from us. You can see why he'd hide one from you if he wanted to get into your pants on the side, but why from everyone else? What possible reason could he have for that?'

I nod. I'm getting really worried now, too.

'Maybe he has mental health issues and needs help,' I say.

'Maybe. I've never seen any evidence of that but actually the colleagues and friends are often the last to know, aren't they?'

I nod. '*Or*' – my imagination's starting to go in all sorts of frightening directions – 'what if he's been involved with serious crime and he's had to start a new life under an alias and cut himself off from everyone for his safety and ours?'

Mags stares at me. 'A Mafia type thing you mean? Like, no? Of course not?'

'Well, there were the ice cream van Mafia wars in Glasgow?'

'Were there?'

'Yep.'

'Oh. Ben, though? Really, no?'

We sit and stare at each other for a bit.

'The Lake District,' Mags suddenly says.

I raise my eyebrows in question.

'He used to go there quite often. I think his parents retired there.'

'Ohhhh.' A memory's coming to me of us talking about our favourite places. 'Yes, he did talk about it.'

He said it was where he liked to go to wind down. The whole being-at-one-with-the-elements-but-knowing-you-could-finish-the-day-in-a-fantastic-pub-and-then-sleep-in-a-comfortable-bed thing.

'I can't believe I didn't think of that before,' I say. I also can't believe it wasn't on Sulwe's list of knowledge-about-Ben questions. 'He could definitely be there. Maybe I'll get a train up.'

'I think the Lake District's quite *big*,' Mags points out. 'You probably need to narrow it down a bit more. Obviously we need to find someone who has his new number and knows where he is, or has his parents' details for example.'

I nod. 'Obviously.' I suddenly have an idea. 'I wonder whose wedding he was at when I met him. Maybe we could find out.'

'Yes, good plan. Also, he's good friends with Fred, the cinema head chef. I'll text him.'

'Thank you so much.' I look at my watch. 'You said you had to meet someone at eight-thirty and it's already eight forty-five. You should go.'

'Are you sure?'

'Of course I'm sure.' I stand up and Mags does too. I hug her. 'Thank you. I've been an embarrassing mess for a few days and it's really helped talking to you.'

'Hey. Any time. We'll find Ben and he'll be okay and you will too.'

As she says this, I actually believe her.

By the time we've hugged again outside the bar and are going off in our opposite directions, I don't believe her optimistic words quite so much, but I do feel better. Not keeping things a secret definitely helps.

On my way home on the bus, squished up uncomfortably close to a double-denim-clad man holding three large bags-for-life full of groceries and many, many boxes of tissues (not a surprise because he keeps on sneezing very snottily; I should not have decided to sit next to him), I get Googling again.

Sulwe's going to be very annoyed that she didn't think of the wedding, because she likes to win; I strike gold quite quickly.

I type in 'wedding Frensham Park Kent Saturday 16 July' and find lots of Facebook posts. There aren't actually any photos of Ben that I can see, but there are men in kilts, some of them the same tartan pattern as Ben's was (it's quite embedded in my memory because it featured quite heavily in the early part of Saturday night's sex). It doesn't take long to find the names of the bride and groom.

I'm so pleased with my amazing detective skills that I smile benevolently and barely gag at all when my seat companion sneezes all over me leaving droplets on my sleeve. I do stand up, though, surreptitiously wiping my sleeve on the side of the seat, which I reason is not an antisocial thing to do, because a) no one actually touches the side of the seat and b) you *expect* bus seats not to be places you could eat your dinner off and c) how long can snot-germs live for anyway? Plus, d) as it turns out he's sneezing messily everywhere anyway so the entire bus is going to be covered in his snot at this rate.

Hanging on to the pole in the middle of the aisle, I realise that in the midst of the detective excitement and sneeze disgust, I missed my stop.

I get off at the next one and begin the walk back, thinking hard about what I should do next. And as I press the button at a pedestrian crossing, I realise that the wedding couple are probably currently on honeymoon, and that I cannot in any case cold-call them. *Hi. I'm a friend of Ben Jones. He does not want to speak to me any more, so much so that he's changed his phone number and left London. Please could you give me his details?* Nope. That's how to get arrested, if anything. Hmm.

Mags texts me late evening, on her way home, with numbers of some friends that she and Ben have in common and descriptions of how Ben knows them, and says she'll call them all to ask if anyone's heard from him in the past week.

'Thank you so much,' I reply. 'Just realised it would be very weird if I contacted complete strangers myself. But I'm worried about him.'

And, selfishly, I want my closure.

'No worries,' Mags texts back. 'Sure he's okay but be good to check.'

On closer inspection, I realise that I do actually know one of the contacts she's sent me, and I think I could phone him and ask about Ben without it being *too* weird, hooray.

I go to sleep neither drunk nor crying, which is an extreme improvement on recent evenings.

Over the next couple of days, I do talk to a few people after introductions from Mags, including some uni friends of Ben's, who have obviously known him for a long time.

I explain the whole story to each one of them, as I did to Mags, so that they don't just think I'm a deranged stalker and refuse to engage.

He hasn't been in touch with anyone I speak to since he (as it turns out) cancelled Wednesday evening drinks during our week together; they've all assumed he was busy with work or away, and before I spoke to them had been sure he'd be back in touch soon, but once they realise that actually he's disappeared and gone non-contact with basically everyone except his lettings agent, they all get worried. And I get even more worried.

From the sounds of it, he's always been a lovely friend.

He's usually good at staying in touch. He works hard. He does not to anyone's knowledge two-time anyone and he has not to anyone's knowledge had a partner this year. He lends people cash when they're down on their luck. He's a devoted godfather. He even bloody remembers people's birthdays and is the life and soul – but not overbearingly-so – of their parties. He has never to anyone's knowledge walked out of his own life before. He is – of course – in a group of friends who sponsor several endangered snow leopards. He couldn't be more perfect if he tried.

Except for the disappear-from-his-own-life-and-break-the-girl's-heart part.

Now that I've spoken to so many people about him (yes, I do feel like a stalker), I'm a lot more worried than desperate for closure, because his disappearance now seems *so* uncharacteristic and it seems *so* unlikely that he had another woman unless he's a professional-level bigamist multi-life type person, which does not seem plausible. His friends are worried and keen to look for him too, so I do think he'll be found soon, and people will make sure he's okay, which cheers me up a little. I resolutely push away the worry that something terrible might have happened to him, because surely someone would have heard if it had.

More than one person mentions the Lake District and eventually, on my ninth call, someone tells me they know his parents' address because a group of them stayed there a few years ago on a short walking holiday. Apparently, during that trip, Ben exhibited excellent first aid skills when one of the group fell and got some nasty gashes. Well, of course he did.

I'm pleased when the friend also mentions that he's a very poor cook and that they all, including Ben, got a little over-drunk that weekend, because there's a limit to how perfect any one person should be.

As soon as I end that call, I get myself straight online to look for train tickets to the Lake District. I haven't ever been before and am completely ignorant about it. It turns out the best way to get there is from Euston to a place called Oxenholme Lake District. The train is a lot faster than you'd think, only about three hours. And it's a lot more expensive than you'd think. Maybe there's a lot of competition for last-minute tickets from tourists.

I'm not at my most flush for cash at the moment, due to my recent flat move after breaking up with Tommy and the large number of weddings this summer, plus I'm ploughing everything I can into my business, but I don't hesitate at all about forking out nearly two hundred quid for a three-hour train journey. I'm really worried about Ben and I have not been feeling good this week, so I'm just going to have to suck up the cost.

I choose a train at just after eight in the morning, and a return for eight the following evening, so that I have nearly the full weekend to search.

About one second after I confirm my payment, I realise that I'm going to need somewhere to stay on Saturday night and some means of transport. And about five minutes after that, I've found out that both accommodation and a (tiny little) rental car are going to cost a fortune.

Well, I'm committed now. I'll just postpone my new sofa purchase.

Wow. I consider how this weekend might pan out. I'm going to go to the Lake District and I'm going to rock up at Ben's parents' house and say 'Hi, Ben, what happened?' or perhaps more likely, 'Hi, Ben's parents, er I'm a friend of Ben's and I was just passing and I wondered if Ben was around, oh you say he isn't here and has actually moved to Prague? No problem, lovely to meet you, bye.'

Yep. Now that my rush of ticket-purchasing adrenalin has worn off, I'm thinking that this weekend is likely to be somewhere on the scale from pretty bad to very bad to devastatingly bad.

I'll just have to hope it's only at the pretty-bad end.

30

LIV

Even when you know in theory that it's a lot colder in the Lake District than in London, you are not prepared for the practice.

I'm just outside the station in the queue for the car rental place and I can see that the countryside is definitely going to be very pretty, but right now I don't care because I'm too busy shivering. I did check the weather forecast and I am wearing a jumper *and* a cardigan, but the jumper is thin and the cardigan's a lot less warm than I thought it would be. What I *need* is a thick woollen polo neck and a Canada Goose-style duvet coat. How is this the predicted fifteen degrees? It feels more like three.

I have a look on my phone. Yep, there are several country clothing stores in the vicinity. I'm going to have to invest even more in this weekend and buy something warm.

The car rental man looks at my London clothing and (I am now realising) not-very-suitable footwear (boots but they are not grippy) and asks me if I'm experienced at driving on narrow country roads, and talks me into buying some extra insurance.

When I'm at the country clothing store (after a little hiccup getting the car started and then lurching and stalling several times as I get used to using gears again), I'm equally weak-minded and am talked into buying both a padded, waterproof thigh-length jacket and some (very comfortable but eye-wateringly-priced) walking boots. In my defence, they are both (despite their high prices) excellent bargains at only forty per cent of their original price.

'That's a lot of money,' I tell the very-good-at-selling sales assistant as I hand over my poor, abused credit card.

'Completely worth it, though,' she says.

Hmm. For the amount I've spent on this weekend I could have gone to New York or Paris or Venice. Somewhere you don't need walking boots or not-that-attractive thick coats in the summer. The coat is orange because the black version was full price and for that I would have had to extend my mortgage.

Anyway, I'm all kitted out now and I have the car, so I'm off.

To Ben's parents' house.

Gaaaaaaaaaaaah.

Now the moment of truth might be just round the corner, I'm not sure I want to arrive at it.

Twenty minutes later, I've discovered that I will not in fact be arriving at it any time soon, because Google Maps and Waze keep trying to send me down roads that are actually tracks with massive holes and no actual tarmac. I don't want to be stranded by myself in the middle of nowhere and I don't want to have to pay the excess on a car insurance claim, so I'm not going down them, and I don't have a paper map, because who has paper maps nowadays, so I'm just going round in circles.

Another fifteen minutes later, I'm back in Oxenholme buying a paper map.

There is literally *nothing* about this trip that isn't expensive. I have to buy an Ordnance Survey one and it costs twelve pounds. I am never going to use this again, I grumble to myself. Google Maps is *free*. Although in this instance, shit.

I can't read a paper map while I drive.

And when I stop to look at the map, I get very confused.

I am not having fun.

Also, the sun's out now and it's *boiling* inside the car, which does not have great aircon, and I need to take off the expensive coat *and* my cardigan, and frankly I wouldn't mind taking my jumper off too but I don't want to give the locals an eyeful.

Eventually, I develop a system where I follow Google Maps on my phone until it gets ridiculous and then I stop and look at the paper map (and on two occasions nearly get hit by two different tractors, so after that I make sure I don't stop on bends), and I stop driving in circles.

At about two p.m., with a very rumbling stomach (no handy sandwich or snack shops anywhere on this route), I arrive at what looks like it must be Ben's parents' house. There seems to be a long drive, the entrance to which is flanked by stone walls and lots of greenery and two tall gateposts with indeterminate somewhat-broken sculpted animals (maybe lions) on each side.

I'm here.

I. Am. Here.

And Ben might be too.

I'm suddenly incredibly reluctant to move forward.

He chose to cut me out of his life. What am I actually thinking? Am I just being a ridiculous stalker?

Well, yes.

I'm worried about him, though. And so's Mags and she's known him for years, and so are his other friends.

And I've spent a small fortune and a lot of effort to get myself here.

Okay, sticking plaster approach yet again. I'm just going to manoeuvre the car into the side of the drive's entrance so I'm not blocking the road, and then walk really fast up the drive and ring the doorbell.

The drive's actually really long. Walking it is literally like going for an actual, mid-length walk. But it's nice. There are hedges and bushes and trees on both sides and it feels very rural.

After a very long time, definitely several minutes, I do begin to wonder if it's just a lane with no house at the end of it.

I'm pondering whether I should go back and get the car, when I round a bend and see the house several hundred metres away in the distance.

I feel like I should have driven, except driving right up to someone's front door across their property seems a lot more trespassery.

Although, I will of course not be able to make a particularly speedy getaway if things don't go well; I'll have to trudge all the way back (I am not a great runner and my new walking boots are already blistering my feet).

As I near the house, I see that it's quite old, wide and low, just two main storeys I think, built from stone, surrounded by lots of flowers and bushes, and with a big circle of grass in front, around which the drive goes.

It's gorgeously chocolate-box, really, really pretty.

And I'm sure that I would *hate* to live here because it's so remote. Like, I'm guessing that if this were your home you wouldn't be able to put on a long trench and boots over your pyjamas at midnight to go to the corner shop for milk and bread and be there and back in eight minutes. Although you *could* wear pyjamas all day long without anyone seeing you, I'm sure. I wonder how far it is to the nearest shop or pub or Chinese takeaway. I feel like it would be a full day trip and you'd have to be careful about opening hours.

When I get to the grass circle, I follow the drive round it rather than walking across the very well-tended lawn, in a ludicrous bid to minimise my unwanted-visitor-ness.

And then I get to the pale bluey-grey front door.

Unbelievably, there's no doorbell, just a knocker. Which is utterly absurd. You can never hear knockers through a whole house, especially one as big as this. If someone's trekked all the way here, would you not want them to be able to make their presence known? What if it's an important delivery? What if you're going out that evening and you *need* some new shoes or a new dress and the postman's here with it but you don't hear the knocker and he takes it away again?

Very ill thought-out.

But whatever. I am now hovering in front of the door and oh my goodness *oh my goodness*. In the window of the room to my right the glass is all dimply in the way that original old glass often is, plus the sun's on the other side of the house, so I can't see very well, but I *can* see the outline of a youngish and large man's shape. It's obviously Ben.

Oh my goodness oh my goodness oh my goodness.

Fuckity fuckity fuck.

Ben is here and I am about to bang the knocker against the front door.

My heart pounding almost as loudly as any knocker could knock, I lift the knocker and drop it, hard.

Ben stands up and begins to move towards the door.

31

LIV

I see Ben's outline, tall and broad, cross the room to my right. Funny how even through a very obscured window you can recognise the way someone moves.

He disappears from view and I hold my breath. Is he going to open the door or am I going to end up kneeling on the doorstep shouting 'I can see you' through the letterbox? I mean, I *will* do that, because my mere presence here, two hundred odd miles from London, is quite clearly massively undignified in itself. I blatantly did not get here by chance and I have blatantly ignored all the please-leave-me-alone signals he's sent and travelled here. So, yes, I will do the shouting through the letterbox thing.

Except... it sounds as though I won't have to.

The door's opening.

It's moving very slowly on its hinges, as if it's extremely heavy.

Finally it's almost open and I'm half smiling, half freaking out in anticipation of seeing Ben.

And then it's fully open, and I reel.

Because although this man has the same physique as Ben and moves in the same way as Ben, he is not Ben.

But I do know him.

And I cannot believe that he's here.

I'm literally shaking my head and screwing my face up in confusion.

This man is my sexual harassing office nemesis from all those years ago. Eight years older but instantly recognisable.

'Max Jones,' I blurt.

He visibly blanches and takes a step backwards, before running a hand over his face and eventually saying, 'Olivia?'

I don't reply because I'm thinking and it's hard work. This is *definitely* the address I got for Ben's parents.

Max Jones. Ben Jones. I've never even considered the idea before, because Jones is a very common surname, and also why would I? But... are they *related*?

They must be. Otherwise how would Max be here where Ben is supposed to be?

'Do you know Ben Jones?' I ask, a lot more bothered about Ben than about coming face-to-face with Max again, as it turns out.

'My brother Ben?'

'Your *brother*?' I just stand and stare. I'm still finding thinking really tricky; my mind's too shocked to work efficiently.

'My brother,' he confirms.

'Is he here?' I'm one-track right now.

'He was here but I arrived with my family so he left.' Max's eyes are kind of goggling.

'Do you know where he is?'

'No.'

'Is he okay, though?'

'Erm, I think so?' Max is still goggling.

I feel hot tears begin to spill onto my cheeks and I don't care at all that I am apparently crying in front of Max-the-arsehole. I'm not sure what the tears are about – maybe just a culmination of recent events and let's face it I've been crying a lot in the last week – but I do know that the thing I'm most upset about right now is Ben. Seeing Max is a tiny little speck of annoyance, really, mixed with extreme incredulity, in the universe of all things related to Ben: worry, fear, hurt, love.

Max is shifting from foot to foot, his demeanour very different from that of the self-confident office dick I remember.

I don't speak because at this moment I don't have the mental capacity to form words.

I also don't move, because having got this far I'm not going anywhere until I have more information on Ben's whereabouts.

My mind's still darting in all sorts of directions, and I'm wondering whether Max and Ben being brothers has any bearing on Ben's disappearance.

Does Ben know that Max was my office nemesis? I try to think but I can't remember whether I told him Max's name. He might have been able to identify him from other things I said, though. Or not. If he *does* know, would that have caused him to disappear? Because the office issue was a good eight years ago now, and I really don't think I mentioned it at all to Ben during the week we were together, and surely he must realise that I'm no longer traumatised by it; it's just something crappy that happened to me once. I think there must be another reason, but *what*?

'I could ask our parents if they know where he is,' Max offers eventually.

My mind snaps to attention. That's on obvious suggestion and it sounds like a good one.

'Yes, please,' I say.

'Okay. I mean, of course.' He half-turns and then looks back at me and says with clear reluctance, 'Would you like to come in?'

As he says it, I hear children's voices from somewhere deep inside the house.

I shake my head and say, 'No, thank you, I'm fine here.' The temperature's plummeted and the bright sun has been replaced by grey drizzle and I left my lovely new warm coat in the car because I'd got so hot, so I'm cold and damp, but of *course* I'm not going in. It sounds as though his kids if not his wife are also in the house.

Hi kids, my name's Liv and I really loathe your dad because he sexually harassed me and then tried to get me fired and caused me to have to move to Paris when I didn't want to and also I've just spent a week sleeping with Uncle Ben and then Uncle Ben scarpered and I'm hunting for him.

I don't think so.

Funnily enough, Max's shoulders visibly drop and he can't help smiling a bit. Yep, in his position I'd be pretty relieved too that I don't want to go in.

'Okay, if you're sure.' He's already half-closed the door in my face. 'Back in a minute.'

He returns in well under the minute, holding a piece of paper, a pen and a phone, and moves outside the house, coming to stand a few feet away from me. He clearly could have made the call inside, in the comfort of the house and with somewhere to lean the paper on. He must be trying to ensure I don't come in. If I weren't all-consumed by the thought that I might be about to see Ben again, I'd be pissed off that he seems to think I might stoop to pushing inside the house and trying to upset his family in any way.

'Hi, Mum,' he says into the phone. 'Do you know where Ben is at the moment – do you have an address for him?' She says something quite long and then he says, 'Okay, thank you very much,' and ends the call.

'Yeah, she was a bit surprised in a good way,' he says. 'Ben and I aren't that close.'

I nod. I don't know why he feels the need to tell me that; maybe he's just over-sharing due to the awkwardness of the situation. I'm not sure whether to be pleased or sorry. If Ben has to have an arse for a brother, I am kind of pleased that he doesn't spend a lot of time with him, but also it's sad not to be close to a sibling.

'Anyway,' he continues. 'She's calling back with his address.'

'Thanks.'

I wonder suddenly if Max was at the wedding in Kent. I try to recall the Facebook photos I saw. I don't think I would have noticed him in any of them because I was so completely not expecting to see him; I was just scouring every image for sight of Ben and then moving on.

Maybe Max *was* there, and Ben didn't want me to see him then and that's why he seemed so keen to go for a walk and get me away from there. Which makes me feel hugely deflated. I'd kind of been thinking, hoping, that the reason he wanted to walk with me was that he'd been feeling unrequited passion for me for all those years and just wanted one more chance.

But, no, when I think about it, of course it was that he was trying to prevent me from bumping into Max.

So, really, I have Max-my-nemesis to thank for my six nights of glorious sex with Ben.

God.

My thoughts are interrupted by the ringing of Max's phone. His ring tone is Bruno Mars's 'The Lazy Song'.

I look at him and the phone, and give him a bit of an eye roll. He *was* very lazy when we worked together, I remember. He shrugs, before saying, 'Hi Mum.'

His mum talks and he writes, leaning the paper against the nearest stone window ledge, and listens a bit more, and then he hangs up, saying, 'Thank you again. See you tomorrow.

'Sunday family lunch,' he tells me, utterly pointlessly.

'Wonderful,' I say, allowing myself a further eye roll.

'Yes, right. So here's the address.' He hands me the paper and I take it gingerly, keen not to touch his arsehole fingers at all.

'Thanks, then.' I turn to make my way back round the outside of the grass circle.

'Olivia.' Max's voice rings out very loudly. 'I'm sorry,' he says, very fast. 'I was a complete wanker back then.'

I turn back to face him. 'Yes, you were.' I look him in the pathetic eye for a long moment without smiling, and then I turn round again and walk off.

I am *very* proud of myself. It would have been so much less good if I'd sworn viciously at him or thanked him for the apology, either of which I might have done at a different moment.

Despite my blisters, I walk really fast back down the drive, firstly because my teeth are chattering and I can't even feel my toes (except for searing heat around the blister areas) and I want to warm up, and secondly and more importantly because I *really* want to go to find Ben now.

Google Maps tells me that the place Ben's staying is twenty-seven minutes away. From my driving experience earlier, I know that Google Maps expects me to drive at actual sixty miles an hour whenever the speed limit is derestricted, with no recognition of the fact that a lot of those derestricted roads are tiny, twisty lanes where city dwellers in strange cars have to drive at max fifteen miles an hour or they feel like they're about to die.

It takes me one hour and twenty minutes to get there. During that time,

I swear a lot and at one point almost cry with frustration when for the fourth time in a row I have to reverse what feels like about five miles back up a country lane so that a rude idiot in a shiny four-by-four (definitely not a local because everyone knows that people who actually live in the countryside don't keep their cars super-buffed) who doesn't know the width of their own car can get past me *and not even say thank you*.

The house Ben's staying in is a cute terraced cottage in a little village near a lake. The lane it's on is narrow (of course) and there's nowhere for me to park the car, so I find a space in a nearby car park next to a row of about fourteen tea shops.

I'm starving, I realise, as I pass one of the teashops, inside which I can see a couple eating what looks like lemon drizzle cake at a red-and-white-checked-tablecloth-covered table. It's nearly four o'clock and I haven't eaten anything since my (slightly stale) train-bought breakfast croissant.

Two minutes later, I'm gobbling up my own slice of the deliciously moist and lemony lemon drizzle. It probably says something bad about me that even in the midst of emotional trauma I'm still hungry, but there you go. Food is my *job*. And I like it. And I think seeing Ben on an empty stomach would be more difficult.

I wash the cake down with water and then pop to the loo. The mirror tells me that I have quite a wild-eyed air, which isn't really a surprise. I can't help giving in to vanity and trying to sort my hair out a bit plus touching up the make-up I did carefully this morning.

It's a fifteen-minute walk to the cottage and the heavens open when I'm about halfway there. This is when my new coat and walking boots massively come into their own. The coat hood's huge – the lady in the shop assured me that the fabric is genuinely waterproof, as are my boots – so while my jeans are plastered to my sodden legs, the rest of me remains totally dry.

I go straight for the sticking-plaster approach yet again and ring the doorbell immediately.

There is no answer.

I ring again.

There is still no answer.

The cottage is not large and I can hear the bell ringing inside. There's no way Ben hasn't heard it if he's in.

He isn't answering. Either he's not in or he is in and he isn't going to come to the door.

I'm going to assume it's the former because there's nothing I can do about the latter. I have more than twenty-four hours left in the Lake District and I don't want to think this has been a completely wasted journey.

I'm going to wait for him.

There's nothing to sit on so I lean against the wall and get my phone out to try to distract myself. Then I worry that if I *am* distracted Ben will get back and see me and I won't see him and he'll just leave without me knowing. So I stand and just look up and down the road into the driving rain.

It's very, very boring.

I'm rewarded, though (eventually), because a long time later, I see a large man who moves like Ben turn into the lane from the opposite end from the car park. He has his shoulders hunched slightly against the rain and is striding quite briskly, like someone who'd really like to get inside. I know that feeling; I am not loving standing here.

After my thinking Max was Ben experience, I'm still not completely sure it's him, but as he approaches I become convinced that it is, and all of a sudden I just want to turn and run away as fast as my sodden legs will carry me.

Coming to the Lake District was a stupid, stupid thing to do. I can see that Ben is safe and sound, and now I should just leave him in peace because he's demonstrated extremely amply that he does not wish to speak to me.

I think I'm going to go. He's physically safe and if he has any kind of mental health issues, who am I to think I can help? And I don't think I *do* want closure now. I don't actually want to know what it was about me that caused him to run for the hills.

I'm going.

At exactly the same moment that I make the decision, Ben stops dead in the middle of the pavement about twenty feet away.

'Liv?' he mouths.

I nod, raise a hand briefly and then turn round and walk off.

32

BEN

'Liv?' I repeat, with some actual sound this time.

She lifts a hand again but keeps on walking away from me and doesn't turn to look back.

What?

Really, *what*?

There can be no way on earth that it's a coincidence she's here. She must somehow have hunted me down. So why in God's name would she then, having found me, walk off? It's truly one of the most ridiculous things I've seen recently.

She's definitely going.

I watch her squelch her way down the road and I debate. I would give anything to be able to run after her, gather her up in my arms and take her inside into the warmth and make slow, perfect love to her forever more. Equally, I can't bear the thought of talking to her, because that fantasy isn't how things would pan out, and the reality is that it would just hurt.

It's properly pissing it down, though, and she looks pretty wet and she's clearly come up here to find me. I mean, she must have.

There's a rumble of thunder, and I realise that I can't watch her walk off in weather like this, so I set off down the road after her.

When I catch her up, I fall in beside her and match my pace to hers, and say, 'Hi Liv.'

'Hello,' she says, looking straight ahead and continuing to walk.

'Bit of a surprise to see you here.'

'Yes.' She carries on walking. I carry on walking next to her.

'You're very wet,' I observe inanely. 'Jeans are not ideal rainstorm attire.'

'Yes, I am wet.' She keeps on walking. I keep on walking next to her.

'Would you like to come inside and get dry?'

She shakes her head inside her enormous hood. 'I'm good, thanks. I have a car parked not too far away.'

'Where are you staying?'

'In a B&B.'

'Oh.'

We get to the end of the lane and Liv turns left. I do too.

I look at her hunched inside her peculiar coat. I love her so much.

'Did you come here to speak to me?' I ask.

'Yep. But I now realise that it was a ridiculous thing to do, so I'd like to apologise for being a stalker and leave you in peace.'

We're still walking.

'Not a stalker, obviously,' I say. Although *how* did she find me? She actually *must* be quite a competent stalker. 'Please come inside and talk?'

'I just...' She stops walking. 'I've been acting on a burst of some kind of misery-filled adrenalin. But now I'm here, I can see that you're okay, and I realise that you did choose to walk away from me and that is entirely your prerogative, and so neither of us – especially you – has anything to gain from a conversation, so I should just go.'

'No, I'd like to talk.' Not really – not at all – but I can't let her just leave now. 'Please?'

'Are you sure?'

'Yep.' Nope.

'Well, that would be nice, then,' she says. 'Thank you.'

And we turn round and make our way back to the cottage, this time almost speed-walking, because this rain is just foul. We don't really say anything during our semi-sprint.

When we get inside the front door of the cottage, I help Liv out of her coat, which is heavy from water.

'Bastards.' She's staring at her soaking cardigan-covered arms.

I raise my eyebrows in question.

'The people who sold me my coat swore blind that there was no rain it couldn't withstand.'

'Is it a recent purchase?'

'Bought it this morning.'

'The walking boots too?' I look down at her feet. I don't really have her pegged as a serious hiker.

'Yep. I haven't been up a single hill on foot and I already have blisters.'

'Sale items?' I ask, clocking how very orange the coat is, even when extremely wet, and knowing Liv's predilection for a (seeming) bargain.

'Yep.'

'Did you go to that touristy shop near the station in Oxenholme?'

'Mmhm.'

'Yep. They're well-known for fleecing tourists.'

'Good to know.'

'Sorry?' I offer.

'Yeah.' She nods and doesn't really smile, and I suspect that she's in that state where you're really upset about something big so you aren't seeing the funny side of smaller things. What am I doing, actually, talking to her about tourist clothing when I should be finding her a towel and dry clothes?

'You need to get dry,' I say. 'There's a heated towel rail in the bathroom upstairs that I can put your coat on, and I can get you some dry clothes.' I'm not sure which dry clothes, to be fair, because there are only my clothes here, and she's only about half my size. 'And I'll put the kettle on and make some hot chocolate.'

'Thank you.'

'Okay.' This feels very awkward now that we don't have sale clothing chat to be side-tracked by. 'Why don't you wait in the kitchen?' I show her where it is at the end of the hall and wave her towards one of the wooden chairs at the table. 'Honestly, you aren't that wet, it's fine to sit down,' I tell her as she hesitates.

'Okay, thank you,' she says again.

When I get back with a T-shirt and hoodie, some tracksuit bottoms and socks, she's at the table with some kitchen paper spread out under the chair.

'I was dripping,' she explains.

Once she's left the room to go upstairs to get changed, I put the kettle on and put the kitchen towel in the bin. Then I sit down in one of the dry chairs and just wait.

She's back a few minutes later, looking traffic-stoppingly gorgeous in my far-too-big-for-her clothes, her hair huge from the damp, and dark, clearly non-waterproof, make-up rings under her eyes.

'I look ridiculous.' She points at herself.

'You look like a very beautiful monochrome clown,' I tell her without thinking, and then regret my words as her mouth forms into a little 'oh' and I catch something like a mix of hurt, hope, wistfulness, I don't know, in her eyes. I shake my head. 'Sorry. I shouldn't have said that.' I realise that I boiled the kettle but did not make our drinks. 'Let me get the hot chocolate.'

I clatter a bit as I make it, to try to pierce the incredibly loud silence that's filling the room.

And then, finally, we're sitting down at the table, opposite each other, each of us holding a mug of chocolate.

We both sip a few times, without speaking.

And then I take the plunge, because this is silly.

'You came to see me,' I state.

'Yes.'

I nod and take quite a long sip.

'The reason that I came' – Liv places her mug down on the table and then takes a second to adjust it so that the handle's exactly parallel to the edge of the table – 'is that I wanted to see you.'

I nod. I mean, yes, obviously.

She nudges the mug a micro-millimetre to the right, and then back to the left again.

Then she says, 'To start off with, my biggest motivation was to get closure on... us, really. I feel as though we've been in each other's lives in big or small ways for a very long time. I wanted to know what *happened*, why you went. And then, as I thought more about it, I got really worried about you, because it seemed so uncharacteristic for you to do' – she gestures vaguely around the room – 'all of this.'

I nod again. She definitely has more to say.

'And *then*, I discovered that you're Max's brother. And I feel like that can't be a coincidence.'

Yep, that's what she had to say. Well, of course it was.

And, out of courtesy, I am of course going to answer her.

'Well, it was a coincidence to begin with. When we met in the shed.'

Liv nods. 'But not a coincidence after that?'

'Well, no. I mean, yeah, no. Okay.' I grip my mug tightly. 'The reason that I lied in the shed that I had a girlfriend was—'

'You lied?'

'Well, yes. I obviously didn't have a girlfriend then, did I, or I'd have been a complete arse to have flirted so much with you.'

'*Oh*.'

'Oh, right. You did think I was a complete arse. And that's why you didn't want to speak to me when we bumped into each other at the Telegraph.'

'I didn't actually,' she says. 'I've never really thought you were an arse. I thought I must have imagined the flirting and read way more into it than there had been, because I *wanted* you to be interested. I didn't want to speak to you at the Telegraph because I knew you had a girlfriend and I really liked you so I didn't think it could end well for me if we became friends.'

Oh.

'No, I was very much flirting,' I confirm. 'If you can fall in love at first sight, that's what I did when we met. But then towards the end of our conversation I realised that the person who'd treated you so badly at work was my own brother. So of course I had to walk away from you, because I was sure if you'd found out you'd have been horrified, and you can't have a good relationship with someone you're lying to about your family. And I figured it couldn't hurt because it wasn't like you were going to have fallen as hard for me as I'd fallen for you.'

'Oh.' She frowns, obviously piecing things together. 'Is that why you were often weird around me when we bumped into each other?'

'Yep. Like when I didn't say I was neighbours with Frankie.'

'And at the cinema.'

'Yep. Every time.'

'What were you doing in your flat when we went back there after the train – while I was in the bathroom?'

'Hiding a photo of Max and his daughters.'

'In the hut... why didn't you tell me you were in the hospitality business when I was talking about my café plans?'

'That was nothing to do with Max. That was just that I thought maybe I could help you in some way but I didn't want to be too obvious because I really liked you.'

'Oh. But you've still been lying to me for a long time.'

'Yup.' I have and I'm not proud.

'Well.' She sits and looks at me and unlike almost every other time I've talked to her, I really can't read her face. 'So you're brothers.'

'Yes.' I take a breath and say, very fast, 'I'm not like him in the way we treat women. I have never thought it acceptable to treat people the way he treated you.'

'I know that,' she tells me, and my heart breaks a tiny bit more with love for her.

'Yeah, so,' I continue, 'we aren't really close. We don't talk a lot. I do spend time with his daughters, my nieces, but not really with him. I found it hard to stomach the way he behaved when we were younger, especially when he'd been drinking. To be fair to him, he seems a different person since he became a father, and I don't think he really drinks any more, but there's a distance between us now.'

'He didn't have your contact details,' Liv states. 'He had to ask your mum for them.'

'Yep.'

'Was he at the wedding in Kent?'

'Yep. Our cousin's wedding.'

She looks down at the table and doesn't look up.

'Oh, no,' I say. 'No, no. Everything that happened between us *happened*.'

Fuck, I can't get any good words out. I *need* Liv to know that I wanted to spend time with her, not just make a diversion from Max. 'What I'm trying to say is that, yes, I did ask you – a little weirdly, I know – to go for a walk with me because I was worried that you'd bump into Max and I thought that would be really awkward for you and selfishly I didn't want to have to explain that he's my brother. And yes, also the drink at the pub, so that you definitely wouldn't bump into him. But also, I wanted to spend some time with you. The walk and the pub were not all because of Max, and obviously the amazing night in the hotel together was nothing to do with him. That was because I have loved you for a very long time and I did not have the willpower to walk away that night. I *wanted* to spend time with you.'

She nods, still looking at the table, and then she lifts her head.

'So has all of this' – she does another one of her expansive arm gestures and knocks a tea towel off the wall to the side – 'been because of Max? Everything that has happened over the years between us? Or not happened.'

'Pretty much,' I lie. Because the answer is both yes, and no.

'And so now I know about Max.' She's half-smiling now.

I nod, not smiling, because I'm starting to sense where she's going here, and I'm feeling stupid because I've only just realised what is inevitably going to happen, and now we're in it.

'And I know you aren't like him,' she says. I nod and then also shake my head, because I know exactly what she's going to say and I don't want her to say it. But she will, and I don't know how to avoid it happening. She smiles this gorgeous, beautiful, heart-breaking, tremulous little smile. And says, 'I love you.'

'I love you too.' I can't not say it. Firstly, it's true, and secondly, I can't bear her to be any more hurt than she will be, and I think it would be worse if I didn't confirm to her that yes I do love her. 'More than words can say.'

Her beautiful, generous mouth is spreading into a proper, wide smile now.

If I were someone who cried, I'd be bawling right now. As it is, my eyes are slightly damp, because I know what's coming, and it's all so much worse than Liv realises.

It's going to be like it was with my ex, Gemma, except infinitely worse, because I *thought* I loved Gemma, but I didn't. This, with Liv, *this* is what love is. And she's about to walk away from me because I can't give her what she wants, needs.

I can't remember the last time I cried. I didn't even cry when I left Liv last week, and that was pretty fucking difficult. But my eyes are feeling very hot right now.

Her smile is faltering, and I'm guessing that will be because she's clocked the despair on my face.

'We can't be together,' I state.

She shakes her head. 'But everyone has dodgy relatives. I mean, my mum and Frankie are amazing, and so was my dad, but my mum's cousin Victor's been in actual prison in Canada for tax evasion. You and Max are not the same person. And it's been eight years and yes, I think he's an arse, but also yes, I've totally moved on. It's just something that happened in the past. I would not make things awkward on Christmas Day.'

I'm shaking my head too. 'I know you wouldn't. It isn't about Max on Christmas Day. It's something else.'

'Oh.' Her smile's gone. She presses her lips together and clasps her hands in front of her on the table.

'Basically.' I check out of the window. I'd rather walk while we have this conversation, so that I don't have to look directly at her, but, while the rain has died down somewhat, it's still fairly relentless, so I'm just going to have to tell her right here in the kitchen. And here I go. 'When Max and I were at university, we were asked to donate sperm for a research study. They had twins, identical and non-identical, plus non-twin brothers, to see what differences genetics, in-utero conditions and upbringing make.'

I can see from her wide-open eyes and the *oh* that her mouth's forming that this is not what she was expecting me to be talking about. I can also see from the way her brow's starting to furrow that her mind's going in all sorts of directions.

'Anyway,' I continue, 'our results were very different.' I force myself not to look down and to keep on looking at Liv, because whatever it might feel like, and however Gemma reacted when I told her, I know I have nothing whatsoever to be ashamed of. 'Max basically has golden balls. Of which he is of course very proud. And I have dud balls. I can't have children.'

'Not dud,' Liv says. 'Even using the word facetiously, that is not a nice way to talk about it.'

'Dud,' I insist, 'if you want kids. Which I know you do.' That's why I had to leave. She's made it so clear, so many times, that she wants children, and she wants her own children. And she's nearly thirty-five. Gemma couldn't cope with the thought of not having her own biological children when she was only twenty-three. 'What would your thoughts be on that?'

'I...' She visibly swallows and pauses for... for far too long, and then opens her mouth again to speak.

But I'm ahead of her, shaking my head and standing up. That hesitation told me everything I needed to know.

'And that is why we can't be together,' I tell her.

'No,' she says, not budging from her chair.

'Yes.' I'm firm. 'We can't. In as much as it ever started, it's over. End of.' We are *way* better off finishing things now before we've even really started than getting further down the line and then having some awful break-up.

And we would split up, because it's very clear from Liv's reaction that I've given her pause for thought. She would have to be all-in right now for there to be a hope of us surviving this as a couple long-term.

I know this from Gemma. She was my university girlfriend and we were going to be together forever. I told her about it immediately after I found out, I thought she was cool about it, we stayed together for a while, and then she split up with me a couple of years after uni, telling me that we had no future because she wanted kids and she did not want to adopt. She told me she loved me and how she might never meet anyone again who she loved as much, but she loved the idea of children at least as much, and she thought it would drive a huge wedge between us. We both cried for a long time. And we used to meet up for a 'catch-up' quite often for years, and then have unprotected sex, and then both (we admitted to each other the last time we saw each other) hope for a miraculous conception. Until eventually, just before the first time I met Liv, actually, I had the self-preservation to tell her that we had to just *stop*, for both our sakes.

And now she's divorced from the man she married on the rebound from me, but she has three children who she adores. And a couple of years ago, not long after her divorce, she asked me if I'd like to get back together. And

I think if I hadn't recently bumped into Liv and known that I no longer loved Gemma, I might have done.

'There have been big advances in fertility treatment since then,' Liv says.

Exactly. She would hope and then her hopes would be dashed and eventually we'd split up. Hoping was not great for Gemma and me.

'Not big enough.' I'm firm, because it's true.

'And there are other ways.'

Yes, there are, but Liv's mind went straight to fertility treatment. In Gemma's words, 'women want the option of being pregnant themselves'.

'No,' I say. There is no point prolonging this conversation. 'It is over.' I enunciate very clearly for emphasis.

Liv looks into my eyes for a moment and then she suddenly slams her hands down on the table. 'Fuck you,' she says. 'Really, fuck you. You have fucked up my life for eight years with your stupid crap. Fuck *you*. I would totally adopt or use a sperm donor. You're a total arse.' She shoves her chair backwards and stands up, knocking a couple of saucepans off their wall hooks. Over the clatter, she says, 'I love you, by the way. I love you so much. But also: fuck you.' And then she marches out.

And about thirty seconds later I see her through the kitchen window marching down the little path to the pavement, wearing her tourist-sucker walking boots and my clothes.

Gone.

It's for the best, I try to tell myself through my immediate pain.

33

LIV

As I stomp up the road, I'm genuinely surprised that the rain has the courage to carry on falling on me and that it doesn't immediately evaporate from the heat of my rage. I'm so filled with burning anger that I feel like if I focused it all into my hand and just held it up, the rain might stop.

I try it, but it doesn't.

Fuck *me*, I'm angry.

Ben is such a *tosser*.

He's lied to me the whole time. He could have told me all of this *right at the beginning*.

It's actually extremely offensive that he didn't think I could immediately separate him and Max in my mind.

And it's even more offensive that he thinks I wouldn't stay with him due to infertility issues.

Yes, I hesitated when he told me, but *not* because I was going to say anything negative, but because I wanted to find the right words to tell him that I love him more than anything else.

Maybe he doesn't love me like I love him.

He can't do because if he did he'd understand that I would never leave him.

I mean, *so many* people have infertility issues. Some people split up because of them, yes, but a lot of people grow stronger together through them. And there are other options. For example. If you really want kids.

What. A. Fucker.

Really.

Also: now I'm thinking about how *fucking angry* I am, why was I so bloody nice to Max earlier? I mean, okay, I wasn't necessarily really nice, but also I think I should have said a little more.

Okay. I'm going back. I'm going to go and see Max and tell him straight that he should *never* treat anyone like that again.

Anger lends me driving wings and I shave ten minutes off the drive back to Ben and Max's parents' house, accomplishing it in one hour ten. It's a mark of the weekend I'm having that I am literally taking note of the length of my journeys.

During the seventy minutes, I cry a lot and swear a lot (shocking a couple of unwitting passers-by in ill-advised shorts and sandals) and also shout a bit (shocking some sheep when I'm stuck in a lane).

When I arrive at the drive entrance, there's no more polite parking and diffidently tiptoeing up the drive. If I want to trespass I'll fucking trespass.

I turn the car into the drive and hurtle up it towards the house, coming to a screeching, gravel-flying halt right outside the front door.

I'm straight out of the car and banging on the door knocker almost before the car wheels have stopped spinning.

A pleasant-looking blonde woman of about my age (not the fiancée who punched me all those years ago, I'm pleased to say) and an adorable little girl (who I recognise from Ben's photos) wearing an apron and a lot of chocolate on her face come to the door.

'Hi?' the woman says.

'I wondered if I could speak to Max.'

'Sure. Let me go and get him. Could I ask what it's about?'

Oh. I should have thought of that. I do want to speak to Max more fully about what happened in the past, but I don't want to ruin this woman's day, let alone her marriage. Ben says Max treats people a lot better now, and I'm not here to mess up anyone's life. I just really, I suppose, want more closure and I also want to make sure he doesn't treat anyone like that again.

'I'm a friend of Ben's,' I say, 'but I used to work with Max. I thought it would be nice to catch up quickly. Liv Murphy.'

'Great,' she says. 'I'll let him know.' She shows me into the sitting room that I saw through the window earlier, to wait.

'Do you like chocolate?' asks the girl – Max's adorable daughter and Ben's adorable niece. I am deeply ashamed to say that for a nanosecond I do have an it's-not-fair thought about the golden balls thing, but in my defence I do then push it away very hard and tell myself that I should never think that again.

I smile at her. 'Yes, I do, and I'm very lucky because my job is working with food so sometimes people *pay* me to eat chocolate.'

'Wow,' the little girl breathes, as her father practically sprints into the room.

'Liv,' he says. 'Alice, go and help Mummy finish making that cake *now*.'

He closes the door behind his daughter and says, 'You came back. You told my wife we were old colleagues.'

Oh, for fuck's sake. Another Jones brother misjudging me. Max is looking at me as if I'm pure evil, as if I'm about to chuck a grenade into his marriage and family life.

'I'd like to talk a little more,' I say. 'Shall we go into the garden so we aren't disturbed?' And so that no-one will overhear us, I hope he understands me to mean. I don't even want to say it because I don't want his wife to misinterpret anything.

I don't care that it's still raining heavily, and clearly Max doesn't either, because he has wellies and an old Barbour on before I can say *guilty conscience*, and we head outside together.

'Firstly,' I say, *so* in control of this, because I still have a lot of rage careening around my veins, and also I spent part of the journey back here planning what I want to say, while Max is just a gibbering wreck of please-let-this-woman-not-be-about-to-tell-my-wife-what-a-tosser-I-was, 'I am not here to tell your wife anything.'

Max relaxes his shoulders visibly. 'Okay,' he says.

'Right. So.' I launch straight into my speech. 'When the whole MeToo thing happened, I remember very well being at a barbecue talking in a group with my friend's neighbour. He was maybe fiftyish and worked in the

City. He was *furious* about MeToo. He basically said there was no harm in pressing a few snogs on unsuspecting secretaries after a boozy lunch. Who in those days were obviously all women.' I think briefly of Amos, the lovely male PA I'm hoping to hire to help me out with my business. 'It made me think of you, of course.'

'Right,' Max says.

'The thing is, there's *huge* harm in those things. Expecting women to put up with that shit as part of their daily lives is subjecting them to constant harassment. *Don't make a fuss about a little un-wanted snog or the best that will happen to you is you'll be shipped off to Paris.* I mean, fuck off. *You* should have been the one who left. For gross misconduct. For serious sexual harassment. Women are not objects. I was in no way at fault. And you treated me appallingly.'

'I appreciate that now.'

'I mean, you should have appreciated it at the time.' I want to finish what I have to say. 'And just to be clear: you were a total arse to force yourself on me, you were a total arse to betray your fiancée, and you were a total arse to compound it all by colluding in me having to leave the London office.'

'Yes.' He's staring at the ground. 'I'm sorry. I really am.'

'*Finally*' – this is my master stroke and I do not feel bad about saying it – 'I'd like to know how you'd feel about men treating Alice, when she's older, the way you used to treat women.'

'God.' He glances up at me before resuming his study of the ground. 'Yes, I would be homicidal.'

'Right, then,' I say. That's it. I don't have anything else to say. Not much, anyway. 'I'm glad you recognise that. You're still a tosser, though.'

'Noted.'

We're some way from the car and we walk back to it in silence.

When we get to it, Max says, 'I am deeply sorry, Liv. I was a twat.'

'Yes, you were. I just hope you aren't any more.'

'Was Paris alright for you, though?' The look on his face tells me that he's been wanting to get that question out for a while.

'Average,' I tell him. Paris itself was actually a pretty good life experience in hindsight, but that is really not the point.

'I'm so sorry,' he repeats.

I resist my ridiculously British urge to thank him for the apology that should never have had to happen, and instead nod and open the car door.

'Good luck with Ben,' he says as I climb inside, apparently imagining that I'm going to see his brother again.

I don't bother to reply.

As I drive away from Ben and Max's parents' property, I'm not really sure what I'm going to do with myself now. There's no reason for me to be in the Lake District but I have another twenty-four hours here.

I register the beauty of the scenery as I follow the Google Maps directions towards the B&B I've booked into, but I don't appreciate it, because I'm too pissed off to appreciate anything.

I don't like feeling like this, I think, as I reverse (pretty expertly actually) into a field's gateway to allow three vintage cars to go past me; I need to rationalise what's happened. Bitterness is an awful emotion.

Ben is a dickhead and it's way better that things ended now than in the future, which they would, given his levels of dickheadery.

I should definitely be grateful that he left me now rather than several months or years down the line.

He's such a dickhead.

He isn't a dickhead, though, I think as another vintage car hoves into view round a bend in the road.

I sigh, stop and put the car into reverse again.

I love him.

He was an idiot not to tell me the truth from the off, but how was he to know that we'd ever see each other again after the shed? I was leaving for Paris. If we'd never met again, his not telling me that he was Max's brother wouldn't have been an issue. And then at what point was he supposed to bring it up? We'd never actually spoken again at any length until the wedding night, so he couldn't and wouldn't have brought it up before then. And obviously he wanted to save me from embarrassment and awkwardness at the wedding, so he wasn't going to mention it then, he just steered me away from any chance of bumping into Max, and that was very sweet of him. And then once we'd started all the sex, it probably wasn't at the forefront of his mind any more.

And his infertility. Well, clearly *no* one would ever say anything like 'Hi, so it seems there's a touch of mutual attraction going on between us. I just want you to know that I can't father kids.' In fact, if he *had* said that in the shed, I'd have been beside myself with terror, because it would have sounded weird and I was stuck in there with him.

And once we were having all the sex, he *should* have told me then, once we'd told each other we loved each other. And we could have discussed and I would have told him that I love him more than I love the idea of us being joint biological parents to any future children. But obviously he has dickhead levels of what he thinks is chivalry, and he didn't think there was a discussion to be had; he just thought and thinks he knows what's best for me.

He is such an idiot. He's a patronising, stupid, moronic dickhead.

I say, 'Fucker,' out loud and then wave at the *really* incompetent elderly vintage car driver and his headscarf-garbed companion as they finally make their way past me, narrowly avoiding scraping the sides of our cars even though there must be a good three feet spare on their left between them and the wall, and start my car up again.

As I drive forward again, I think he really is a fucker, but if I'm honest, I can see how it all happened and, at every step along the way, in his head he must have been doing the right thing. I mean, I can actually see his point of view almost entirely. Except for blowing his infertility up into such a big issue. *That* is just stupid. It would be a deal-breaker for some people, I think, but not for me. And instead of walking out – and I mean, how stupidly over-dramatic actually – he should have told me then and discussed it rationally. Walking away with no discussion was not the right thing to do.

Maybe it's understandable, though. He mentioned an ex, Gemma. I wonder if they discussed this and she reacted badly and that hurt him. Maybe he has a moderately understandable reason for being this dramatic about it all. Maybe he wasn't entirely being stupidly chivalrous but was also trying to stop himself being hurt again.

I make a sudden decision. I have twenty-four more hours here. Maybe it was fate that I booked that train. To give us more time to sort this out.

I'm going back. I'm going to give it one more shot.

I might also apologise for all the fuck-yous. They were quite rude.

And oh for fuck's sake. There's obviously been some kind of vintage car rally. There are vintage cars bloody everywhere and it looks like I'm going to be stuck for hours reversing over and over again so that yet another shiny old car can get past me.

I actually love a vintage car. They're beautiful. Especially the ones that have clearly been lovingly restored, because there's all that human love as part and parcel of them. But now, surrounded and hemmed in and prevented from moving by them, I am not admiring them.

I just want to *go*, get back to Ben *right now*, and hope that he'll talk more.

34

BEN

Nothing of Liv's reaction to my revelation was a surprise to me, I think, as I aim a vicious kick at some mud on the path I'm trudging.

'Oy, mate.' Two oncoming hikers who I hadn't even noticed are now splattered in dark brown sludge.

'God. I am *so* sorry. World of my own and taking it out on the ground. And you, apparently.' I reach into my pocket for my wallet. 'Can I pay for dry cleaning or something? Or buy you a drink?'

'I recognise you,' the muddier of the couple says. 'You're renting Skylark Cottage, aren't you?'

'Yep.'

'Long let?'

'Not sure yet. I took it for three months initially.' I came up here to avoid seeing Liv any more and to lick my wounds. Work-wise it's fine – with what I'm doing at the moment I could live anywhere – and friend-wise I'm not feeling too sociable right now. I'll send all my friends my new number soon and keep in touch that way for a while.

'We live a couple of doors down. Badger Cottage. Always good to meet neighbours. We'll take you up on that offer of a drink. Tonight?'

'Er, yes, I think so.'

I do *not* want to go to the pub with complete strangers this evening. I want to... well, I want to kick mud, basically. I am so far from being the life and soul of a pub evening it's untrue.

'Ring O Bells at about eight?'

'Great.' I try for a smile but I think my face muscles have forgotten how to form one.

'See you there. Cheerio.' The muddy man sticks his thumb up at me, his female companion smiles and off they go. Cheerily.

I wait until they've gone, thinking I'm going to kick more mud, and then I don't bother, because I don't think toddler tantrums are going to help me here.

I thought it was painful when Gemma split up with me over my infertility, and I've carried that pain for a long time. As it turns out, Gemma was clearly not the love of my life, because I know once and for all that Liv is; and the pain of that break-up was nothing compared to this. It isn't even pain, it's just emptiness, like what actually is there for me in life without her?

Which is stupid. I'll be okay. I'll recover from this.

Right now, though, I feel like total, total shit, utterly hopeless.

I do not want to go for a drink with anyone this evening.

I nearly twist my ankle on a tree root and am surprised that I'm not too numb to feel the pain that shoots up my leg.

By the time I get back down into the village, the heavens have opened once more. I am so very much not in the mood to go to the pub. I'll make an excuse, I decide. Buy them an expensive bottle of wine instead.

But as I go past Badger Cottage, the muddy woman waves at me from the window. Cheerily.

I wave back, not so cheerily.

'See you later,' she mouths.

'Great,' I mouth. I think I'm going to have to go. I don't need to feel like an un-neighbourly arse on top of everything else.

35

LIV

It takes me forever to get through the immense number of vintage cars. I've never driven one or really been up close to one before, but I now feel like when it comes to classic cars I'm bordering on expert.

Most of them are lovely and shiny with amazing features: running boards, bench seats, starting handles, no roofs and cool mirrors. Aesthetically, pretty much every single one of them is to die for.

Practically, however, not so much. Vintage cars are either hard to manoeuvre or every single vintage car driver is so incompetent they should never have passed their test. I've had the most two-steps-forward-three-steps-reversed journey of my entire life.

Finally, I'm past them all (after I wiggle round the last one, I see a big sign at the entrance to a field advertising a classic car rally today and think *oh*) and am actually driving forwards – for about a mile and a half, that is, until I come across a herd of cows crossing the road from one field to another, very, very slowly, the crossing administered by two men and a boy who look like they could happily spend not just the rest of the evening but the rest of the *month* in the middle of this road. And straight after that I get stuck behind a very large farming vehicle which is yellow and has a big, wide, spiky thing behind it.

By the time they've gone, I'm totally resigned to spending possibly the rest of my life on this journey. Time is dribbling away and I can do absolutely nothing about it.

And then suddenly I'm on a road that's actually wide enough for two average width cars and I'm sailing along.

I get back to Ben's village at about eight o'clock.

It takes me a long time to find a parking space because the car park's closed and there are very few spaces on the road. Eventually I fit the car (slightly diagonally) into a tiny space opposite the village church, and climb across the car (scraping my shin really hard on a broken little drawer handle on my way across) and let myself out of the passenger door.

I make it down to Ben's cottage a few minutes later.

The cottage is entirely dark; it's dusk and there are no lights in any of the windows. There's no sound either, no TV or radio.

Right. Clearly, he is not in.

I am such an idiot. I should really have thought of this.

It's nearly half eight. I have a very sore shin and I'm really hungry and Google Maps tells me that the B&B's about forty-five minutes away, which in the real windy-vintage-car-and-cow-filled-lanes world means anything up to about three hours away.

Okay, I'm just going to head to the B&B and go to bed.

I don't know what I'm going to do tomorrow. Maybe I should take this as a sign that Ben and I are not, and never have been, meant to be. Maybe the vintage cars and the cows (and the bit where I got lost and ended up halfway up a mountain before I could find a turning point) *were* meant to be, to stop me seeing Ben.

I trudge back up the road. As I go round the corner of the chocolate box pub, the Ring O Bells, my stomach almost *heaves* with hunger, stimulated by lovely garlicky and curry smells coming out of a back door that must lead on to its kitchen.

This is very much not London and there's every chance I'll struggle to find any kind of food shop open at this hour.

I go inside the pub to buy myself a couple of packets of crisps to take away. I can't face sitting eating by myself right now, even if they have a table.

The pub's quite busy with several groups of people and a few couples. Everyone, without fail, looks happy to my miserable eye.

I heave a big sigh, and the barman says, 'Cheer up, love, it might never happen.'

I resist the urge to yell *Piss off* and instead give him a big fake smile and say, 'Ha.'

'What can I do you for?' he asks.

'Crisps please. A packet of salt and vinegar and a packet of crispy bacon please.'

'Drink?'

'I'm good, thanks.' I still have some water in the car. 'I'm just going to take these away if that's okay.'

'Using us like a convenience store?' He smiles at me.

'Yep,' I tell him and smile back, pleased and slightly surprised that, after what has felt like a huge trauma with Ben, I can still interact with other human beings without bursting into tears.

As I take the crisps, I think I hear Ben's voice from the group over by the window. I glance over but can't see him. Honestly, I've immediately regressed to the way I used to be years ago when I used to think I glimpsed him in all sorts of places. Really, really annoying.

I shoot another smile at the barman before leaving with my crisps.

I walk round the corner of the pub and then, of *course*, because apparently now I'm right back in my spot-fake-Bens-all-the-bloody-time thing, I think I spy him sitting in the window, holding a pint of beer and chatting in a group.

I am *so* pissed off. I do not want to keep on imagining that he's there, like his ghost is following me everywhere I go. I mean, he obviously might move back to London, and I obviously might therefore bump into him again, and I obviously therefore am going to *imagine* that I see him all the bloody time. And I do not want that to happen.

I look again, because I can't help it, and oh. No. This is not my imagination. It *is* Ben.

Okay. I'm even more pissed off now. He's chatting and laughing and he looks like he's having bloody fun. Who does that straight after a conversation like we had? He must have a heart of stone.

I'm *furious*.

No. I shouldn't be pissed off. I'm being unreasonable.

Of course Ben can come to the pub if he wants to. He's looking cheerful – there's nothing wrong with that, is there? It's actually entirely his prerogative to mess with my head – my heart – for over eight years and sleep with me for nearly a week and then be over me immediately. If he was even *under* me in the first place.

I mean, a week is not that long. It's shorter than a lot of holiday romances.

Arguably, it's all my fault for reading too much into things.

Although he did say that he loved me.

But maybe not everyone means the same thing when they say they love people.

He *did* say he loved me, though.

And I love him so much.

And I have really nothing to lose at this point. I actually cannot feel any sadder or any more humiliated or anything else.

I'm going back in.

'Hi, Ben,' I say a minute or two later.

He does one of the biggest comedy jumps I've ever seen and spills his beer all over the man next to him.

'First mud, now beer,' the man says. 'Do you hate my trousers or something?' Then he laughs uproariously at his own joke and so does the woman sitting on his other side.

Ben isn't listening, though; he's just staring at me.

'Liv?' he says.

'Here, space for a little one.' The man sitting in the beer spillage moves his chair and pulls another one over so that I can squish in between him and Ben.

'Er, thank you.' I sit down, awkwardly, my thigh pressed right up against Ben's. I'm not really sure right now whether I'd rather be pressed against his lovely, hard, muscly and probably never-again-available-to-me thigh, or the other man's already-sticky beery (and not as lovely and hard and muscly looking) one.

'Let's get you a drink.' One of the other men in the group waves the barman over.

The barman makes his way towards us but I shake my head and say, 'No, honestly, I'm fine, actually. I was just popping in.'

Ben's been statue-like but he unfreezes and says, 'Actually, yes, I think Liv and I are going to have to get going. It's been a great evening, thanks, everyone.'

'Pub quiz Tuesday evening, remember,' the man covered in beer says.

'Definitely.' Ben stands up.

'Liv, you're very welcome, too,' the woman next to him says.

'Thank you so much.' I stand up too.

'Liv, what's your area of expertise?' someone else asks. 'In a quiz?'

'Um, food?' I say.

'What about Geography and History?'

'Average.'

I'm not bad at world capitals, actually, but I'm really not up for discussing that right now.

'Yes, so great, then. Goodnight.' Ben gestures with his hand for me to walk towards the door ahead of him.

We pass a family – parents and a little boy and an even littler girl – just finishing a pub dinner. I didn't notice them before because when I came in for the crisps I was just kind of focused on getting to the bar, and when I came in to speak to Ben, I was only focused on him.

The boy and girl are *so* cute. Even in the midst of the Ben turmoil going through my mind, I can't help smiling at them. I feel Ben's eyes on me and look up at him. And the expression in his eyes makes me gasp. It's a look of real despair.

I'm torn: I hate to see him look like that because I don't want him to be sad; but also strangely it gives me hope that there's still something big between us to fight for.

'Lucky you're leaving,' hollers the barman as we reach the door, 'otherwise I'd have had to charge you extra for eating those crisps inside.'

'Ha, ha.' I fake a laugh. Ben says nothing.

The pub was warm and it takes me a moment to adjust to the straight-to-the-bone chill outside.

'I presume you came back for your clothes?' Ben asks.

'Oh.' I look down at my trackie-bottom-clad legs. Oh yes. My clothes. 'No. I didn't.'

I came back for you.

'So...?'

'Um.' Yep, I should really have prepared something to say. I certainly had time while I was tucked in country lane passing places watching classic cars go past.

Okay. I'm going to get my things. I might as well because there's no point losing perfectly good clothes, but mainly, going back to Ben's cottage will buy me time with him.

'Yes, please,' I say.

'Yes, please?' he queries.

'Yes, please, I would like to get my clothes.'

'Oh, of course.' He looks around and then says, 'Why don't you wait in the pub while I collect them for you.'

He says it a bit like a command. I don't want to stay in the pub, though. I want to go back to the cottage with him. I want to talk to him one more time.

'No, no.' I start walking. 'I don't want to inconvenience you. I'll just pop to the cottage with you so that you don't have to come back out again.'

'Where are you going now?' Ben calls after me.

I turn round. 'To the cottage.'

'It's this way.' He indicates with his head in the exact opposite direction from the way I've set off. He's smirking a little, which I love and which defuses things a little. There are not many situations that Ben can't find the humour in, even when he isn't that happy. 'You taking the scenic route?'

'Now you mention it, I'll go directly there.'

We set off down the road together and within about ten steps I'm panicking. Ben's quite a fast walker and the village is small, so it won't take long to get to the cottage and realistically he isn't going to invite me in for another chat, he's just going to gather the clothes up fast and pretty much chuck them at me and then that will be that.

'I didn't really come back for my clothes,' I blurt out. 'I came back because I wanted to tell you that I love you and the reason that I hesitated when you told me about the infertility is not that I was in any way hesitating but because you looked upset and I was searching for the right words.'

'You aren't normally at a loss for words.' He is so stubborn. Like a mule.

'I'm not normally having huge conversations,' I counter. I'm feeling mule-like too. I do not want to give up until he understands that I love him and that for me infertility does not affect that.

He switches tack. 'The look in your eyes when you saw those children in the pub. Adoring.'

I say the first thing that comes into my head to try to convince him. 'I think I look adoring when I see cute kittens. I don't want to give birth to one though.'

'Hmm,' he says.

'I hear that pregnancy is not a lot of fun,' I continue. 'There are other ways of having children.'

Oh, shit, we're in the lane of his cottage. I need to fire all my ammo right now. Ben's clearing his throat but I'm just going to plough on with every point that comes to me.

'Also,' I say, 'there are a lot of people in the world, and we're all putting a lot of pressure on resources and contributing towards climate change. And simultaneously there are a lot of children who need loving homes. *Also*, Sulwe's adopted and she's extremely close to her adoptive family. And I don't want to be rude or intrusive but it does seem to me as though you aren't *that* close to Max, so I don't think the blood-thicker-than-water thing holds.'

'You sound like you're trying to convince yourself,' he says as he opens his front door.

'Oh, for fuck's *sake*,' I say, going in ahead of him whether he likes it or not. 'I am not trying to convince myself. I am already convinced. I *began* convinced. I am trying to convince *you*.'

'Of what?'

'Of the fact that I love you and I would like to be with you irrespective of your fertility. And from my side I don't even know if and when I would like children, I mean, I would like at least one, but there are other ways to make that happen.' I suddenly think of another good point. 'When Frankie and Nella were planning marriage, and their kids, with sperm donors, it didn't even enter anyone's head to suggest that they shouldn't get married because they can't have a child that they are both the biological parent of.' I think about the bigoted arse Frankie told me they got accosted by a couple of weeks ago on the Tube when they were on their way home holding hands after an anniversary dinner. 'Okay, *some* people have a problem with gay or queer people having children, but those people are total dickheads. Most people do not.'

'You said that Frankie and Nella only wanted to have two children but after Frankie had twins they had a third because Nella wanted to be the biological mother of a baby.'

'And that is Nella but I am not Nella. Not everyone feels like that. And not every woman *can* be the biological mother of their children either. I've never been pregnant. For all I know, I am not able to be pregnant. And if I *can* get pregnant, there are sperm donation options. *Or*, as I mentioned, adoption. Or no children. I *would* like kids, yes, but not in a be-all-and-end-all way.'

Ben's staring at me, frowning a bit.

'I love you.' I feel like I'm on a roll now. 'I would like to be with you and I don't know whether I think we could end up together forever or whether it's just for now but I do know that I love you more than I could ever have imagined I would love a man. I want you to be happy. I want to be with you. I want to convince you that apple and cumin *is* a good combination.' We've bickered about flavour combos a few times. 'I just want to talk to you. I. Just. Love. You.'

I've never been so open with a man about my feelings in my entire life. And actually, while I have known Ben for a long time in a small way, I've only known him in a big way for a couple of weeks, and that is a very, very short time. I might just have gone mad. I feel like I've practically just proposed marriage to a complete stranger.

But also I feel like I've just told someone I've known for a long time now that I love him and I'd like to start a relationship, and surely that isn't that stupid?

Ben swallows visibly, his Adam's apple moving quite hard.

He looks down. And stares.

'You've hurt yourself,' he says.

I look down too. Wow, there's a lot of blood seeping through the tracksuit bottoms from that scrape on my right leg. And actually now I think about it it's stinging a lot. But I really don't care. I flap away his concern with my hand.

'I love you,' I repeat.

Fuuuuuuck. What if he doesn't feel the same way about me?

Actually, I don't care. It will not make me feel any worse if he doesn't. It's binary: if he loves me and wants to be with me and can get over the infertility thing, I'm happy; if he doesn't, I'm going to be devastated. That's it.

And, suddenly, I'm over this whole thing. Over it. Totally over it. It's been going on for over eight years now. Too long.

'Ben, I've loved you since the day I first met you in the shed. I feel like this is it now. The end or the beginning. And clearly it's down to you.'

36

BEN

'I love you too much to be able to let you make a sacrifice,' I tell Liv, drinking in her beautiful face with my eyes for what could well be the last time.

And then I jump as she yells, 'Not a sacrifice, you fuckwit. I just bloody love you but apparently we can't go on a single date because you're an idiot.'

The yell pierces something inside me and suddenly, I don't know how or why or what or anything at all, but I do know that I believe her.

'I believe you,' I state.

'What do you believe?' she asks, still shouting.

'That you love me and would like to be with me.'

'Right.' She yells the word, which makes me laugh. 'Why are you *laughing*?'

'All the shouting.'

'Right,' she says at a more average volume.

And then we stand where we are, about six feet apart, and just stare at each other.

And then I say, 'So, to clarify...'

What? Clarify? We're having what feels like an enormous conversation about our feelings, and I'm *clarifying* things, like I'm possibly the most anal man ever born.

I start again. And, actually, it's really simple. Seconds have passed since I began to believe that Liv's love for me might indeed be bigger than the infertility thing, and I still believe it.

So I open my mouth and say, 'Liv, I love you. Could we date? And would you like to stay here tonight?'

Liv nods and shakes her head at the same time, and unfolds the arms I now realise she's had folded across her chest as if she was trying to protect herself.

I open my own arms, and she walks straight into them.

'I love you so much and I always have,' I tell her before, very slowly, because now I feel like I finally have time with Liv, I bend my head and begin what is the best kiss of my entire life.

EPILOGUE

LIV

Exactly four years later

'We're here,' Ben tells me, as I feel the car draw to a halt.

'Can I take the blindfold off?'

'Nope.' His voice has just become a bit more distant and I can feel a light breeze. He must have got out of the car. 'Hang on. I'm just going to get the kids into the buggy.'

I settle back into my seat. I'll be waiting for some time, because the double buggy's a tricky one, and Ben is not gifted with it. It isn't looking like he's going to get better with it, either, because it's been five months now since the children came home with us, and we've both put the buggy up and down a lot in that time (me a lot more quickly than Ben, every time, and with no injured fingers in my case).

I close my eyes under the blindfold and allow myself to drift off into sleep. If I'm honest, I'm so sleep-deprived at the moment that whatever present Ben has for me cannot possibly be as good as an unexpected little snooze under an eye mask.

The kids – biological sister and brother Ella and Jack – were twenty-one and four months old when we adopted them, and had both been in foster care from birth. They're both great at sleeping *if* one of us is in the room with them, but not so great when we aren't – maybe because their early months were unsettled.

The five months since they've been with us have been difficult in some ways – the sleep and the constant nappies (Jack had diarrhoea for ages amongst other symptoms until the doctors worked out that he had a dairy allergy) and the various worries that you suddenly have when you become a parent, plus I've taken maternity leave and I do actually miss work a lot and I'm not sure I'll manage to go back for a while because I really want the children to be fully settled with us and sleeping well before I do – but also indescribably wonderful and one hundred per cent worth it. I mean, more than a hundred per cent. Infinitely worth it.

'Mummmyyyyyy,' Ella hollers, penetrating my doze, and I smile. It is *the* most gorgeous thing to hear her call us Mummy and Daddy. Jack just says Mamamama and Dadadada still.

'Two seconds, Ella,' Ben pants, and I smile some more, imagining him wrestling with all the straps.

Eventually, he says, 'Okay, ready. I'm standing next to the car with the kids in the buggy and I am not at all hot and bothered and I didn't come at all close to losing any of my fingers or thumbs.'

'Well done.'

'Do you think you can get out of the car by yourself? I don't want to let go of the buggy.'

He *still* doesn't trust the brake.

'Yep, course I can.'

Ouch, ouch, ouch. It's more difficult than you'd think getting out of a car blindfolded.

Eventually I'm out, though, and we're making our way across the grass, Ben pushing the buggy with one hand and guiding me with the other, which is seriously impressive, because a double buggy containing a baby and a toddler is not light.

I smell something.

'What's that?' I ask. 'It smells like we're standing in the middle of a lot of traffic.'

'Very good sense of smell.' Ben approves. 'That'll be part of the reason you're so good with flavours.'

We keep on walking over very tufty grass and I only trip and nearly break my ankle once, which is good going, and then Ben stops us.

'Here we are. Blindfold off.'

He takes it off and I blink a few times in the bright sunlight, and then stare.

'It's the hut,' I say.

We're in the bus terminus where we first met, opposite the shed-turned-kebab-hut.

'Yep.' He grins at me.

'Um, great,' I say. And it *is* great. I mean, it's nice to be back here, remember where we first met and so on. But I'm not loving the fact that the kids are getting facefuls of petrol fumes – I turn the buggy so that they're facing the other way – and also I'm not *massively* up for a kebab right now. But it's very sweet that he wants to remember our first meeting. So I give him a big smile.

He leans forward and plants a big kiss on my lips and then leans back. And there's that big grin again.

'I love you,' he says. 'I've brought you here so that we can go to the hut.'

'I love you too.' I wonder if he'll be offended if I don't have a kebab.

Maybe I could get a veggie one. I don't think that would give me food poisoning.

'Pretty sure I know what you're thinking right now.' Ben's still grinning. 'You're thinking about the time you got food poisoning from one of their kebabs.'

'That is true.'

'So let's go inside.'

'Let's what?'

'Check out their little kitchen area.' He starts pushing the buggy towards the hut.

'What?' I run after them.

Ben's walking towards the hut very purposefully.

As we get closer, I see that its shutters are down, which I have to say is quite a relief, because I'm not sure that I want to risk even a veggie kebab from them. I don't think they would necessarily be totally scrupulous about ensuring that they cook their veggies and meats separately.

'It's closed,' I point out, just as Ben – very confusingly – inserts a key into the door. The key came from his shorts pocket I think. 'How come you have that?' I am *really* bewildered.

'Imagine if I'd had this key when we first met,' he says as he pushes the door open.

'We wouldn't be here now and we wouldn't have Ella and Jack,' I say, bending down to the buggy to give them each a quick kiss on the nose. 'So thank goodness we didn't.'

Then I stand up, fast, and say, 'But how *do* you have the key now, and why?'

'Well.' Ben shoots me yet another grin and then pushes the door wider.

I can't see anything inside because it's all dark. My bewilderment is growing.

And then Ben switches a light on and I do not see what I'm expecting to see.

I do see a background of health-hazard-level scummy kebab kitchen, but I also see way more people than you'd think would fit in here: my mum and Declan, who she married last year, Frankie and Nella, Sulwe and Lewis, and Ben's parents. They're all squished round a couple of makeshift tables and in front of them are flasks and cakes on picnic plates. In the corner behind them, lying in a tangle of limbs on a gigantic outdoor bean-bag, are Ben's nieces, Sulwe's daughter, and Frankie and Nella's three girls.

I just stare. Ben has obviously organised a little tea party for us, and that's lovely, and it's very romantic that he's organised it in the place we first met, *but*, being honest, I'd have to say there are better venues. I mean, yes, it *is* romantic to come back here, but it does smell very kebabby and it's fairly small. There's a lot of elbow knocking going on round that table.

'Surprise!' Mum stands up, not without difficulty – she's very hemmed in between Declan and Nella – and reaches behind her and pulls out a long rectangle of metal.

I am *still* bewildered.

'What?' I'm kind of over this now.

Mum turns the metal over and I see that it says *The Hut* on it.

Cute. I love that Mum managed to keep the slightly weird secret metal present secret. During the dark years after Dad died, she told me and Frankie absolutely everything – couldn't keep any secrets – because basically her best friend (Dad) had gone and she needed someone to confide in. But since she and Declan became serious, he's become her best friend and she tells him instead of us about things like sex (thank goodness) and presents and surprise parties in kebab huts.

'Great?' I say. I'm always grateful for presents, but, also, it's a large bit of metal. Where am I going to put that in our house?

'Seriously.' Sulwe's staring at me. 'How sleep-deprived *are* you?'

'Um, very?'

'You numpty,' she says.

Ben reaches an arm round me and pulls me in close and – like every single time ever since I first met him in this hut – I get a shiver from the proximity to him.

'I've bought the hut for you so you can set your café up in it,' he says. 'If you'd like to. Otherwise we can just carry on selling dodgy kebabs and see how often we get taken to court.'

My hands are on my cheeks. 'Oh my goodness. Oh, Ben.'

It's perfect. I could hire people to work here but I could manage it round the children. And I *know* this is the perfect spot for a café. Like I said all those years ago.

'It's perfect,' I tell him out loud. 'Thank you so very much.'

'No, thank you.' He squeezes me even more tightly against him. 'Thank you for being in my life and, just, thank you for being you.'

Tears are leaking out of my eyes now. In my defence, as already mentioned, I am *really* tired at the moment. But also, I do feel extremely emotional.

'I'm so *lucky*,' I say.

'I think you two earnt your luck,' Sulwe says. 'I mean, all those years before you got together.'

'Mmm.' I'm not *totally* paying attention, because Ben's kissing me and whispering very deliciously naughty things in my ear about how maybe there'll be some payment in kind required later.

'This is nearly as good as our wedding day,' I tell him. That was a wonderful day – we got married in the Lake District and had the reception at Ben's parents' house and it genuinely only rained for half the day – and at the time I couldn't imagine ever feeling happier.

But now we have the kids, and life continues to grow better and better.

'I love this shed,' I tell Ben. 'And I love you.'

And he kisses me again, and everyone cheers, and I can't think of a better place to be right now than this smelly kebab hut.

ACKNOWLEDGMENTS

I've loved writing Liv and Ben's story, and am enormously grateful for the help I've had throughout.

Huge thanks to my agent, Sarah Hornsley at PFD, for all her support and advice as the ideas that became 'Another Time, Another Place' took seed and grew to fruition; and to Sam Brace at PFD for her continuing enthusiastic and amazing support during Sarah's maternity leave (congratulations again, Sarah!).

The team at Boldwood have been truly lovely and have made me feel so welcome. Emily Yau is a fantastic editor and it's been such a pleasure to work with someone so collaborative, who 'gets' Liv and Ben and who has the ability to suggest small changes that have a very big impact! Thank you also to Eleanor Leese for her exactly-right copy edits, to Clare Stacey at Head Design for designing such a beautiful cover and to Rachel Sargeant for her forensic proofreads.

And last but obviously not least, thank you so much to my family and friends. Much of the story is set in Putney in South-West London; thank you to all my Putney friends for many happy memories. And thank you to Fiona MacLennan and Liz Gale (they know why!) and to my (remarkably tolerant) husband and children for putting up with my weirdly-timed bursts of writing and all the pizza (you can get a lot more words written fast if you don't bother with vegetables). You're all wonderful; thank you.

MORE FROM JO LOVETT

We hope you enjoyed reading ***Another Time, Another Place***. If you did, please leave a review.

If you'd like to gift a copy, this book is also available as an ebook, large print, paperback, digital audio download and audiobook CD.

Sign up to Jo Lovett's mailing list for news, competitions and updates on future books.

https://bit.ly/JoLovettNews

Explore more from Jo Lovett.

ABOUT THE AUTHOR

Clare Swatman is the author of five previous novels, which have been translated into more than twenty languages. *The World Outside My Window* is her seventh novel. A former journalist, she spent the previous twenty years writing true life stories and health features for *Bella* and *Woman & Home*, amongst many other magazines, but now writes fiction full-time. Clare lives in Hertfordshire with her husband and two teenage sons.

Visit Clare's website: https://clareswatmanauthor.com

Follow Clare on social media:

facebook.com/clareswatmanauthor
twitter.com/clareswatman
instagram.com/clareswatmanauthor

Milton Keynes UK
Ingram Content Group UK Ltd.
UKHW041848090823
426579UK00001B/6

9 781785 134968